THE S
BRIEF

Volume 1 of The Silk Tales

A NOVEL BY

JOHN M. BURTON QC

EDITED BY KATHERINE BURTON

Books by John M. Burton

The Silk Brief, Volume 1 of The Silk Tales

The Silk Head, Volume 2 of The Silk Tales

The Silk Returns, Volume 3 of the Silk Tales

The Silk Ribbon, Volume 4 of The Silk Tales

The Silk's Child, Volume 5 of The Silk Tales

The Silk's Cruise, Volume 6 of The Silk Tales

Parricide, Volume 1 of The Murder Trials of Cicero

Poison, Volume 2 of The Murder Trials of Cicero

The Myth of Sparta, Volume 1 of The Chronicles of Sparta

The Return of the Spartans, Volume 2 of The Chronicles of Sparta

The Trial of Admiral Byng, Pour Encourager Les Autres, Volume 1 of the Historical Trials Series

Treachery, The Princes in The Tower.

TABLE OF CONTENTS

CHAPTER 1.

DRINKS WITH THE SENIOR CLERK

David Brant QC awoke to the sound of rain falling upon the windowsill outside his bedroom. It was Saturday morning, 7th July 2012 and yet it felt almost like winter. He should have been used to it by now, after all, the weather forecasters had helpfully informed the public that June 2012 was supposed to be the wettest for over 100 years and he assumed that July would break a similar record. Strangely that was not a comforting fact to him. He began to regain some of his functions as sleep fell away, one of the first things he noticed was the awful headache he had and a mouth that felt so dry that the drinking of a river would not have quenched his thirst. He was 55 years of age and the first question he asked himself that Saturday morning was the same question he had asked himself on many occasions, "Why did I drink so much last night?" He was a great believer in moderation in all things, unfortunately he had never been able to apply this to red wine.

He was a practising Criminal Barrister and, the night before, he had been out with his Senior Clerk. They had shared four bottles of red wine in, El Vinos, the wine bar close to his Chambers. He had been at the Bar for over 30 years but was only awarded Silk in 2010. "Awarded" was probably a strong word to use in the circumstances as it had cost a fortune to make the necessary application to become a Silk and he had completed a 49-page application form and required references from the last 12 Judges in front of whom he had appeared, also six Barristers against whom he had acted or had lead as a Leading Junior Barrister, and further references from six Solicitors who had instructed him. Having made five such applications in the past, he had finally been awarded the title.

He recalled with fondness the day he received a letter from the Lord Chancellor's office telling him that he had the required "Excellence" to become one of Her Majesty's Queen's Counsel. The second paragraph of that letter had then reminded him that he owed another £4,500 for being awarded this position. This was the amount payable because of the cost of the selection process. Along with the £3,000 he paid when he made his application, it was definitely an expensive procedure and not one to be lightly entered into. He had recalled the ceremony when the then Lord Chancellor, Jack Straw, presented him with his letters patent declaring he was one of Her Majesty's Counsel, Learned in the Law. Jack Straw had attended the meeting of the new Silks in Parliament where they were all sworn in. David remembered Jack Straw's speech which had started off with the words, "I had wondered whether to say this." David's experience was like that of most people, if you wondered whether to say something it was better not to say it, but Jack Straw had continued and effectively told the new ranks of Silks just before their swearing in, there was little work out there that was publicly funded any more. Despite this remarkable introduction to the ceremony to those who had spent so much of their time and money in order to become Silks it did not dampen the day and David enjoyed the festivities and the Party later when he consumed copious amounts of Champagne purchased for himself and his guests. Now, on Saturday morning, he felt like he had done the morning after that party. Often described as "tired and emotional", in reality he was suffering the full force of alcoholic poisoning. Why oh why had he consumed so much the night before.

He knew the answer of course, most of the socialising a Barrister does, requires drinking copious amounts of alcohol with Solicitors, other Barristers, or Clerks. Last night, David had taken his Senior Clerk, John Winston, for a drink to ask why there was so little work around at the moment. The first bottle of red wine they had consumed was a house claret from El Vinos. This had been consumed without any comments about practices or work and had been a general chat about families, how John's family was doing well and his two sons were doing well in their private school, how he was looking forward to taking his customary three weeks off in August to take his family to his large villa in the south of Spain. David listened to this conversation with feigned enthusiasm and even heard himself say the words, "You deserve a break, it's been a hard year."

Of course in reality he meant it had been a hard year for him. The Senior Clerk was still receiving his large salary and his percentage bonus meaning he received far in excess of £120,000 per annum regardless of the fact that there was less work at the Criminal Bar and many of the Barristers were struggling. David himself had much less work this year than he had for a long time. Of course the quality of the work was much better and the fees were higher for the work that he actually conducted but he had spent a lot of this time looking out on the rained out garden of his ground floor flat. By the time they had started the second bottle of house Claret, the conversation had moved on to the true purpose of the meeting and he had asked his clerk, John, where all the work was. Other Silks in Chambers appeared to be busy why was it that David wasn't. John Winston would listen to these complaints from many of his Barristers and was ready with an answer. There is no Silk work out there he said. He continued and said,

"Don't worry though Sir I'm not concerned about your practice at the moment, I have no doubt that there is a big case around the corner."

David looked at him and smiled and thought to himself I have no doubt that you are not worried about my practice, you can still afford to send your sons to private school and take your family on holiday to your private villa in Spain whereas I'll be lucky to persuade my bank manager to lend enough money to pay next month's mortgage!

David continued to smile throughout the conversation and by the time of the third bottle of Claret he was still smiling although now his smile appeared wider than normal due to the staining effect the claret had on his lips and the corners of his mouth. By the time of the fourth bottle he had changed and become slightly maudlin and he had announced to John that if this lack of work continued he may be forced to leave Chambers. He had been a Member of Temple Lane Chambers for about five years, like many of the members of the Bar he had moved Chambers a number of times, the grass always appearing to be lusher elsewhere though in practice it seldom had been. He had known John, for those five years and they had got on reasonably well although David never felt he had made his way into the "inner circle" in Chambers, those Barristers who were well fed with work. John had been a Clerk in Temple Lane Chambers since he was a pimply youth of 16. He had left school and gone straight into Clerking having been given the job by his uncle David Winston, the then Senior Clerk of Temple Lane Chambers. John had progressed from his position of Gopher, making tea and running around with briefs, making a steady rise through the clerking ranks. He had been appointed to a new position each time a Clerk had retired or moved on, either voluntarily or with encouragement from Chambers. He became a Second Junior Clerk, then the First Junior Clerk and finally some 30 years later, the Senior Clerk. David had always wondered at the career progress of clerks, how it was that someone who left school with very limited qualifications, if any at all, could progress to becoming the Senior Clerk earning more than most Barristers in his own Chambers, all of whom were technically his employers.

John had reacted well to the implied threat that David would leave Chambers. He had similar conversations with many Barristers over the years. Some he had considered troublemakers, and he was glad to see the back of them, others he had thought were rainmakers who could produce a lot of work from good-quality Solicitors. Others were good Barristers, some of whom he considered to be friends, at least as friendly as a Clerk could be with a Member of the Bar. He did not want to lose David from Chambers. He knew David was a good Barrister, he knew David could attract work from good-quality Solicitors and he knew that David had an excellent reputation in the profession. David was one of the few Barristers who did not think he knew more about Clerking than John. It never ceased to amaze John how most Barristers from Pupils, (namely Barristers in Training), to Silks thought they knew how to Clerk a Chambers better than he did when he had spent all his working life as a Clerk. Losing David would not be good to Chambers or himself but his problem was that there was very little Silk work out there. He had tried to get work for David and other Silks in Chambers but there were less Silk certificates around these days. About 95% of all Criminal Court work was legally aided and in order to instruct a Queen's Counsel the court has to award a Silk certificate. Due to the recession and the constant comments by Parliament that the legal aid bill was rising each year, Silk certificates were not being awarded in court and there simply was less Silk work to go around. Also, John had to admit, he was not as hungry as he had been in his earlier years. He had paid off the mortgage on his home and his Spanish villa. His children were coming to the end of their school careers and hopefully soon paying the private education fees would be a thing of the past and University would not cost him as much. He no longer felt the need to go the extra mile to get work for his Barristers. After all, he had seen the erosion in Clerks salaries over the years. Originally Senior Clerks had been paid a percentage of Chambers turn over, up to 10% in some cases. That had been reduced to larger "basic" salaries and small percentages of 1% or so. The erosion of the percentage element meant to him there was erosion in the incentive to work hard. In the past in a Chambers this size he might have been able to earn £250,000 per annum. Last year his salary and percentage paid him about £150,000 a year and this year it would be less, probably around £130,000. Nevertheless it was enough for his needs and he did not need to work any harder even if he had many Members of Chambers breathing down his neck. He had been offered two new Silk briefs by a Solicitor who had even mentioned David's name although John believed he would inevitably be able to steer the briefs the way he wanted. He toyed in his mind whether he should recommend David for one of them even though other Silks in Chambers had been out of Court longer.

They had been well into their fourth bottle of house Claret when John made up his mind about the briefs and said to David,

"I don't want to lose you Sir, since joining us, you've been one of the most loyal Members of Chambers, I also think over the last few years, you and I have become friends. I am doing my best to get you some work but you know it's not easy at the moment. However, I do know that the Solicitors, Rooney Williams and Co picked up a murder case that is to be tried in the Bailey. It's listed the first week of September I've been told. They want one of their in-house advocates to act as Junior Counsel and they want a Silk from Chambers to lead her. They were suggesting that they'd like Mr Wontner QC to lead on this case, but I can suggest that you do it instead."

David looked at him through increasingly glassy eyes. James Wontner QC was his Head of Chambers. He was a very capable advocate although he did not seem to attract much work for himself and had been nicknamed "Want More QC." Generally in Chambers the Tenants (Members of Chambers) thought that John Winston provided all of James's work. David was torn by the offer. He did not want to be seen to be taking work from other Silks in Chambers particularly if the Solicitors had asked for them, but equally in order to ensure that he could pay his mortgage on his flat in the Barbican and eat, he wanted this brief. He had once owned a large house in Kent, but school fees and a divorce from Sarah his Barrister wife who practised Family law, had seriously eroded his capital and made significant in-roads into his income. It had not assisted that, over the years, he had invested large amounts in Lloyds TSB bank shares, once owning £200,000 shares. At that time he received an annual dividend of 7% and that £14,000 a year had been very helpful in paying the bills. However, he had seen his Lloyds TSB bank shares collapse with the banking crisis, from a value of close to £7 a share to just 30 pence a share. The dividend had disappeared at the same time and eventually he had to sell his shares at a considerable loss just to pay his tax bill.

"John, you know I don't want to take work away from anyone else. If the solicitors want James Wontner QC and he is available to conduct the case then he should do it."

David listened to himself as he made his comments, inwardly screaming at himself not to be an idiot but he at least had to pretend that he didn't want to steal work from others.

John Winston had been around 30 years, he had trained under his uncle David Winston who had been an old-style clerk. As his own career had proved, there is always a Junior Clerk waiting to step into your shoes. In order to survive you have to ensure you have a loyal Junior Clerk (well as loyal as can be) and that you keep the top four or five Members of Chambers happy. He had learnt the secret of being a Senior Clerk. Keep all your senses operating all the time, keep your eyes and ears open and develop a good sense of smell. He could smell bullshit a mile away. He smiled over the table, putting his glass down, he lifted the bottle of Claret and emptied the remains into the two glasses, ensuring, as he had throughout the night, that more went into David's glass than his own.

"Don't you worry about that Sir, I have another case that Mr Wontner will want to do that will clash with this one. Even Mr Want More QC cannot be in two places at once and we both know that you will be the man for this job."

He winked at David as he said this. David was in two minds at that moment. He had not really wanted to take a brief away from his Head of Chambers but equally he wanted the brief. The fourth bottle of claret had certainly affected him, although he still noted that at a time when his

Senior Clerk said there was no Silk work around he had managed apparently, to find two Silk briefs. He had also noticed the conspiratorial wink when John used the Head of Chambers nickname. He put his limited feelings of guilt aside and left El Vinos feeling better about his immediate future, he had his first Silk brief in months. Having paid the bill with a generous tip to the waitress, thank God for credit cards, he had shaken hands with John outside and caught a cab to his flat in the Barbican. He was more cheerful entering his flat that night than he had been when he left it that morning. He went straight to his kitchen and picked a bottle of Claret from his wine rack. He decided one further glass would not go amiss before he made his way to bed. Now he awoke on Saturday morning remembering consuming just one glass of wine at home the night before. He was somewhat surprised to see in his kitchen an almost empty bottle of Claret standing next to a half empty glass of red wine. Or was that a glass half full? He wasn't entirely sure these days.

CHAPTER 2.

THE BRIEF ARRIVES.

The weekend came to a close without David doing much at all. Sunday had been one of the rainiest July days he could remember and he had stayed in his flat watching the Wimbledon final between Roger Federer and Andy Murray. Having watched Andy Murray lose in four sets he decided to spend the rest of the day reading. He decided that he ought to take a few days off wine and booze generally, so he had poured the remains of his bottle of good Claret down the sink and drank cups of coffee, tea and orange juice throughout the day. He read his correspondence with the usual disdain he had for the large number of red bills that he usually had to wade through. He had learnt throughout his career as a Barrister to ignore the first bills and wait until they were red and then check the deadlines that they gave for payment. Then pay them a week or two later. On this occasion all the bills were at an early blue stage so they did not need any attention and he threw the lot of them in his kitchen bin.

Monday came and as he had no Court work or even other work such as advisory work he chose not to visit his Chambers. He knew if he did he would see the familiar faces of the Tenants and

Pupil Barristers in his Chambers. The Pupils were trainee Barristers running around between Magistrates Courts eking out a meagre living with just hope to rely upon as a substitute for a real income. Once they completed Pupillage the young Barrister could apply for a Tenancy in Chambers. Technically the work should get better but often it was of the same quality with the added problem that now the young Barrister had to pay rent to his or her Chambers. Once the Barristers had survived for the first few years they usually, but not inevitably, reached the next level, meaning they were busier with better quality of work. However, even they would stop David to moan about the dwindling fees from legal aid, the bleak future of the Criminal Bar and the Legal Services Commission's apparent refusal to pay fees for cases that had been concluded less than three months ago. There was the highest level of Barristers, they were the Senior Juniors and the Silks, few of whom would be around as they would either be in Court or at home, preferring not to leave the comfort of home if they did not have to. David also knew that when he went into Chambers, someone would always ask what work he was doing at the moment, any interesting cases? His answer for the last couple of months had been he was working on some advisory work at the moment but that answer wore thin when he had given it a number of times. No Barrister liked to say he had no work as it almost seemed an admission of failure, so David deflected questions about the current state of his Practice, and moved on to make enquiries of the work his questioner was conducting. He had no interest in the answers but it was better to move on in such discussions than concentrate on his own stagnating career.

By Monday night he had relapsed from his self-imposed drinking ban and he opened and consumed a bottle of Spanish Rioja Reserva 2006 which he personally preferred to the heavy Claret he drank in El Vinos. He was at home, his two children, a girl and a boy, had left home years ago and were more ensconced in their Mother's camp rather than in his after the divorce. It probably had not helped that he had an affair with one of his Instructing Solicitors, Alison Wright of Johns Solicitors. They had conducted a serious Robbery case in Leeds together when he was a Leading Junior Barrister. The client was a regular villain from London who had contracted out his services to a Leeds gang of Bureau De Change Robbers. A gun had been used in one of the Robberies and David had been asked to conduct the trial in Leeds. David had not been able to travel daily from his home in Kent for the trial and so had stayed in the Hilton in Leeds. Dinners out in the heavy romantic air of Leeds had led to one evening when they had shared a bed. The romantic night had been a disaster as had his need to confess to his Wife. The romance ended after the return from Leeds and needless to say he had never been instructed again by that Solicitor. More importantly his Wife had decided that enough was enough, she had not felt the need at that stage to point out that she was having an affair with a Barrister in her own Chambers and David only found this out many months later. Divorce had followed his confession with him being branded the Home wrecker. His children had readily taken his Wife's side in the divorce, presumably his Wife had not felt the need to confess to them about her own affair. His children did occasionally contact him when they needed help with finances but, as he was having problems with his own finances he had not been able to assist them as often as he had in the past and this had meant his children's' contact with him became increasingly irregular.

He often thought to himself, if he had been a Queen's Counsel ten years ago when there was plenty of Silk work around, he would be a millionaire by now. He then remembered he had been a Leading Junior during this period earning in excess of £150,000 a year and he had been a millionaire until the divorce. Sarah had taken the matrimonial house, its contents and a large amount of cash and endowment policies and he had taken the flat in the Barbican, a much smaller sum of cash, and the Lloyds TSB shares. He had been allowed to keep his meagre Pension policies which may pay a pittance when he retired. He had to admit Sarah's knowledge and practice of Family Law was excellent!

David poured himself another glass of Rioja Reserva and stared at the TV. He had recorded an episode of the new TV programme "Silk" for his own entertainment and he started the recording to see if it was as entertaining as he had heard.

He started with the typical Criminal Barrister's approach to such programmes. Firstly criticising the mistakes in legal procedure and laughing at the concept of a brand new Silk turning down Silk work because she did not like the Solicitor, but soon, despite himself, he started to enjoy watching the character Martha Costella QC fighting against the male dominated world of Barristers and getting yet another client acquitted after making a rousing defence speech. In spite of himself he enjoyed the episode and decided to watch others when they were on.

He soon finished the bottle of Rioja Reserva and decided that was enough for the night. Tomorrow he must start his own personal campaign to improve his practice. It would mean meeting and socialising with a lot of Solicitors but he had always enjoyed that despite the effect it had upon his wallet and perhaps more importantly, his liver.

Monday night came and went in a bit of a blur. It had not helped that having consumed one bottle of Rioja, having decided on his strategy to regain his practice, he had decided to open another bottle to celebrate just by having one or at most two glasses. After he had finished that bottle he had felt immensely tired and he had gone to bed only to be woken up on Tuesday morning by Mary, his 40 year old well-endowed cleaner, who, not expecting him to be home, had opened his bedroom door to find him sprawled naked across his bed. After exchanging apologies with her, he had decided to shower, get dressed and go into Chambers leaving Mary behind with a large smile across her face, readying herself to tell her husband and her friends the horrors of what she had seen. She would practice the shocked look later on in the mirror until she had perfected it.

David finished showering, thanking the designers of his flat for putting a lock on the bathroom door, so that there were no more surprises in store for him, or for that matter, Mary. He then received a call on his mobile phone from Chambers. This surprised him. It was a long time ago that he got regular calls from his Chambers. Now it seemed he could go for days without them contacting him unless it was to ask whether his standing order had gone through for his rent to Chambers this month.

More surprisingly, it was his Senior Clerk on the phone.

"Hello Sir, just thought I would ring to tell you I have persuaded Charles Rooney of Rooney Williams LLP to instruct you on a Murder. The case is listed to start on Monday 10th September and has a three week listing. You will be leading Charlotte Williams, who is the Junior in-house Advocate. The papers have been delivered to

Chambers this morning and are in your tray. There's a conference in Belmarsh Prison this week on Friday 13th July at 6pm. The Solicitors couldn't get an earlier time. It's a "meet and greet" conference so they don't expect you to know all the papers by then."

David mumbled a few thanks and an "I owe you a good lunch", even though he privately thought that the Clerk was receiving an excellent salary in order to get work like this. He then put the phone down and mused to himself, so it worked. He had heard long ago that Clerks tend to brief those who shouted at them most recently. He had made a half-hearted comment that he may have to leave Chambers and here he was instructed on a murder case. He must try this again the next time his diary emptied in front of him.

He got dressed with renewed vigour. He decided to put on his Silk clothes. As a Junior Barrister following the dress code expected of him over the years he had worn three piece or double breasted dark suits. Now as a Silk he did not have to wear these any more. Junior Barristers wore these because they put their gowns over their suits when they went into Court. As Courts expected dark clothing, they wore dark suits. However, Silks had special waistcoats which they wore under their gowns instead of their suit jackets. It meant they could wear any type of jacket they fancied to Court as they would not wear it in Court and often Criminal Silks could be seen sporting light coloured linen jackets and dark trousers for this reason. He had purchased such a jacket and a pair of dark trousers. Ironically these had been a lot cheaper than the suits he had been forced to purchase over the years as a Junior Barrister.

He travelled into Chambers having consumed just one glass of orange juice for breakfast. Mary was still wearing a massive grin on her face but he had decided to ignore it and with a "Cheerio" he had left the flat. He did wonder to himself why he employed Mary. She was not a particularly good cleaner or conversationalist and she clearly had little regard for him. He recalled a few years ago when his then 20 year old son, Robert, had made one of his rare visits to the flat after the divorce. It had been a warm dry summer, unlike this one and Mary had chosen to wear one of her tight fitting T shirts which displayed her most visible assets prominently. She had flirted with his son and he was not sure whether his son was embarrassed or actually enjoyed it. He later learnt from Robert that she had asked him what career he was aiming at and upon Robert saying he wanted to be a Doctor she had applauded him in not following in his father's footsteps and then dismissed David's thirty years at the Bar with the simple comment, "oh your father only gets guilty people off." He liked to think that in his thirty years he had got the odd innocent person "off" as well. He had certainly represented a large number of guilty who had been convicted despite his best efforts. He supposed he continued to employ Mary because it was "better the devil you know." He had tried to hire other cleaners over the years, the best had been a young Polish cleaner, Agnita he hired for a few months when Mary was busy giving birth to her fourth child. Agnita had been an excellent cleaner and the flat had never looked so good, he was going to hire her full time until one day she just disappeared without a word never to be seen again. He assumed she had just returned to Poland so he had been forced to take Mary back after her maternity leave.

He had only been gone five minutes when Mary felt that she had worked long enough for now and she put the kettle on and sat down ready to have her first half hour break in her two hour cleaning session. She did not miss the opportunity of using her iPhone to text all her friends about the horrors of what she had witnessed that morning, adding, less than charitably, how surprisingly small a certain part of David's anatomy was!

David arrived at Farringdon train station, bought himself a coffee and made his way down on to the platform. He was travelling to Blackfriars Station and he would then walk down Tudor Street to his Chambers in the Temple. He had drank half of his coffee before the train arrived and looked into it deciding that today it was definitely half full.

He arrived in Chambers and was greeted by John and the other Clerks, Tony the First Junior who always seemed to have a phone glued to his ear,

Asif, the Second Junior who was always staring into his computer screen and Ryan, the Gopher who was constantly trying to look busy and moving papers around Chambers. Daphne the bookkeeper was there, apparently chasing fees for the Barristers and there was Mike the Administrator tapping away at his keyboard no doubt with some further important message to the Tenants in Chambers about the urgent need to purchase a Chambers' kettle.

It never ceased to amaze David throughout the thirty years of his practice that he had never seen a Clerks room that did not seem busy. Privately he wondered if it was all a show put on every time that Barristers walk into a Clerks room like when the light comes on in your fridge when you open the door and that normally the Clerks just sit there with their feet up. Despite the hive of activity in the Clerks room, there was still a lack of work, fees just did not seem to come in, papers were constantly getting lost and the administration of Chambers made the High Street Banks look efficient. Then again, he wondered, he could be doing them a great dis-service, maybe they really were this busy he wondered hopefully.

On this day he did not really care. There was a murder brief waiting for him which would occupy up to three weeks in September. He would probably be paid for it in January 2013 just in time to meet the first of the two tax payments he had to make each year as a self-employed Barrister. That would be a great relief and also he had some work which meant he was doing the job he loved.

John pointed out where the brief was in his pigeon hole. This was rather pointless really as David had visited his pigeon hole over a thousand times since he first joined Chambers. Even though of late it was empty, he still checked it whenever he came in. Nevertheless, he picked up the brief with an appropriate thank you and went to his room which he shared with four other Criminal Silks, including the Head of Chambers.

He placed the Brief on his desk. Four lever arch files of papers containing about 1,200 pages. This was not a lot by the standards of the cases he had conducted before he had become a Silk. His largest case to date had been when he was a Junior Counsel and his brief contained 120,000 pages, albeit the pages had not been served on paper but were served on an iron key, a special type of flash drive that erased its contents if you put in the wrong password. That had been an MTIC VAT fraud, otherwise known as a Missing Trader Intra Community fraud. It had involved the alleged sale of mobile phones between traders in this country selling to another country in the European Union who had then sold on to a number of other traders. The final European Union trader then sold and exported the phones to a trader in the United Kingdom who then sold them on to original seller. These used to be known as "Carousel Frauds" because the goods were allegedly sold in a complete circle or Carousel. The fraud worked because of the complexities of VAT rules. VAT was charged when sales were made in this country but not when the phones were sold to the EU therefore a seller to a customer abroad could claim back his VAT that he had paid to his UK seller from Her Majesty's Revenue, Customs and Excise. The Revenue were not supposed to lose out because someone in the chain who purchased from abroad then sold on in the UK and should account for the VAT they charged their customer. Of course in practice these individuals disappeared, hence the term "Missing Trader" and the Revenue lost millions. It had taken David a long time to get to understand the nuances of such frauds and the issues involved. Of course having finally understood the issues in the case, he had not been instructed on an MTIC VAT fraud again. He really wished he could have one of those cases again but he would settle for a 1,200 page murder at this stage.

He opened the pink ribbon around his papers that signalled that this was a defence brief, prosecution cases had white ribbon and he had not seen one of those since becoming a Silk. He took out his instructions. They amounted to ten typed pages giving a short analysis of the issues in the case. There was a proof of evidence, eight pages long and comments on prosecution witnesses another eight pages long. There were also 20 pages of notes made by his Junior, Charlotte Williams which summarised the evidence of the Prosecution witnesses and the Exhibits. The rest of the papers consisted of Prosecution Witness statements and Exhibits including interviews of the Defendant. In the past, the instructions, the proof and the comments would have consisted of far more pages but Solicitors, even in murder cases, were now paid a "litigator's fee" based on the number of pages of Prosecution evidence rather than the actual work conducted and so instructions became gradually reduced in size. Indeed, David had noted how some firms provided little more than the Prosecution papers and brief instructions that effectively said, "get on with it."

David began as he always did by reading the Prosecution summary of the case. In his experience it always helped to know what was being said by your opposition before you heard the explanation given by your own client.

The Defendant was called Damien Clarke, he was a thirty year old man living in a flat owned by a Housing Association situated in Thamesmead Way, Woolwich. He still lived with his mother and her two daughters although they rarely saw him because of his fondness for smoking crack cocaine late at night. Damien referred to this as "social use" although David wondered how anyone could smoke crack cocaine on a social basis.

Damien was apparently friends with the fifty two year old Usman Hussain who had a flat nearby in a block of flats in Cambridge Gardens, Woolwich. Usman was, according to Damien, a social smoker of crack cocaine. He was also a "runner" a person who knew who to contact and where to get hold of crack cocaine in the Woolwich area. Usman apparently let people come to his flat to smoke with him and when the supplies ran out he would obtain money from them and then visit one of his contacts to provide a further few hours smoking.

The Prosecution papers stated that on Saturday 4th February 2012 at about 7:00 am the Fire Brigade had been called to Cambridge Gardens near Woolwich. It was a purpose built block of 12 flats on three floors and was relatively modern. One of the occupants of the flats, Mr Leonard Feeley, who lived on the first floor in flat number eight, had heard a smoke alarm go off outside flat number six immediately across from his flat. When he had gone to see what was happening he had seen smoke pouring out of the door of the flat. He knew that the occupant was a man in his late fifties or early sixties although he did not know his name. He had nodded to him in the past, but did not want to get friendly because of the large number of undesirables who seemed to visit that flat at all times of the day. Also a great deal of noise came from that flat and often he would hear people shouting up from the ground asking for Usman to throw his keys down to them or press a buzzer to release the outside door.

Mr Feeley had gone over to the flat to knock on the door to see if anyone was there but as he heard no noise he had immediately phoned 999. The

Emergency call service had logged his call at 6:57 am and the Fire Brigade, an Ambulance unit and Police were called and arrived at 7:07am.

The Fire Brigade broke down the door to flat number six and went in and put the fire out. The flat had two bedrooms and in one of the bedrooms the Fire Brigade Officers discovered a body. It was Usman Hussain. Fortunately the fire had not destroyed much of the flat and the body was still intact, wrapped in a duvet soaked with blood and covered with a layer of soot. The paramedics entered the flat at 7:15am but immediately knew that Usman Hussain was dead and from their experience and the look of the body he had possibly been dead for a couple of hours. They could see multiple stab wounds. A Doctor was called who made the formal pronouncement that Mr Hussain was dead and then the police cleared everyone out of the property and brought their Scenes Of Crimes Officers (SOCOs) in to search the premises and take large number of photographs.

The Prosecution case statement continued to state that the body had eventually been removed and a Pathologist had confirmed the cause of death as multiple stab wounds. From a measure of the depth and width of the wounds the knife had a blade of probably about 12 or 13 cm in length and 2-2.5 centimetres in width. There were 12 separate stab wounds and considerable force had been used in some as the sternum, (breast bone), had been fractured.

It was clear that Usman Hussain was a man with many visitors to his flat but he had one person who stayed with him. She was a young Prostitute called Gillian Banks. Usman had taken a shine to her and given her free accommodation in return for her favours. Police attention was immediately focussed on her until it transpired that on the Friday 3rd February she had to appear at Woolwich Magistrates Court in relation to a theft charge she faced. She had not appeared at the stipulated time of 10:00am and a bench warrant had been issued for her arrest. She had strolled into Court just after 12 noon on the Friday with some story that her mini cab had been late collecting her. As she had failed to appear on a number of occasions and given similar poor excuses the District Judge had refused her bail and she had been locked up over the weekend, which had the unintended advantage of providing her with the perfect alibi.

A more favourable development from the police point of view had occurred on Saturday 4th February 2012 at about 2pm when Damien Clarke had entered the police station. He was dressed in a clean pair of jeans and T shirt, wearing a thick Hoody referring to the band "Mindless Behaviour" printed on the front.

He had spoken to the Desk Sergeant and stated he was aware there had been a murder in Woolwich. His friend had been killed by two men and he was a witness.

The police had taken him into an interview room and provided tea and sympathy as he was crying a lot. He kept saying "why him, why did it have to be him?"

The Police had then interviewed him about the killing as a prospective witness. The interview had been taped so that an accurate version of what he said could be obtained. His story was that he had been out on the Friday with an ex-girlfriend Jenny Jones. They spent the day together but had a falling out in the evening and at about 11:30pm he had made his way to Usman's for a social smoke of crack cocaine. He had shouted up to Usman when he arrived at his flat and asked to be buzzed in which he was. He went up to the first floor and into flat number six where he was greeted by Usman. Usman told him that he was concerned that Gillian Banks had gone out just before 12 noon saying that she would be back in the afternoon but he had heard nothing more from her.

Damien had seen two other men in the flat with a girl. He had been introduced to them but had never seen them before and could not remember their names. He thought the girl was called Babs or maybe Babe although he thought that was probably her nickname. He could remember that one of the men was Scottish and the other Arabian but he could remember no further details. All of the occupants of Usman's flat were smoking crack cocaine and Damien started smoking it as well. Within a few hours they ran out of drugs and the men, including Damien pooled their resources and gave Usman the money to go out and collect more from one of his contacts. Damien was unaware what time this was but he recalled feeling tired and falling asleep in an armchair in Usman's lounge. He awoke to hear muffled screams coming from Babs who he saw was lying down on the sofa in the lounge and was now only partially clothed. Damien saw that the Scottish man was holding her down and the other man was trying to rape her. At that stage Usman came into the room and started shouting at the two men. Damien was just stunned and kept sitting in the armchair. The Scottish man moved away from the sofa and went towards the kitchen which was next to the lounge. He then returned brandishing a large kitchen knife. Usman was holding onto the other man pulling him away from Babs when suddenly the Scottish man started to stab him repeatedly. Damien remembered there was blood everywhere and some splashed onto his clothes. He tried to get up from the armchair but was forced back down by the Arabian man. Babs left the flat screaming, she was wearing few clothes as most had been torn from her but she managed to get out of the flat and run away. Usman had screamed when he had first been struck but had soon collapsed and lay silent in the lounge.

Damien could remember all of this in a blur, made worse by the combination of shock, alcohol and crack cocaine in his system. Eventually the Scottish man had told him to get up from the armchair, collect a duvet from a bedroom, put it round Usman's body and move the body to the bedroom. The Scottish man was still holding the knife and Damien through fear had done what he was told. He had then been told to take the knife, clean it and return it to the kitchen.

The men then threatened that if he said anything about what he had seen they would find him and kill him just like they had killed Usman.

They had been collecting their coats and other items when Damien saw his opportunity. He grabbed his jacket and rushed to the door, he got through, ran down the stairs, pressed an exit button next to a side door and left. He ran to his mother's house getting there 15 minutes later. There he buzzed to get in and his elder sister, Christine let him in. He was terrified of what he had seen and the threats from the two men. He stripped off and washed his blood stained clothes in his mother's washing machine. He had been too afraid at that stage to approach the police but finally just before 2pm he had showered and gone to his local police station to tell them what had happened.

Not revealed in the papers was the reaction of Detective Sergeant Monkton when he heard Damien's version of events. He put his pen down, took another bite of his digestive biscuit and a sip from his cup of tea and said he would switch off the tape so that refreshments could be consumed. He had been a Police Officer for twenty years and prided himself on knowing when someone was lying. His first questions of Damien had been about his date of birth and his full name and address. This was simply in order to check with the Police National Computer whether he had any previous convictions. The results had been provided to him when the tea and biscuits had been brought in by a female Police Officer, Angela Walters. DS Monkton had then turned to Damien and said,

"Damien, I hope you don't mind me calling you Damien, there are just a few questions I want to ask you about what you've told me. Now it's more a matter of formality, but I think we should caution you and then we will start the tape again to record what you have to say. Of course you can have a Solicitor present, that's a matter for you but it does mean that we will have to wait for some time until we get one."

Damien readily agreed to being interviewed without a Solicitor present and DS Monkton smiled thinking to himself he had scored a great success. He had solved a murder within seven hours of the body being found. Having looked at Damien's criminal record for drugs, possession of a flick knife and wounding, using a knife, he knew he had the murderer in front of him.

This was all referred to in the Prosecution case summary as the Police were concerned at inconsistencies in Damien's version of events and at 14:30 they decided to arrest him on suspicion of murder and interview him under caution. He was offered the services of a Solicitor but had declined the offer.

The Case summary revealed that the interviewing had taken place over the next six hours, with two short breaks for refreshments to be consumed. During that time DS Monkton had raised the fact of Damien's criminal record, had raised questions about why had he washed his clothes after the murder, why had he showered, why had he not gone to the police straight away. He had asked how he managed to get away from the flat, didn't the men follow him. The Police had also started to make separate enquiries and having visited his mother's flat they had spoken to his mother and sisters. His elder sister, Karen remembered hearing a noise at about 5-00 in the morning which sounded like someone entering the flat and then about an hour later a similar noise which sounded like someone leaving the flat. As far as she was concerned this could only be Damien as he was the only one who tended to come in or go out of the property at that time in the morning. She said her mother and sister, like her, rarely got up before 7am. His sister Christine Clarke remembered him coming into the flat again at 7-30 that morning. She was up at this time and she let him in. According to her, he was not out of breath and did not seem to have been running. She noticed nothing out of the ordinary about his clothes and certainly had not seen any blood on them.

This information was fed back to DS Monkton throughout the day and slowly he introduced each new fact into the interview. Eventually towards the end of the six hours he put his theory to Damien that in a drug fuelled craze he had killed Usman. He had moved the body and made some basic attempt at cleaning up. He returned to his mother's flat sometime around 5am and washed his clothes and showered. He was no doubt worried about what he had done and worried about having left something behind in Usman's flat that might incriminate him. He had then left his mother's flat at about 6am and returned to Usman's flat where he had set fire to it to destroy all such traces. He had then returned to his mother's flat at about 7-30am being let in by his elder sister Karen.

Damien denied all these allegations and it now dawned on him for the first time that the Police did not believe his story and suspected him of the murder. He finally asked if he could have a Solicitor and an hour later at 9-30pm he was seen by Charles Rooney of Rooney Williams, who upon hearing that this was a murder investigation, had come to the police station himself rather than send a junior member of his firm.

Upon his arrival DS Monkton, now clocking up the overtime hours, disclosed to Charles Rooney the basic facts about the case and a summary of the statements made by Damien to the police. He then saw his client in the Police cells and asked him for his version of events. It did not take him long to form the impression that his client had said more than enough, putting forward a version of events that was riddled with problems. He firmly advised that Damien should make no further comment in interview. Two further interviews were conducted by DS Monkton that night between 10-30pm and 12-10am. Damien chose to follow the advice of his Solicitor and this time made no further comment. The following day at 10-00 in the morning he was charged with murder, he was cautioned and simply stated, "I didn't kill him."

David Brant put down the case summary and commenced reading the statements of the Prosecution witnesses. At once he saw the great difficulties his client was facing. He started to put together a brief Chronology of times and events that the evidence disclosed. The police had interviewed Jenny, Damien's ex-girlfriend who accounted for her day with him. They had met on Friday 3rd February 2012 just after 12pm. They had gone straight to a pub and consumed several pints of lager. They had moved on throughout the day and consumed large amounts of alcohol in different pubs, supplemented by cans of lager purchased in off-licences. The day had become a blur to her but she had remembered she and Damien had a falling out very late in the evening. He had demanded sex from her for "old time's sake" and she had refused. He had punched her and started to tear at her clothes but stopped and ran away when a passer-by shouted at him. She had not seen him since nor did she want to, but she did not want to bring any charges in relation to the incident.

One witness, Graham Storey, from flat number five did recall someone shouting up to Usman's flat just before midnight on 3rd February 2012. He lived next door to Usman's flat at number 6 and often heard loud noises from next door. He had taken to wearing ear plugs because the noises became unbearable at times. He had heard noises in the early hours of 4th February and recalled hearing Usman, whose voice he recognised, a single male's voice and a girl's voice. He had put his ear plugs in after that and heard no more until the next morning when he heard very loud knocking on his door as the Fire Brigade were clearing his building.

Annabelle Lyons was a neighbour on the same floor at flat number 7 and she was sure she had heard screaming coming from the flat. It sounded like a female voice but it could have been a male voice, she could not be sure. She thought it occurred at about 4:30am as she recalled looking at the clock in her bedroom at that time.

Alexander McDonald was a downstairs neighbour who occupied flat number 2, directly underneath Usman Hussain's flat. He described himself as retired in his statement. He stated that he had been woken by loud noises at about 2am on 4th February 2012, coming from the flat above. He had looked at his bedside clock which is why he knew it was that time. He knew an Asian gentleman lived there but he did not know his name. He had often heard loud noises coming from this flat so this was not unusual. He was just falling asleep again when he heard someone screaming. He was sure it was the Asian gentleman. He had gone back to sleep as it was not the first time he had heard such noises from this flat and indeed he had not thought them the loudest or the worst noises he had ever heard coming from there.

David stopped reading the brief for a few minutes as he went to the Chambers kitchen to make himself a coffee. He could of course have asked Ryan, the Chambers Gopher, to make him a coffee but from experience he knew it would take about 30 minutes before he received it and it would be cold and taste awful.

He returned to his room with a steaming mug of coffee and continued with his reading. The Police had taken Damien's phone and downloaded its contents and obtained cell site evidence of its location. The Police considered four phone contacts to be important in this case. Firstly on 3rd February 2012 at 11:37 he had phoned Jenny's phone for 34 seconds presumably in connection with their meeting at 12pm that day. His phone was located in the vicinity of Woolwich High Street. At 23:17 he sent a text to Jenny, "You fucking bitch you led me on." He was cell sited in the vicinity of Cambridge Gardens. On 4th February 2012 at 05:21 he had called a phone that the Police discovered belonged to a friend of his called

Christopher White. The call was for 2 minutes and 10 seconds and the phone was cell sited to the vicinity of Damien's mother flat. At 12:32 he phoned Christopher White again. The Police spoke to Christopher White who stated he could not remember the first call but remembered the second call when Damien told him he witnessed a murder and was wondering whether he should go the police. Christopher advised him to go.

David took a sip of his fast-cooling coffee. It was probably time to make another. He mused for a moment, might there be any challenge to the cell site evidence? He had learnt a great deal about cell site evidence as it appeared in a large number of cases these days. He recalled one case when he was a Junior, when what was alleged to be his client's phone had been cell sited to the locations of 13 robberies on Security vans at about the time the robberies had taken place. The client had been acquitted simply because he had been arrested with a known criminal and the police had emptied the contents of their jackets onto the ground in order to photograph them. This had the potential for mixing up the phones and as the other phone was cell sited away from the robberies the jury had concluded that there was a doubt about whose phone it was. Two weeks after release the client had been arrested in the act of committing a robbery on another security van.

There was a popular misconception about cell site evidence that it involves some kind of triangulation so that a phone can be pinpointed to an exact location. In fact it cannot and the highest that cell site evidence can go is to indicate which mobile phone mast a phone used when a call was made and usually, due to most cell site masts providing signals in three directions, the direction the phone was situated at the time of the call. As David knew, sometimes in cities like London, a mobile phone does not necessarily use the nearest mobile phone mast for a number of reasons such as the signal being masked by a large building, so it is not a precise science. Could there be such an issue here, particularly as the papers indicated that Damien's mother's address was only 15 minutes away from Usman Hussain's address. Was it possible that on some occasions a mobile phone in either location could use the same mast? He flagged this as a point for consideration depending upon what Damien's instructions were.

He made himself another coffee and went back to his room to read more of the papers. Just as he opened them his phone rang which he answered. It was Asif telling him that Charles Rooney was on the phone.

"Charles, long time, how are you mate?"

He answered in his usual friendly and wholly un-silk-like way.

"David, good to hear your voice, I understand you are going to help our Damien Clarke with the little problem he has at the moment."

David thought how wonderful it was that Solicitors could describe an allegation of murder as a "little problem."

"Of course Charles, happy to assist, it will be good to work with your firm again, we haven't worked together since I conducted that murder case of Stan Connelly last year."

He thought it would not hurt to remind the Solicitor that it was a long time between briefs, particularly as the case of Connelly where the Defendant was charged with murder, had resulted in an acquittal. There was a great belief amongst members of the Criminal Bar that it was much better to lose cases than win them because an acquittal usually and ironically resulted in no more work from that firm. Psychologically, it was probably something to do with the fact that you got more credit for being seen to fight hard in a losing case than achieve an acquittal in what was, by the fact of the acquittal, a winnable case.

"Yes, David, I don't think I ever thanked you for your sterling efforts in the Stan Connelly case. I don't know if you know but after he was released, Connelly was arrested and convicted of rape. He used the duty Solicitors' firm to represent him. Strange how ungrateful clients are."

Never a truer word thought David, you have been entirely ungrateful for all the times I have worked for you and obtained results. He then thought for a moment that if Connelly had been found guilty of murder, he would have been in prison and unable to commit the rape and some poor victim would not have suffered. David dismissed the thought as soon as he had it, if he thought like that he would never be able to continue as a Barrister.

"I know what you mean, but I suppose we should be happy they instruct us in the first place and that we get the result for them."

"Yes, yes, anyway David, I don't expect you've had a chance to read the papers yet as I know how busy you Silks are. I just wanted to give you a quick call to touch base with you. We have a conference fixed in Belmarsh on Thursday at 6pm. No worries, I don't expect you to have read all the papers by then. It's just a "meet and greet" so that you can see Damien and so that he sees he has a Silk working on his case. I suspect you have been told that Charlotte is your Junior on this case. She will not be able to make Thursday's conference but we will all meet up soon to discuss the case once you've had a chance to read all the papers."

"Thursday, oh, I thought the conference was on Friday."

"No, I told your Clerks, it's Thursday 12th July at 6pm."

"Thanks Charles, it was probably a mix up in the Clerks room, glad you've phoned and I'll see you on Thursday. I should have had a chance to look at the papers by then."

They said goodbye, David thinking to himself, "Useless clerks, they can't even get the date of a Murder conference right."

He carried on reading the papers. There had been no point in telling Charles Rooney that he had read a significant amount of the brief to date, if he knew that David had time to read it straight away it would look like he had no work at all and Charles might begin to doubt his ability. He was not surprised that Charlotte would not be at the conference. She was a Barrister who like David had practiced at the independent Bar. She then took a job with Rooney Williams and became an employed Barrister. In the now distant past, only Barristers in independent practice, practising from Barrister's Chambers, had been able to conduct cases in the Crown Court. Now, to the horror of the independent Bar, Solicitor Advocates and employed Barristers were allowed to conduct such cases which had meant an erosion into the work of the independent Bar. The Criminal Bar, long used to being unable to organise itself to do anything other than enjoy a few parties, had not mounted any rear guard action against this attack on its work and had been forced to satisfy itself by moaning about the quality of in house advocates whether they be Solicitors or Barristers. If they were Solicitors they were not properly trained to conduct Criminal cases, if they were Barristers, they were incompetent and had failed to make it at the independent Bar. Of course the truth was different, there were very good Solicitor Advocates and good employed Barristers, there were bad ones too, but then the independent Bar had its fair share of poor Advocates. David had worked with Charlotte Williams on two previous occasions. He thought she was a perfectly competent Advocate and able when she was willing to work! She was able to draft perfectly good advices and applications for Silk certificates and could draft an excellent Defence Statement. She was also very attractive and excellent company and he knew he would enjoy sharing the odd bottle of Claret with her. She did of course have some failings. One of her major failings was her air of pessimism with clients that did not endear her to them as she appeared to think and express to them that they were all guilty. She had also changed her attitude to work since joining the employed Bar and she had a great reluctance to do any work even when she was requested to assist. David remembered the case of Connelly when he had asked her if she could draft a few pointers for his final speech. Her response had been,

"Surely you are able to think of enough points yourself without getting any assistance from me!"

She now seemed to think that working after 5pm was not part of her contract or professional duties. He never expected to see her at a conference in Belmarsh at 6pm on any day of the week.

He continued to delve into the papers. He read the statements of the Fire Brigade Officers who referred to arriving at the flat, putting out the fire and finding the body. Thomas Wardle, a fire fighter described his investigation of the flat and that how he considered there were two seats of fire. One was on the sofa in the living room, the other was also in the living room but in the area of the carpet by the window. The statement said that no accelerants could be detected. David had dealt with many Arson cases during his career and knew that the Prosecution would rely on the fact that there were two "seats of fire", as this suggested that the fire had been started in two places which tended to rule out an accidental fire. Most arsonists used an "accelerant" usually a fluid that burns easily, to help a fire start and take hold. The lack of an accelerant did not rule out arson but it made it less likely.

David continued with reading the papers and came across the statements of the paramedics who attended the scene as well as the Doctor who certified death at the scene. He then moved on to the report of the Prosecution pathologist. Dr Alistair Forsyth. He was aware of Alistair Forsyth's reputation as a no-nonsense type of witness. He was very able and tended towards being fair although he was slightly dogmatic in his approach. His 15 page report started in the usual way with a declaration about his qualifications and experience. He had the following degrees; Bachelor of Science, Bachelor of Medicine and Bachelor of Surgery and he held a Diploma in Medical Jurisprudence in Pathology and was a Fellow of the

Royal College of Pathologists. He was a Foundation Member of the Faculty of Forensic and Legal Medicine of the Royal College of Physicians of London. He had been involved in the study and practise of forensic pathology since 1997 and was admitted to the Home Office Register of Accredited Forensic Pathologists in 2002. Now he was working from an independent laboratory and he conducted work for both the Prosecution and the Defence. David knew his qualifications were unassailable and no one would seek to challenge his expertise. He had conducted a post mortem at 14-00 on 6th February 2012 and he listed in his report details about the height and weight of the body and then gave the names and the weights of all the organs that he removed. He concluded that Usman Hussain had not suffered from any natural disease that could have contributed to his death. There was no evidence of burns or inhalation of fire fumes and no "carboxyhaemoglobin was reported in the toxicological analyses", which meant that Usman Hussain was dead by the time the fire was started. He listed any old injuries that were discovered and then listed the 12 stab wounds and cuts that were found. Some of these were on the arms and hands and were "classic defence injuries" no doubt caused by Usman Hussain trying to protect himself against a knife-wielding assailant. From measuring the depth and height of the wounds he had concluded that the knife used to cause them was between 2 and 2.5cm in width and 12-13cm in length. He pointed out that this was an approximation because of the tendency of tissues to compress so deep wounds could be made by knives with short blades. He had been shown a knife produced by the Police from Usman Hussain's kitchen. He stated this knife could have caused the injuries. He noted that a number of the wounds were to the chest and had penetrated the chest cavity puncturing the left lung. One of the wounds showed that the knife had fractured the sternum and was then deflected through the rib-cage into the heart. He determined that this would have required severe force. One wound had penetrated the neck. Any one of a number of these wounds would have proved fatal. He concluded the injuries were consistent with one assailant using one weapon. He gave the cause of death as:

a. Shock and haemorrhage
b. Stab wounds to the chest and neck

David decided there was little headway to be made in relation to this report. In any event, the report merely indicated that a single person used a knife to kill Usman Hussain, it did not say who the killer was and it was equally consistent with both the Prosecution account and the account given by Damien in interview.

He continued reading over lunch as he wanted to get to grips with the papers and quite frankly he was enjoying the challenge after so long without a brief. A junior tenant, Wendy Pritchard, put her head round his door and asked if he wanted a sandwich as she was going out to get something to eat. He asked her for his favourite BLT sandwich and an orange juice and she kindly brought one for him which he ate as he continued reading his brief.

Now it was 4pm and he was beginning to tire a little from reading the papers. He decided to stretch his legs and go for a cup of tea and a carrot cake. He was firmly of the view that he deserved such luxuries on this day. He was leaving Chambers when he bumped into Wendy Pritchard again. She asked him where he was going and once he said he was going out for tea, she asked if he minded if she joined him. He could hardly refuse and as she was attractive and pleasant company and he could now answer questions about his practice as he was working on a murder, and he readily agreed.

They walked together down Middle Temple Lane and turned left into Crown Office Row opposite the Inner Temple Garden and then went to the Pegasus Bar where he ordered tea and toasted tea cakes. It was only a few minutes into the conversation when Wendy asked him what he was working on at the moment. He mentioned the murder case as if it was a daily occurrence that he was instructed on murders.

"Oh I'm just working on a murder at the moment. It's not particularly exciting, the Police say it's one crack addict killing another."

He gave her a rundown of the facts which he had learnt that day and told her he was leading an in-house Junior Advocate. He pointed out that he would rather lead a Junior from Chambers but had no choice in the matter. He then moved on to ask what Wendy was doing at the moment.

Wendy was 32 years of age, she had come to the Bar after first qualifying as a Solicitor and practicing in Criminal work in the Solicitors firm Thatcher and Cook. She had decided that she would rather be a Barrister than a Solicitor Advocate and when she was 25 she had converted from being a Solicitor to become a Barrister. She had still had to conduct a pupillage for 6 months but shortly after the completion of her pupillage she had been offered a tenancy in Temple Lane Chambers when she was 27. It had certainly assisted her application that Thatcher and Cook were one of the main instructing Solicitors to Temple Lane Chambers but David noted that in any event she had an excellent reputation in Chambers for someone so junior. She was rather busy as a Barrister and although the work was not of a very high quality, it was excellent for her call at the Bar, as she had been sensible enough to retain a good relationship with her old firm of Solicitors and they instructed her regularly.

Having consumed a pot of tea Wendy announced that she had to return to Chambers to prepare an Actual Bodily Harm (ABH) trial in Inner London Crown Court for tomorrow. David had actually enjoyed the interlude and was slightly reluctant to return to Chambers. Not only had he enjoyed Wendy's company, he had quite enjoyed the feeling seeing heads turn when he entered the Pegasus Bar with her. He had forgotten the last time that had happened to him, although the feeling of pleasure was slightly diminished when he heard the sotto voce comment about. "punching above his weight", that came from one corner of the bar.

He returned to Chambers with Wendy and they parted with her thanking him for the tea. She added,

"If you need any help on your murder case please do ask. I'd be really interested in helping out. It sounds to me like your man committed the murder and his best hope would be to plead to manslaughter on the basis of the new "loss of control provisions" under sections 54 and 55 of the Coroners and Justice Act 2009. I was reading the recent case of R v Clinton and others the other day and would love an opportunity to do some research for you."

He thanked her for her offer and decided that either she was sexually attracted to him and wanted to spend more time with him, a thought he dismissed almost immediately, when he looked at himself in the mirror and saw his bulging torso, or she was just a genuine decent person wanting to assist. More cynically he thought, she might simply want to progress in the profession and saw his patronage as useful.

In any event he would consider her offer. Charlotte Williams would only be willing to work from 9am to 5pm and would no doubt be incredibly busy in court during most of that time. Wendy's knowledge on "loss of control" may be useful. He knew the law of Provocation had changed as the Government had decided that the centuries old concept of Provocation was no longer relevant and needed replacing with a new concept, but he had not bothered to study it, nor would he bother until he had a case in that area. After all the Government seemed to enjoy bringing in new laws and then repealing them or amending them, there seemed little point in learning anything about them in detail until he had a case in that area as the law would probably change again soon.

He carried on reading the brief. He now reached the final witness statements which were mainly those of police officers. These were the officers who attended the scene in the early hours of 4th February and noted the position of the body. There were statements from the SOCOs who had visited Usman Hussain's flat and Damien's flat and there were statements from DS Monkton who had arrested and interviewed Damien. DS Monkton had made a number of statements starting with when he first met Damien, the account Damien gave, his doubts concerning inconsistencies in that account and the "rambling" nature of how Damien gave it and finally he had told Damien he would need to caution him as a suspect and interview him under caution. He stated that he had offered Damien a Solicitor but Damien had declined the offer until almost six hours into the interview. Further statements were provided from Police officers who had handed out questionnaires to people in the area over the next two weeks to see if they had seen Damien leaving the flat. Finally there were statements from Officers who had trawled through CCTV footage taken from cameras in the area between 23:00 on 4th February 2012 until 07:00 on 5th February 2012. They had done this to see if they could see Damien but had been unable to identify him. Finally he read a statement from an FME, a Forensic Medical Examiner, actually Dr Adrian Monkton a GP who had considerable experience in attending Police Stations and seeing injuries to detainees. He had attended the police station to see an injury that Damien had complained about in custody. He had a burn mark on the palm of his right hand. Damien had told him this had been caused the night before when he accidentally burnt himself smoking crack cocaine. Dr Monkton gave an opinion in his report to the effect that he had seen many burns in his life and he considered this was unlikely to have been caused by smoking crack cocaine but was more likely to have been caused by someone trying to start a fire and accidentally burning themselves in the process.

Having read these statements and added a few handwritten notes to Charlotte Williams' notes, he decided to call it a day and make his way home. He had missed most of the rush hour as it was now just after seven in the evening. He would return to Chambers the following day to read through the exhibits. Now all he needed was to get home, put his feet up and open another bottle of his favourite Rioja Reserva to toast his good fortune at being instructed on another murder case. From what he had read so far, he could see that his client Damien had several problems with his case. He would probably call on Wendy Pritchard's assistance, mainly because he had enjoyed her company, even though he could not see from what he had read how, "loss of control", could possibly be a defence in this case.

CHAPTER 3.

DELIBERATE FIRE?

He returned to Chambers on Wednesday morning having consumed a bottle and a half of red wine the night before. He had a slight hangover and decided that he really must limit himself to at most a bottle a night otherwise people might start to think he was an alcoholic. He had no doubt that quite a few already did! He got himself a coffee on the way to Chambers, he felt he could afford that expense and he went into Chambers, passed what appeared to be an incredibly busy Clerks' room and went to his room where he sat down at the desk and began to trawl through the Exhibits and the "Unused" material. This was more tedious than reading the witness statements but had to be done. In this case there were about 250 pages of Witness Statements and 450 pages of Exhibits and about 500 pages of "unused" material. "Unused" material simply means that it is "unused" by the Prosecution as part of their case and is served on the defence because it contains material that may assist the defence or may undermine the prosecution case. It was always a concern to members of the Criminal Bar that in some cases the unused material was the most voluminous material served. This was because the Graduated Fee payment system under which Barristers are paid, no payment is made for reading the Unused Material. Nevertheless it had to be read because often a Statement or an Exhibit would be found buried somewhere in the middle of these documents that really assisted the defence. Normally he would have expected his Junior to make a note of the most relevant documents but he noticed that Charlotte had not made any notes on this occasion.

David started by reading the Exhibits, these consisted of: the transcripts of 999 calls made by the various Tenants in the flats at around 7:00 am 5th February; pages of maps of the area and where the various CCTV cameras were located, diagrams of Usman Hussain's flat and where various items were found, photographs, "event logs" which had been compiled by Police officers who had viewed the CCTV footage from the various cameras at the scene and finally almost 400 pages of the original note of Damien's version of what had happened and transcripts of the interviews he had with police.

By lunchtime he had finished reading about half of the Exhibits. No one had offered to buy him a sandwich today so he decided to stretch his legs, leave the Temple by the Fleet Street entrance at the North end of Middle Temple lane and grab a sandwich at one of the many sandwich shops.

After a brief walk through the streets he came back to Temple Lane Chambers to continue with the reading of the Exhibits. By just after 6pm he had completed reading most of them. He had skim read quite a few as he had not needed to read them in any detail at this stage. He had noted how repetitive the interviews were with DS Monkton asking the same question time and time again. He decided to complete all the reading the following day in time for the 6 pm conference and he returned to his flat. This time he decided to take the night off from any drinking, to prove to himself, more than for any other reason, that he did not need alcohol. He decided to use the time fruitfully and put together a Chronology of useful times based on what he had read to date and which he knew would help with his preparation of the case.

CHRONOLOGY

03.02.2012

11:37 DAMIEN PHONES JENNY IN THE VICINITY OF WOOLWICH HIGH STREET

12:00 DAMIEN MEETS JENNY

12:00 GILLIAN BANKS ATTENDS MAGISTRATES COURT AND IS REMANDED IN CUSTODY

23:17 DAMIEN SENDS TEXT TO JENNY, "YOU FUCKING BITCH YOU LED ME ON." DAMIEN'S PHONE IN THE VICINITY OF UMRAN HUSSAIN'S FLAT

23:30 TIME DAMIEN STATES HE HAD FALLING OUT WITH JENNY; JENNY CLAIMS ATTEMPTED RAPE; DAMIEN ATTENDS CAMBRIDGE GARDENS

04.02.2012

ABOUT 00-00 GRAHAM STOREY HEARD A MAN SHOUTING UP TO USMAN HUSSAIN ASKING TO BE BUZZED IN OR HAVE THE KEYS THROWN DOWN

02:00 ALEXANDER MCDONALD HEARS LOUD NOISES FOLLOWED BY A SCREAM FROM USMAN HUSSAIN'S FLAT

03:00 – 04:00 AM GRAHAM STOREY HEARS LOUD NOISES COMING FROM USMAN HUSSAIN'S FLAT, SOUNDS LIKE USMAN HUSSAIN, A WOMAN AND A MAN.

04:30 ANNABELLE LYONS HEARS A SCREAM COMING FROM USMAN HUSSAIN'S FLAT

05:00 KAREN CLARKE HEARS WHAT SHE THINKS IS DAMIEN RETURN TO HIS HOME

05:21 DAMIEN'S PHONE CALLS CHRISTOPHER WHITE'S PHONE; DAMIEN'S PHONE IN THE VICINITY OF HIS MOTHER'S FLAT

06:00 KAREN CLARKE HEARS WHAT SHE THINKS IS DAMIEN LEAVING HOME

06:57 LEONARD FEELEY PHONES 999

07:00 FIRE BRIGADE AMBULANCE AND POLICE CALLED TO CAMBRIDGE GARDENS (BY WHOM?)

07-07 FIRE BRIGADE AMBULANCE AND POLICE ARRIVE AT CAMBRIDGE GARDENS

BODY FOUND

07:-15 PARAMEDICS CHECK THE BODY, BELIEVE HE HAS BEEN DEAD FOR POSSIBLY A COUPLE OF HOURS

07:30 ACCORDING TO CHRISTINE CLARKE, DAMIEN RETURNS HOME AGAIN

ACCORDING TO DAMIEN HE WASHES CLOTHES AND SHOWERS

12:32 DAMIEN PHONES CHRISTOPHER WHITE; PHONE IN THE VICINITY OF HIS MOTHER'S FLAT

14:00 DAMIEN CLARKE ATTENDS POLICE STATION AND GIVES HIS VERSION OF EVENTS "WHY HIM, WHY DID IT HAVE TO BE HIM?"

14:30 DAMIEN ARRESTED ON SUSPICION OF MURDER AND CAUTIONED

14:30 -20:30 INTERVIEWED BY DS MONKTON

21:30 CHARLES ROONEY ARRIVES AT THE POLICE STATION AND ADVISES DAMIEN NOT TO ANSWER ANY MORE QUESTIONS

22:30-00:10 DAMIEN CLARKE INTERVIEWED, MAKES NO COMMENT.

05.02.2012

10:00 DAMIEN CHARGED WITH MURDER, CAUTIONED AND SAID "I DIDN'T KILL HIM"

On the Thursday he returned to Chambers in the early morning and by lunch he had completed reading all the Exhibits and the Unused material. There had been little of much use in the Unused material save for one statement from a Forensic scientist, Helen Forster who specialised in the seats of fires. She stated that it was possible that there was only one seat of fire rather than two. She believed from her examination that the fires had started on the sofa and spread to the curtains rather than there be two seats of fire. She referred to the fact that the smoke detectors in the flat were disconnected (he had wondered why the smoking of crack cocaine had not set them off). She also stated that all the internal doors of flat number 6 were open at the time of the fire and this had allowed the smoke produced by the fire to spread freely throughout the flat. Importantly she noted that fires can either flame or they may smoulder. A smouldering fire can be caused by a carelessly discarded cigarette. This would smoulder for some time before taking hold and producing flames. The process could take between 30 minutes and a few hours depending on the material the sofa was made from and the amount of the ventilation. The more ventilation the quicker the fire would take hold and here there was a lot of ventilation because all the internal doors were open. A flaming fire on the other hand such as a deliberately started fire would soon take hold and develop rapidly particularly if there was an accelerant and good ventilation from open doors. She concluded that from her examination she could not say whether the fire was a smouldering or a flaming fire and therefore could not say whether it was accidental or deliberate.

David knew this was an important statement for the Defence. It was interesting that the Prosecution were putting forward a fire officer to give evidence that there was a deliberate arson with two seats of fire and discarding a Forensic Scientist who stated that the fire may have one seat of fire and have been accidentally started.

Having found this nugget of information he moved on to consider Damien's statement to his Solicitors, contained in a "proof of evidence" and his comments about Prosecution witnesses.

CHAPTER 4.

THE FIRST CONFERENCE WITH THE CLIENT

At 4:25pm David left Chambers armed with just his Witness Statement bundle and a selection of Exhibits including the Unused statement of Helen Forster. It was only to be a "meet and greet" conference but he wanted the client to know he had read all the papers and knew all the issues in the case at this early stage. He had a bad experience in the distant past of a Silk who had not even bothered to read any of his papers when he attended a murder consultation with David and a client in prison. David had been instructed as a Junior Barrister on a murder case and had read the papers and drafted an Advice on Evidence and an Advice stating that legal aid should be extended to cover Junior and Queen's Counsel at trial. He had thought that in the circumstances of the case they should have their own Forensic scientist instructed to give an expert report on the blood spattering to see if the Defendant's account was plausible. The Silk had attended the conference and said in front of the client that he did not consider such a report would assist at all, dismissing David's hard work in a few words. He had then demonstrated that he had not even read the papers when he said to the client, "this is a Murder where the victim was killed under a railway arch." David had looked at him aghast as the killing had taken place in a private house, miles away from any railway line. The Silk had simply smiled and asked a few anodyne questions. Then, just three weeks before the trial the Silk had phoned David to say that he thought, "this was a case where a forensic scientist should be instructed to give an expert report on the blood spattering to see if the Defendant's account is plausible" and could David draft such an Advice to extend legal aid to cover such an expert. David had pointed out as politely as he could that he had drafted such an advice two months earlier and sent a copy to the Silk. The Silk had replied "so you did my boy, so you did", but I suggest we update it and put both our names on it. An expert was duly instructed and his evidence helped secure the acquittal although there was considerable criticism from the Trial Judge as to why such an expert had not been instructed earlier. The Silk had explained to the Judge that he was not sure why that was and then turned to David sitting behind him, almost pointing to him to suggest it was David's fault. David had decided as a result that he would never advise any Solicitor to use that Silk again however good he was in Court. He had also decided that when given the opportunity he would read everything he could in a case to ensure he was never put in a similar position and have Junior Barristers refusing to recommend him to Solicitors.

He made his way towards Blackfriars station and then travelled to London Bridge where he changed trains to go to Woolwich. There he caught a cab to Her Majesty's Prison Belmarsh and started the lengthy procedure to get in to the maximum security prison. He got there well in time for the conference and then waited for Charles Rooney. Charles Rooney nonchalantly walked in at 6:15pm.

"Hello David, long time!"

David smiled at him and returned the greeting. There was no apology for being late but then he had not expected one. The Prison Guards made various noises about them being too late to get into Belmarsh now, but Charles' affable smile soon disarmed them and they were allowed in. However, after they had taken their jackets and shoes off to be x-rayed, had a rub down search and been transported through the various parts of Belmarsh to get to the legal visitors area, it was already 6:35pm and they only had 25 minutes or so with Damien before the Prison officers told them it was time to go.

Damien was already seated in the conference room when David and Charles Rooney arrived. David immediately introduced himself before sitting down.

"Good evening, Mr Clarke, my name is David Brant QC and I will be representing you at your trial. I'm sorry we won't have much time to discuss the case with you tonight as we have only been allotted a short time by the prison service and you know how long it takes to get through security at Belmarsh."

He thought it pointless to add that, "It's even shorter because your Solicitor was late!"

He continued,

"We all thought it important that I see you as soon as possible so we meet and briefly discuss the case and where we go from here."

There were then the pleasantries asking Damien how he was, was he getting enough social visits, how was his health, any problems he would like to share, before David decided to show off his knowledge of the case.

"Mr Clarke, or hopefully I can call you Damien?"

Damien nodded and smiled and David noted how he was missing all of his front teeth and what was left amounted to two brown little stumps at either corner of his mouth. He also noted the spider web tattoo on Damien's neck and the fading homemade tattoos on his arms, probably inflicted with a biro and a sharp point.

"Good, well Damien as you probably know I have been instructed by your Solicitor, Mr Rooney here of Rooney Williams to lead in your defence. I will be leading Ms Williams from Rooney Williams who I have worked with in the past but who unfortunately cannot join us tonight."

Again he decided it was best not to add, "because you can't get her to work after 5!"

He noticed how Damien grimaced a little at the name of Charlotte Williams and concluded she had probably already told him he had no chance of an acquittal and his best chance would be to plead.

"I have just received the papers in the last few days so I have not had an opportunity to consider them in as much detail as I would have liked but I have been assisted by Mr Rooney and by some very helpful notes that Ms Williams has drafted."

He noticed the grimace again when he used the name.

"I understand from your statement that you pleaded not guilty when the case came before the Court for a Pleas and Case Management Hearing, what we lawyers call a PCMH for short. I have read most of the papers in the case including your interview and the comments you have made to Mr Rooney here. I understand it's your case that you had nothing to do with this murder and in fact you were an innocent witness to a horrendous assault on your friend Usman Hussain."

Damien replied that was correct, he had not killed anybody nor had he set fire to the place and then he added.

"I hope you believe me, unlike that last brief who thought I was guilty."

David decided it was clear Charlotte had seen Damien and was up to her old tricks again. He also decided that there seemed little point in discussing the potential defence of "loss of control" so he would not be calling for Wendy Pritchard's assistance.

"Damien, I am sure Ms Williams was not expressing an opinion to you but pointing out some of the difficulties you may face at trial. It is better to be aware of these matters in advance, so that you are ready to deal with them."

Damien uttered some wholly incomprehensible grunt which David thought was probably better not repeated.

"Damien I have noticed one matter from the unused that I think is really quite helpful to you and it's a statement from a forensic scientist called Helen Forster. She states that the fire may have only started in one place and could have been accidental."

He noted how Damien's eyes looked up at this. Clearly no one had brought this unused statement to his attention so David was happy to obtain brownie points for being the first to spot this and bring it to Damien's attention.

The rest of the very short meeting went smoothly and the "meet and greet" appeared to have gone well from David's point of view. He and Charles Rooney then left the prison after travelling back through the various parts of Belmarsh prison. As David had travelled by train, Charles Rooney offered him a lift to Woolwich station from Belmarsh. They had a brief opportunity to discuss cases in the short drive to Woolwich, David pointing out that he had had a quiet patch but was busy at the moment. (He did not point out that the reason he was busy was because of this one case). He then turned to Charles Rooney and said,

"Charles, I was thinking, we never really celebrated our success in the Stan Connelly case. We should have a lunch together soon and perhaps celebrate this one as well."

David had thought it might be a good idea to mention a lunch now in the hope he could discuss any other Silk case Charles Rooney might have.

"Capital idea David, actually I am seeing a client in central London next Tuesday, 17th July in the morning, it's a fraud case and he has difficulty getting to my offices. Why don't we meet then."

David was actually taken aback, he meant a lunch sometime in the future, possibly even after this case was concluded. A lunch now and Charles Rooney might forget all about him by the end of this case. Still he had made the suggestion so he had no choice but to carry on with it.

"Excellent, I'll book a booth in Chez Gerard, in Chancery Lane for say 1pm on 17th July."

"Thanks David, I look forward to it."

David was dropped at Woolwich station and he caught the over ground into London and then home. He knew from previous experiences with the remarkably wealthy Charles Rooney, that it would be David's credit card that received a real bashing the following week.

CHAPTER 5.

LUNCH WITH THE INSTRUCTING SOLICITOR.

Tuesday 17th July started like most days in this remarkably wet July with moments of dryness sandwiched between drizzle and torrential rain. David went into Chambers and saw his Senior Clerk and mentioned that he had arranged lunch today with Charles Rooney. Then in an effort to ensure that John did not invite himself he said,

"John, I'm very grateful for this brief, you and I should enjoy a decent lunch soon as my treat, just have a look in your diary and mine and let's arrange a mutually convenient time."

He thought to himself, anytime was suitable for him as his diary was empty of cases until the Clarke case, but he had least had to pretend he might have some important appointments.

John thanked him and taking the hint that he wasn't invited, said,

"It's a pity you hadn't said before, I've arranged to see an important Solicitor who is down from the North today. I've been meaning to take Charles Rooney out to lunch as he has been kind to us recently. He's sent that Murder to you and he sent a Fraud in to Mr Wontner."

David, pricked his ears up at the word "fraud." Fraud cases which required Silks were invariably long, had a lot of documentation and often fell into the Very High Cost Cases (VHCC) category meaning that a Barrister got paid an hourly rate rather than a fee simply calculated on page length. He decided though that it did not seem appropriate to ask what the case was and look desperate so he simply smiled and left.

He had intended to book a table at Chez Gerard in Chancery Lane but when he tried he found it had closed down for refurbishment and had reopened as Brasserie Blanc. It demonstrated that he had not been out for many lunches recently. Nevertheless he decided to book the Brasserie Blanc and he arrived just before 1pm and was promptly seated at one of the tables on the ground floor. He seated himself facing the door so that he could see Charles Rooney when he came in. As he knew that Charles Rooney was always late he decided to order himself a drink whilst he waited, although diplomatically, he decided to order a sparkling water rather than anything alcoholic. He also ordered bread and olives so he had something to nibble on.

At 1:25pm Charles Rooney entered and gave him a wave. On this occasion he did give a half-hearted apology for being late, his meeting had gone on longer than he anticipated. David smiled and told him there was no problem. They then decided on what to order. David took the wine list and suggested that they have the Château Maris Old Vine Grenache. It was not the best wine he had ever ordered for a lunch with a Solicitor but he thought it would be impressive enough for this lunch. They both ordered Burgundian snails to start and rare fillet steaks for their main courses and then they settled down to the usual pleasantries. They asked about each other's families, they asked each other about the work the other was conducting. David gave his customary line about conducting a lot more Advisory work these days but how he still enjoyed the cut and thrust of a good murder.

"That's why I thought of you for this case David."

David, put his glass down of Chateau Maris Old Vine Grenache down and responded,

"You asked for me?"

"Oh yes, I rang your Senior Clerk John and told him that I had a couple of Silk briefs that needed placing. I mentioned the murder first and he jumped in and suggested your Head of Chambers, Wontner. I told him that I wanted you because you're a blood and guts man and you did an excellent job on Connelly last year. He kept on about Wontner being the man for the job until I told him that I had a Fraud case with a Silk certificate and I was thinking of Wontner because Fraud is his field."

David kept smiling at this revelation although inwardly he was annoyed. His Senior Clerk had pulled yet another stroke on him. The Solicitor was briefing him anyway on the case. There had been no directing the brief away from Wontner, quite the opposite, there had been an attempt to direct it away from him and he had promised to take his Senior Clerk out for a meal as a thanks!

He felt the corners of his mouth strain as he kept his false smile in place. He then relaxed it a little as he gripped his glass of wine just a shade more tightly than normal and took a large sip of what was described as the quintessential Grenache warmth. He decided to move on from this revelation and think how to deal with it at a later stage.

"Thanks for that Charles, although I don't want you thinking I only deal with blood and guts, I do have a considerable amount of experience in Fraud cases."

"Oh I know", replied Charles, finishing off his snails with relish and desperately trying to mop up all the garlic sauce with a small piece of bread.

"But I know how much you like blood and guts and I thought of you as soon as this chap was charged. In any event you've worked with Charlotte before and she really rates you. You know she can be a little difficult with a few leaders now and then and I always think it's important to put the right team together. Wontner is going to be leading Andy

Saville, who's a bright lad but doesn't have Charlotte's, shall we say, "feisty" temperament."

David thought, great, I lose out on a decent Fraud because I'm the only one who can get on with Charlotte. I wonder what would happen if I fell out with her, would I be busier?

"Of course Charles, you know I am always delighted to work with Charlotte. She brings a sound no-nonsense attitude to a case."

Charles Rooney paused before answering,

"Yes ...pity we can't get her to work more than 9-5 though."

David decided that there was no point in answering this criticism even though he had expressed the same to other Barristers, a knowing smile was all he managed.

The meal continued in this vein. Charles Rooney stated the firm was busy but apart from these two cases, the major work was simply not there anymore. The Police were not charging criminals, if they were they were charged with lesser offences in order to obtain a quick plea and all his other Fraud work involved "bail backs", clients being arrested and their documents then seized whilst they were released on bail to come back in say 6 months' time. He had despaired as to whether the client in the Fraud was going to be charged or "bailed back" again although he believed that the Police had to charge him as the case was getting very old.

They continued discussing the difficulties as a Criminal lawyer these days and whether there really was any future in either side of the profession.

"There's always going to be work David, people are going to commit crimes, people are going to get caught, people are going to be tried. My concern with this Government is that they have squeezed us dry with their austerity programme and I'm not sure what the future holds for any of us."

David agreed, although he noted he had received a lift in Charles Rooney's brand new Jaguar XJ motor car which he knew from brochures he had seen and rapidly discarded, cost in excess of £56,000. Charles had also told him about his four bedroomed villa quite near to his clerk John's villa, near Marbella, in Spain. Charles Rooney did not look like he would be appearing in a bankruptcy court anytime soon.

David offered a second bottle of the Chateau Maris Old Vine Grenache which Charles readily accepted. The lunch was pleasant and in view of the fact that Charles had instructed him on a murder and was showing an interest in instructing him in the future, he was happy to pay despite being close to his spending limit.

They said goodbye outside the restaurant and went off in separate directions. David wondered if there was any point confronting his Senior Clerk about taking credit for a case that went to David when in fact he had tried to steer it away from him. He decided, as he so often had in the past, that there was no point. John would simply deny it and he could hardly start an investigation as nothing would be achieved particularly as the Head of Chambers was being fed his work by the Senior Clerk. He thought it best to store this one up to be used in the future if that ever became necessary.

CHAPTER 6.

RENEWING AN ACQUAINTANCE.

It was 4:30pm on Friday 20th July, traditionally a time when most businesses are winding down for the weekend. In Temple Lane Chambers the Clerks room was actually at its busiest. Solicitors were phoning in about work for Monday, the Clerks were checking the latest lists to see if Crown Court trials had remained in the earlier lists or been moved to earlier or later times or removed from the lists altogether. They were also checking the Crown Court "warned list", cases that had no fixed dates for trial and were placed in a one week or two list meaning they could be called on any time during that period. Asif, the second Junior Clerk was sorting out work for the Pupils including checking who was on the Saturday rota. Some unlucky Pupil would be giving up a Saturday to spend in some Magistrates Court somewhere in the South East of England. They were phoning Tenants with the time of their cases listed for Monday and Members of Chambers were also coming into the Clerk's room checking to see if they were in Court on Monday or to check who was covering one of their cases on Monday whilst they were conducting some other case.

John Winston was on the phone, busy in conversation with Graham Martin, a Senior Tenant and would frown every time a Member of Chambers came into his room. He had specifically asked that Barristers did not come into the Clerks room and bother the Clerks at the busiest time of the day. The Head of Chambers had sent a global email to everyone in Chambers telling them not to go into the Clerks room between 3-30pm and 5-30pm on Fridays unless it was a matter of urgency and yet Members of Chambers were still coming in to make ridiculous requests, such as could a Junior Clerk go out and buy some milk so they could have a cup of tea. Ignoring the Member of Chambers who had just made this request he continued with his conversation,

"Yes Sir, I appreciate they owe you a lot of money. I spoke to Alan, the Senior Partner and he said he knows he owes you a lot but he said he is going to sort payment out for most of the cases next week, he wants you especially to cover this case because he believes it's going to be a big one and he wants you to lead on it once the certificate is changed to two Juniors. No, I know you've heard all that before but this time I think he means it. Well Sir, I haven't got anyone else who they will accept, I know Northampton Crown Court is a long way to go for a Mention but I'd treat this as a loss leader. I really think he means it this time. OK, thanks for that Sir, the papers are in your tray."

John put the phone down and said to no one in particular, but now in the absence of any Barristers,

"The trouble with some Barristers is they actually believe they are good at what they do."

Tony smiled, he had learnt a lot from John over the years and he believed he was ready to take over from him when the time came for his inevitable push into retirement. Here was another example of John's considerable advocacy being able to persuade a Senior Member of Chambers to go all the way to Northampton on a Monday, on a "bog standard" Mention for a dodgy Solicitor who never seemed to pay private fees, but who provided Chambers with a relatively significant amount of good quality legal aid work. He thought that John should have been a Barrister with such advocacy skills but then John would never have been willing to take the pay cut.

Tony finished his conversation on the phone and spoke to John.

"John, Mr Brant's case is in on Monday in the Bailey for a Mention. Apparently the CPS has not served documents they promised to serve and the Solicitors want someone to chase them up. Charlotte Williams has a case in the Warned list so she can't do it and they have no one else in the firm available. They don't want us to instruct a Junior to cover it and they've asked if Mr Brant is available."

"Shit", was John's somewhat laconic and unhelpful reply.

He then added, "I've just spent a huge amount of my time persuading a bloody Junior to cover a Mention. Am I now expected to use what little energy I've got left persuading a Silk to do a Junior's Mention. Won't they accept a Junior Counsel?"

"No, something like they don't want to be responsible for the fees."

John now understood the problem. Under the Graduated Fees system there was no payment for these Mentions. The Barrister who conducts the trial has to pay a sum out of his fee to anyone who attends on his behalf. As the Solicitors were using in-house Counsel they would lose up to £100 if a Junior went along whereas if David Brant QC turned up they would lose nothing.

"Alright Tony, could you get Mr Brant on the phone and I'll break the good news to him"

Tony managed to get David in a few minutes. Unused to many calls from his Chambers these days, David answered the phone quickly just in case it was news of some major case for which his services were required. After a quick hello Tony immediately put him through to John. He could have dealt with the issue but as far as he was concerned that was the job of a Senior Clerk and he was not on that pay grade yet.

John started off with a few pleasantries and then moved on to discuss Charles Rooney.

"I hear Sir that your lunch went very well. He was quite happy you paid for him and bought him a good lunch. He told me he is certainly going to bear you in mind for future Silk work and indeed he told me there are one or two potential cases brewing at the moment."

Interesting, thought David, he never told me about any brewing cases.

"Anyway Sir, the situation is this. There's been a bit of a cock up at the Solicitors. They've listed your case on Monday for an argument on disclosure. Obviously it needs someone who is involved with the case to attend. Charlotte Williams was lined up to do the appearance but she's gone part-heard in a trial and can't get out even though she has tried. They really want a heavy weight application and they have asked you if you would mind doing it as a favour. I think it's an excellent opportunity. They really will be grateful and I'm sure they will think of you next time they have a Silk brief. In any event you'll finish before lunchtime and we can have that lunch we mentioned."

David wondered at modern science and that an apparatus as simple as a telephone designed purely with hearing in mind, could also activate his sense of smell! It was giving off a distinct odour now! Here he was, thirty years at the Bar, he was being asked to do an application which realistically should be done by his Junior, he would not receive a fee for it and worse, he would be forced to buy his Clerk an expensive meal as a token of gratitude for a case that the Clerk had tried to steer away from him!

However, he had nothing in his diary and it might not hurt to be seen down at the Old Bailey and do a favour for the Solicitors even though he doubted they had anything "brewing" and he doubted they would even recall the favour five minutes after the appearance had finished.

He agreed to appear at the Mention on Monday and asked which Court and who the judge would be.

"It's Court 10, first on at 10:00am, His Honour Judge Tanner."

"Tanner", replied David.

"You know him Sir, he's not been sitting long in the Bailey."

"Yes, I know him, he used to be my Pupil-Master."

John thought for a minute, he had remembered the names of all the Judges invited to David's party when he got Silk and he did not remember HHJ Tanner being invited.

"I didn't know that Sir, did he come to your Silk party?"

"No he did not. He was not invited."

"Oh, I see Sir."

Suddenly John became interested, here was an interesting nugget of information. David Brant and his Pupil Master had not got on, he wondered why?

They arranged lunch for Monday at the Savoy Grill. David put the phone down. Another expensive day ahead, thought David, and I have to deal with HHJ Tanner.

It had been thirty years ago that David did his Pupillage at the Chambers of Lord White QC, at Boswell Chambers. He still remembered his six months there as an awful time full of horrible memories. Most people who have taken A Levels spend many years suffering from nightmares about turning up late to examinations or not having revised enough. In fact, David still occasionally had nightmares about taking his Geography A Level even though he had never taken Geography A level. However, for the first few years of practice at the Bar, his worst nightmares had been about his six month pupillage at Boswell Chambers.

The main way to become a Barrister in his day back in the 1970s had been to take a Law Degree for three years, hopefully obtain a respectable 2(2), or "drinking degree", then do the one year Bar Course at the Inns of Court School of Law. After obtaining the qualification of "Barrister" he then had to conduct a 12 month pupillage before he could become a "Tenant" in a set of Chambers. The pupillage was formed of two parts, the first six months involved following a Barrister around and watching what he did in Court, learning from the hands of an experienced Barrister. The second six months he still had to follow a Barrister around but was allowed to conduct cases and so hopefully would spend more time learning on his feet rather than beneath the feet of another. He had been given a 12 months pupillage in Boswell Chambers. His first six months was to be with Henry Tanner, a young up and coming Barrister. He had then been told by Henry he would have a further six months with another member of his Chambers. He had attended his first day of pupillage full of hope and believing that he had managed to get onto the first rung of the ladder.

He had arrived in Boswell Chambers one September morning to discover that his Pupil Master was conducting a case in Norwich and he was not expected to follow him but could get on with some papers on his desk. He was directed to Henry Tanner's desk and left there. The first week passed and next to no one had said anything to him. He had read all the papers he could find on Henry's desk and had put pen to paper in relation to a few, but in three days he was bored. There had been no communication from his Pupil Master and virtually no communication from anyone else in Chambers. This surprised him a little as the Chambers had a reputation for being left-wing and he assumed that left-wing sets would treat Pupils better than the Establishment sets. He soon decided that this was not the case. Before joining the set he had watched Lord White QC on television talking about how proud he was representing the common downtrodden man in the battle against the full weight of the State. After a short time in Chambers he decided that Lord White might be proud to represent the common downtrodden man, he certainly did not want to socialise with one though! As a Pupil in those Chambers David likened himself to a box of growing mushrooms, which had been shoved into a dark corner and fed a diet of manure.

By the end of the first week he had started to sneak out of Chambers and go to Niblett Hall, the student hall for Members of the Inner Temple, the Inn he had joined when he was at University and where he could purchase sandwiches and/or coffee cheaply. No one had actually seen him leave and he presumed no one would notice that he had gone. There he met the Inner Temple Student Officer who politely asked him how his Pupillage was going. He told her truthfully that it seemed a complete waste of time. He had not seen his Pupil Master, he had exhausted all the work he had to do, only a couple of Members of the Chambers had spoken to him and their conversations had been limited to the word "Hello." He pointed out his only hope was to survive six months of boredom and then he could conduct cases himself.

After the only enjoyable conversation he had during the week he returned to Chambers. He had not been gone for more than two hours but when he returned he discovered that Henry Tanner had returned from Norwich with a conviction in his case and was in a foul mood and was looking for him.

He returned to Chambers to be treated like he was being Court-Martialled for stealing the army silver. Why had he left the chambers without checking with the Clerks? Why had he been away so long? Why had he not checked with the Clerks to see if there were any papers in the Clerks room for Henry that he could have worked on? If he wanted to have a future at the Bar he would have to pull his socks up.

Having taken this dressing down in front of other Tenants and Pupils, he wanted to fight back and point out that he had been left on his own for a week without enough work, no one had talked to him, no one had told him that there were papers in his Pupil Master's pigeon hole that needed looking at and he had only popped out for lunch. However, he could see that Henry, member of the National Council of Civil Liberties, Member of Amnesty International, left wing supporter of the common man was not particularly interested in the concept of a fair trial for Pupils and he decided that his best course would be to apologise which he did.

His pupillage had got off to a bad start and it got worse over the next three months. He followed his pupil master around from Court to Court, travelling to St Albans in Hertfordshire, Ipswich in Suffolk, Canterbury in Kent and Aylesbury in Buckinghamshire. He had to fund his travel himself even though he was not earning any money in his first six months Pupillage and Henry, despite his left wing ideals was not renowned for his munificence. He recalled Henry buying him a coffee once when a Solicitor had been present. It had probably not been helpful that he had looked shocked by this sudden act of generosity and the Solicitor had of course noticed.

At the end of three months when they were both in Henry's room in Chambers, Henry had suddenly turned to David and said,

"Have you sorted out a second six months pupillage?"

This was the first time this had been mentioned since his first interview and he said,

"I thought I was going to do my second six months here."

Henry looked at him with as much scorn as he could muster, and that was a lot and he said simply,

"No, no."

David was horrified. He had planned to conduct a second six months pupillage in Boswell Chambers, then apply for a tenancy there and hopefully start his career there, but all that had just been dashed. He asked if Henry minded him leaving for the day as he now had to sort out a second six months pupillage. Henry, who was clearly glad to get rid of him, readily agreed.

David had no idea where to start looking for a second six months pupillage but fortunately he met a Senior member of the Bar called Jeremy Hines at a student party who said if he ever needed help, just contact him. He phoned Jeremy that day and by one of those happy coincidences that occasionally happen, Jeremy had been in Court with Simon Peters, another Senior member of the Bar who had said he was looking for a Pupil. An interview of sorts was arranged that day and within ten minutes of meeting, David was offered his second six months pupillage. He could have gone home but David could not resist returning to Henry's Chambers the same day to announce that he had sorted his second six months pupillage.

Henry looked shocked at this announcement that anyone could arrange a pupillage in just one day and all he could say was,

"So soon?"

To which David proudly replied, "Oh yes" which had no doubt caused Henry to detest him even more than before.

Within three months David left Henry's Chambers and had little further contact with him. He recalled sending him a letter a couple of years later when he was still looking for a tenancy and asking if Henry could assist. Henry just ignored the letter. He then bumped into Henry at Court three weeks after sending the letter and Henry told him he had received the letter and was wracking his brains as to how he could assist. Of course no assistance was forthcoming and David later discovered, when he was finally offered a tenancy, that Henry had been giving him bad references for the last two years! As a result he had steadfastly ignored Henry Tanner whenever he had met him in the future. He noted when Henry became a Judge and thought it amusing to see that a renowned far left wing lawyer, who had refused to Prosecute whilst in practice, was now a Judge whose reputation was that he was incredibly Prosecution-minded.

Now, having avoided Henry Tanner for over thirty years, he would have to appear in front of him. Perhaps more galling, he would be expected to show him due deference by calling him "My Lord" as all Bailey Judges had to be addressed. At least it was only for a Mention that would take no more than about half an hour but he did not relish the prospect of seeing him.

CHAPTER 7.

THE POINTLESS HEARING.

On Monday 23rd July 2012 at 9am David arrived at the Bailey and queued outside the main entrance with the other Court users, namely, Counsel, Solicitors, Police Officers, Witnesses and Defendants who all use the same entrance. The weather had changed recently and it was a pleasant day. He went through Security and made his way to the 4th floor where he signed himself in on the Court computer and went into the Silk's robing room. He changed into his Silk robes and as he had an hour before the hearing he decided to treat himself to a Bailey breakfast and a coffee in the Bar Mess on the fifth floor. He saw a number of familiar faces who asked how he was doing and made the usual complaints about the state of the Bar and legal aid fees. He joined in the conversations with the usual enthusiasm as he finished his cooked breakfast. He did not see his opponent in the Bar Mess and so when he finished a second coffee, he made his way to Court 10 at 9:40am.

There he met Prosecution Counsel, who was dealing with the hearing before starting a trial at 10-30pm. It was Timothy Arnold, a Barrister of about 15 years call who had been appointed a

Junior Treasury Council a few years earlier. Treasury Council are appointed by the Government to prosecute serious cases, especially cases in the Bailey. It was a prestigious position and was much sought after as it invariably guarantees a good quality and quantity of Prosecution work.

"Hello David, what are you doing here? You're not covering this Mention are you?"

David smiled at him, noticing the implicit criticism of any Silk attending such a pointless hearing.

"Hi Tim, yes I am covering it, my instructing Solicitors and I consider issues of disclosure to be very important in cases like this and thought it appropriate that I attend to deal with the outstanding issues."

"I'm a little surprised David as the CPS wrote to your Solicitors early last week. We have complied with the vast majority of their requests and have told them we will be in a position to deal with the rest by 4pm Friday of this week. They even acknowledged our letter."

David smiled again, trying to demonstrate that he was aware of all these matters even though in fact his Solicitors had merely sent him copies of the requests they had made three weeks earlier and had not supplied any replies from the Crown nor even indicated there was a response.

"Tim, I understand all that, but we are concerned at how long this disclosure is taking. All of the items on our list should have been disclosed well before our request and we just want to set a timetable that the Prosecution will adhere to."

Tim Arnold had no problem with this and as he was keen to get back to his trial he agreed a timetable for the disclosure.

At 10:10am His Honour Judge Henry Tanner came into Court. David smiled at him a pleasant smile even though inwardly his mind went back thirty years to the day he thought his career had ended.

Tim Arnold made the necessary introductions to the Judge and David made a perceptible nod of his head when his name was introduced. His Honour Judge Tanner looked at him with his usual world weary scowl, without a single hint of recognition.

Tim Arnold outlined the brief facts of the case and pointed out how it was agreed between the parties that there should be an Order for the service of the outstanding disclosure and then sat down.

His Honour Judge Tanner, turned to David and said,

"Mr Brent, sorry Mr Brant is it, I don't usually expect to see Queen's Counsel on applications like this. Was your attendance really justified on a Mention that has been agreed between the parties?"

David of course stood as he was addressed and answered shortly,

"My Lord, should rest assured that as no fee is payable for today's appearance, there has been no strain on the public purse by the Defence. In any event we have agreed a timetable but disclosure is, as my Lord knows, an important issue, particularly in a serious case like this and there may well have been matters that needed to be aired in front of your Lordship. Fortunately, due to Mr Arnold and myself being able to agree matters, we do not need to take up any further of your Lordship's time by asking my Lord to rule on any matter."

His Honour Judge Tanner's scowl never left his face. He never acknowledged David's presence or showed any recognition of him, although David felt that the deliberate mispronunciation of his name was probably some acknowledgment that he remembered David.

David returned to Chambers after the hearing to discover that lunch had been cancelled with John Winston because he had to see a Solicitor and deal with a "pressing matter." David wondered why he had even bothered to get out of bed that day. The hearing had been totally unnecessary despite what he had said and it surprised him that no one had bothered to tell him that the Prosecution had agreed to disclose the items the Solicitors requested. He almost felt that he had come full circle from his Pupillage days when half of his Court appearances appeared unnecessary.

He remembered in the early days of his Pupillage he was told by his Clerks to go to a place called Godstone Magistrates to conduct a remand hearing, effectively a simple hearing where the parties would simply turn up so that the Court could see the Defendant. He had never heard of Godstone Magistrates Court and neither had anyone else in his then Chambers. There was no Court Guide or Internet in those days and the brief was simply a piece of paper typed by the clerks saying, "In the Godstone Magistrates Court", giving the name of the client and the Solicitors details and nothing else. He had tried to find out where Godstone Magistrates Court was the night before by looking on a map for Godstone. He discovered that there was an Upper and a Lower Godstone but could not see where the nearest railway station was so he phoned British Rail. They suggested he catch a train to a place called Oxted. He was concerned about arriving miles away from the Court so he checked the map again and found a station called Lower Godstone and he decided to travel there hoping the Magistrates Court would be nearby.

The next morning he set out early in case he had problems finding the Court. He recalled it was a bright hot Summer's day and he was wearing the only suit he possessed. It was a thick woollen suit which kept him lukewarm in winter and boiling hot in summer. He arrived at Lower Godstone and left the train at about 9am. He was surprised to find he was on a platform in the middle of the countryside with no buildings visible. He left the "station", which in fact was just the platform and walked down a slope feeling he was in the middle of fields. Fortunately, he saw a Newsagent in the distance which appeared to be the only shop around and he made his way towards it. He went in and joined a short queue of people who were buying newspapers. He wondered where they had all come from because there did not seem to be any houses around. After what seemed ages he came to the head of the queue and asked where the Godstone Magistrates Court was. The proprietor looked at him quizzically as though he had asked where the Great Pyramid of Giza was located. She then announced she had never heard of it. The sole remaining customer in the shop asked if he was looking for Upper Godstone as the Magistrates Court may be there and he politely asked how to get there. She announced there was one bus an hour and pointed him to the nearest bus stop in a nearby country lane. He quickly ran to the nearest bus stop and was gratified to see that the next bus was in 20 minutes, at least he had not missed it. He waited about 40 minutes with mounting panic, there were no mobile phones and there was no telephone box around and he dare not leave the bus stop in case he missed the bus and had to wait another hour. Eventually the bus arrived and he asked the driver where Godstone Magistrates Court was. Again he was met with a bemused look and the answer was the driver did not know but would drop David off at the bus station in Upper Godstone so he could ask someone there. David was now seriously beginning to panic. He recalled all the stories he had been told on the Bar course that there was no excuse for lateness at Court and he could be reported to the Bar Council if he was late. He was already late for a 10-00 hearing and he still had no idea where the Court was.

After what seemed like hours to him but was probably only 20 minutes or so, the bus arrived at Upper Godstone bus station. He got off, thanking the bus driver and found a ticket inspector in the bus station and immediately and breathlessly asked him where Godstone Magistrates was. He announced with a look as if, how anyone could not know, that it was in Oxted, 3 or 4 miles away. Now in desperation, he asked him how he could get there. The Inspector, smiled at him and helpfully stated that there was a bus that went straight there which started at this bus station. David, feeling perceptibly relieved asked him when the next bus was and the Inspector stated,

"Oh, you've just missed one, but there is one in another hour."

David, was now panic stricken, thinking his career was over, Chambers would never forgive him for being late and letting a client down and the Bar Council was probably already drafting disciplinary proceedings. It was about 10-15am and he decided he had better try and make his way to Oxted. He could not wait another hour for a bus so he started walking then running towards Oxted. His heavy woollen suit was now making him feel like he was in a mobile sauna. He noticed a car passing so he decided to thumb a lift for the first time in his life, thinking no one would take pity on some idiot in a dark suit running up a country lane in the Middle of Summer. However, much to his surprise a kind driver stopped. David asked him if he knew where Godstone Magistrates Court was and met the by now usual response that he did not know, but the driver would give him a lift to Oxted Police station and the Police would undoubtedly tell him where he was. David inwardly cursed himself. If he had phoned the local police station the night before he would have found out where Godstone Magistrates Court was and saved himself the agony of the last hour or so. Nevertheless, he felt better, his career was saved, he would arrive in Oxted in the next 15 minutes or so and only be about 30 minutes late to Court.

About 15 minutes later the kind driver dropped David at the police station and to his delight he could see that the Magistrates Court was part of the same building. He had made it. It was only just after 10-30 and he was sure that there would be other cases and his would be reached later. He slowed down, pulled at his jacket, tried to calm himself down and look more like a Barrister than some demented mad man and he walked towards the Court entrance. He arrived and stopped dead in his tracks. There were iron bars across the entrance and they were padlocked. He hoped the Magistrate Court had not sat, found he was not there and then adjourned for the day and he went next door to the police station to find out what had happened. There he saw a Police Custody Sergeant, who looked up quizzically as David came up to him. He was clearly not used to seeing people in heavy dark woollen suits in this Police station. David asked if next door was the Godstone Magistrates Court and the Police officer told him it was. David then asked him what time the Magistrate Court opened. The Officer looked at David as if he was mad and told David the news that Godstone Magistrates Court only sat a few days a week and was not sitting again until the next day!

David almost collapsed at the news. He had almost killed himself trying to get to the Court and now he found some idiot had given him the wrong day. He found a telephone box and called Steve, his then Senior Clerk about what had happened. Steve in a completely offhand way said, "Well, the solicitors told us it was today.", and then apparently turning to the Junior Clerk, John, he said, "Isn't that right John." David had no need to wait for an answer as within a few weeks of joining his new set as a Pupil he knew the Junior Clerk would always agree with the Senior Clerk. It seemed to be an unwritten term of employment in a Junior Clerk's contract. David had no idea whether it was the Clerks' fault or the Solicitor's fault and of course it did not matter. He was only a Pupil and no one was going to apologise to him and of course he was not going to be paid for a pointless day nor would his expenses be reimbursed to him.

David, smiled at this memory, although today had been a waste of time at least it was nowhere near as bad as his experiences had been when he was a Pupil.

CHAPTER 8.

FURTHER EVIDENCE.

The following Monday, 30th July, David rose at 10:00am, getting used to the lack of trial work, he was spending longer in bed. At 10:30am, having finished a light and unappetising breakfast he received a call on his mobile phone. It was from Charlotte Williams, his Junior in the case of Damien Clarke. He got over his shock that she had phoned him at all and answered her call.

"Hello Charlotte, how are you, it's been a long time."

"I'm fine David", she replied, immediately dispensing with pleasantries.

"Have you seen the latest Unused Material served by the Crown."

David was pleasantly surprised that Charlotte had considered it part of her job description to read the Unused Material.

"No Charlotte, anything interesting."

"Yes, the Police have apparently located the girl called "Babs" or "Babe" and interviewed her. She has a string of convictions for drugs and prostitution and a couple for violence. She says she was at the flat the night Usman was killed. There were two other men there as well at one stage and she says there was an attempt to rape her but that it was Damien who tried to rape her. She claims she fought him off and left the flat with her clothes torn. She says the other two men actually tried to help her! "

Great, David thought, Babs/Babes corroborates his story about two men being there but alleges Damien is the rapist and claims that instead of attacking her, the men tried to help her!

"Charlotte, you said it's Unused Material, why are the Prosecution not using it."

"Apparently, according to the notes of the officer who interviewed her, she gave three different versions of what happened that night during the first thirty minutes of questioning. First she claimed she wasn't at the flat, then she claimed that Damien had attempted to rape her outside the flat and finally she said, she remembered clearly that Damien tried to rape her in the flat. They don't think she would make a reliable witness so they've decided to put her in the Unused Material, kindly offering us the opportunity to call her if we wish."

"Oh right, well that's kind of them! We're really going to call someone who is unreliable and alleges our client tried to rape her!"

"Obviously, David. More interestingly, the Prosecution has also served two further expert reports. It's another reason they are probably not relying on Babe's statement. It doesn't fit in with their latest Forensic evidence. They've served an expert on bloodstaining named Roger Allbright who points out where the blood stains were throughout the flat. He concludes that the Murder took place in the lounge as there were very few stains in the bedroom and a great deal in the lounge. They've also served a statement from an expert in "footwear intelligence".

"Really", David replied, it never ceased to amaze him, how every time he conducted a case there was a new name for some area of forensic expertise.

"Yes, his name is Geoffrey Turnton. He studied all the footprints found in the flat. He was supplied with copies of the footprints of the Fire Officers, the Paramedics and the Police and he eliminated any footprints he found in sooty deposits from the fire. He then checked for footprints he found in the blood stains or any footprints that left bloody stained marks under the soot level. Obviously he concluded that any footprints in the soot layer came after the fire and would be from people entering the flat after the fire. Any footprints found in the blood stains or any bloody foot prints found under the soot level must have been created after Usman was stabbed and therefore must have been created by the assailant or someone who was present during the murder. He found that there were twelve such prints. Two of those prints were too smudged to make out any marks but the other ten all contained the same marks, namely a star or part of a star pattern. These he has traced to a style of trainer called "Star 'D' Sprints." He concludes from measurements that it is likely that only one pair of such trainers made all these marks by someone whose shoes were in the range of size 7.5-9.5. He therefore concludes there was only one person in the flat after the murder had taken place and guess what? Damien Clarke's shoe size is an 8."

"Why is there such a range in the size of the shoe?"

"He says that this particular manufacturer uses the same sole size on different sizes of upper so that there can be a range of different shoe sizes leaving roughly the same size sole print."

"Thanks Charlotte, that rather hurts our defence that there were two other people in addition to Damien present at the time of the Murder. Were any of these types of shoes found at Damien's flat when a search was made?"

Charlotte paused before answering, "I've checked through the Exhibits list and the search record and there is reference to one set of trainers being taken from him on arrest but there is no reference to what type they were or what the soles look like."

"Thanks, we could of course ask the Prosecution to tell us what they were but that might result in a bit of an own goal!" "I agree David, I can always look at the Exhibits at Court although I can't believe the Prosecution would not have checked Damien's trainers."

David remembered his days of prosecuting as a Junior and the occasions when the Crown Prosecution Service not only forgot to check important pieces of evidence but sometimes forgot to instruct Counsel to attend Court. It tended to be on minor cases but he remembered frequently attending Isleworth Crown Court at 9:00 am to pick up papers for a Crown Court trial that was starting at 10:15am. He remembered that just as frequently he would wait until 9:30am before anyone attended from the Crown Prosecution Service with papers and how he then had less than 45 minutes to read all the papers, prepare an opening speech to the Jury and decide what order to call the witnesses. At least in those days he had not had to spend most of the night preparing a case.

"I know Charlotte, it's hard to believe that such a basic mistake could be made but then we've both witnessed bigger mistakes being made."

It was agreed that David would receive a copy of these papers shortly and they would have another conference with Damien (Charlotte's first) to raise this new evidence with him.

On Tuesday 31st July David made his way into Chambers at lunchtime in order to pick up the new papers that had been served and also to avoid his cleaner Mary, who still grinned at him every time she came to visit the flat on Tuesdays. The London Olympics had started and, for added security during this period, the Inns of Court had insisted that the front doors of each Chambers be locked. He also noticed that quite a few Belgians were using the Temple because their team was staying there. This had the advantage that more Belgian beer was being stocked in the local bars, a tipple that David thought was so much better for him than El Vinos Claret.

He went into Chambers, said "hello" to the Clerks, who looked as busy as ever, glued to their computer screens and then having picked up the newly served papers he went to his room to read them. He found little of interest in them save for Bab's statements to the officers. He also read the forensic evidence of Roger Allbright and Geoffrey Turnton which he found more interesting. Charlotte had given an accurate summary of the evidence although she had not mentioned one or two interesting facts.

Roger Allbright described the positioning of blood staining, pointing out the different types of bloodstains he found in the flat. He had found; "transfer bloodstaining" caused by a bleeding person or object wet with blood coming into contact with another surface, "drip bloodstains" caused by blood dripping from a person or off a weapon which creates drip bloodstains on floors or other surfaces, "spattered bloodstains", caused when force is applied to wet blood which can cause the blood to break up and form into droplets that become airborne and fly away from the source of bloodstaining, "cast off pattern bloodstaining" caused by a bloodied object such as a hand being swung through the air and causing blood spots to land on walls, ceilings and furniture. The soot deposits in the flat had been removed by the use of liquid latex which had been applied to areas and then lifted when dry, removing the layer of soot and allowing bloodstains to be seen and measured. David noted his conclusions were that the Murder took place in the lounge but that there were significant spots of blood found in the hallway which suggested to the expert that force was applied to a source of wet blood resulting in airborne droplets which hit the walls. It suggested that some blows into an already bleeding Usman may have taken place in the hallway. David noted that his instructions to date from Damien could not account for this.

Geoffrey Turnton's statement contained a couple of plan exhibits showing where the blood stained footprints were found. Noticeably, six were found in the living room including the ones without any discernible marks, two more were found in the hallway, two more in the main bedroom and two in the kitchen. All had been treated with chemicals to trace small amounts of blood. Leuco crystal violet which reacts to small amounts of blood not necessarily visible to the eye had been used. This produced a deep purple colour when it reacted with blood. Acid violet was a dye that was used to stain the proteins in blood and produce a violet product when blood was discovered. Finally, Luminol a chemical reagent was used which reacted to non-visible blood stains and produced a blue green glow that could be seen in dark environments. Photographs were produced of the various areas before the chemicals were applied, photographs were then taken of the areas with the chemicals applied and finally composite photographs of the area before and after the chemical was applied were produced. It was noticeable to David that it looked like the footprints left a trail from the lounge to the bedroom where Usman's body was found.

He turned to the rest of the evidence that had been served which was mostly continuity evidence from the police, statements showing which exhibit was found and by whom, where it was taken after it was found and who then passed it on to Forensic scientists. He then found a further statement from a Doctor Wakeley at Queen Elizabeth Hospital who saw Damien a few days after his arrest when he was complaining about the burn to his hand. According to the Doctor, Damien told him that the burn had been caused by someone holding his hand over the naked flame of a lighter. The Doctor stated that from what he saw, the injury could have been caused in that way.

Clearly he would have to see Damien and see whether he had any explanation for this new evidence.

CHAPTER 9.

THE FURTHER CONFERENCE AND THE "ART EXHIBITION."

On Thursday 2nd August at 1pm David made his way to Belmarsh prison again. He arrived in time for a coffee and a Cheese and Ham toastie in the Visitor Centre, which would have to be a substitute for lunch. He noted that a Conference had been arranged for 2pm today, no doubt so Charlotte could get home sometime around 5pm.

The first to arrive was Charles Rooney, who was surprisingly early arriving at 1:50pm. Charlotte arrived a few minutes later. David offered them both a coffee which they declined and they all signed in and went through the Security checks to see Damien.

After Charlotte was introduced and the usual pleasantries about how Damien was, locked up in a maximum security prison. David mentioned that new evidence had been served and they would need some instructions. Damien said he had seen the material and was happy to deal with any issues raised.

David noticed that, although Damien was sporting a "prison tan", which is the distinctive pallor of someone who does not see the Sun often, he was generally looking a lot better than when they first met. Prison was almost agreeing with him, possibly because, although drugs are available in most prisons, Damien would not have been in a position to consume as much as he had on the outside and his health appeared to be improving. It never ceased to amaze David how some people, usually those addicted to hard drugs, were actually in better health than those out on the streets.

"Damien, I want to deal firstly with a statement from a Doctor that has been served. Doctor Wakeley is the Doctor who saw you at the Queen Elizabeth Hospital when you went to see him a few days after your arrest. He states that you told him that the injury to your hand was caused by someone holding your hand over a naked flame."

"It was, I remember it. When the Scottish bloke had got me to clean the knife he took Usman's lighter, grabbed my hand and burnt it and threatened me that if I told anyone what I'd seen he'd come back and kill me."

"Damien, when you spoke to the police doctor on the day of your arrest you told him that you burnt your hand accidentally when you were smoking crack cocaine."

"Yes I know, I lied to him. He was telling me it looked like I'd burnt my hand setting fire to the flat. I couldn't remember then how I'd burnt it but I knew I didn't set fire to the flat so I just told him I'd burnt it smoking crack. It was only a few days later that I remembered the bloke holding my hand over the flame and threatening me."

David looked at him to see if there were any obvious signs of lying but he could not see any so he moved on.

"Were there any other statements that you made to the police or anyone else that weren't true? Obviously it is better that we know now rather than find out during the trial."

"No, I swear to you on my mother's life, everything else I've said is the truth, the whole truth and nothing but the truth, so help me God."

David looked closely at Damien after this statement. Was Damien practicing for when he was before the Court, when he would make a similar statement although avoiding the use of "so help me God", which is not used in British Court rooms.

"Very well, Damien, I have to ask you these questions because we need to know what you are saying about the evidence in the case. Further statements have been served by Forensic scientists in this case and I would like your help with their evidence. One called Roger Allbright deals with bloodstaining found in the flat. He concludes that the major assault took place in the lounge ..."

"Yeah it did like I said, that's where the Scottish man killed Usman."

"Yes, but the Forensic scientist then goes on to say that there were blood spots in the hall which are consistent with force being used into an already bleeding Usman. It suggests that someone hit him in the hallway when he was bleeding."

"No that's wrong, he was already dead and I'd covered him in the duvet when I took him through to his bedroom. There's no way he was hit in the hallway."

"Damien, have you any idea how that blood could have got onto the walls?"

" I've got no idea."

David decided to move on as it was clear he was not going to get any assistance on this issue from Damien and Damien was clearly beginning to get agitated.

"Alright Damien, we'll look into that, and possibly instruct our own expert. There is one further piece of new evidence I want to deal with before I move onto the Unused Material."

David smiled and Damien became clearly less agitated.

"The Prosecution have served a statement from a Forensic scientist who is an expert in footwear. He states that 12 prints were found that can be linked to the time after Usman had been stabbed. This is because the prints were in blood and had a layer of soot over them which means they must have been caused before the fire and therefore before any police officer, fire officer or paramedic arrived on the scene. He points to twelve such prints, both right and left foot. Ten of them have the same footprint, a star made by a trainer called a "Star 'D' Sprint."

Damien looked up at this information.

"I've never owned any trainers like that, I've never even heard of any called that."

"Damien, some of those prints were found in the lounge, some in the hallway and some in the bedroom where Usman's body was found. Two more were found in the kitchen. Now you have told us that you travelled between all of those rooms. You were in the lounge, you carried Usman's body in a duvet through the hallway to the bedroom and you washed the knife in the kitchen. There were two other footprints found where the prints could not be made out. These were found in the lounge."

"They could be mine", interjected Damien, hopefully.

"The difficulty Damien is that the only prints found in the hallway, bedroom and kitchen belonged to the same trainers with a star pattern. No other footprints were found anywhere except possibly the foot prints in the lounge that have no pattern."

"I'm telling you the truth, I didn't kill him. I don't know why there's only one type of fucking print but it's not fucking mine!"

Charles Rooney decided to inject at this point.

"Damien, try and calm down, Mr Brant is not passing any judgment on you. He is merely explaining what the evidence is to see whether you can assist us."

David noticed Charlotte's face at this stage. She was giving a look of complete disbelief in what Damien was saying. David decided it was necessary to support Charles Rooney's comments.

"That's right Damien, NONE of us are here to judge you, quite the opposite, we are all here as part of your team of Defence lawyers whose job is to represent you. However, we would be failing in our duty to you if we did not explain the strengths of the evidence and ask for your assistance to see if you can help us on any particular area."

David gave Damien a smile at the end of this speech which he had given on many occasions in the past to clients when the evidence was beginning to look overwhelming against them, and the client had no interest in pleading guilty.

Damien visibly calmed down and David decided to move on, although the next area he wanted to cover was the Unused Material. He appreciated that discussing that might cause even more problems but he had to raise Bab's statements with Damien.

"Damien, the last matter I wanted to raise with you relates to the Unused Material the Prosecution has served. As I've told you before, Unused Material is evidence that the Prosecution have decided they must disclose to the Defence because it may undermine or weaken their case, or it may assist your case. They have located Babs. She has given three versions of events claiming firstly, that she was not at the flat, secondly that you attempted to rape her outside the flat ..."

Damien became discernibly angry at this statement.

"Thirdly, that there were two other men in the flat with you and you tried to rape her in the flat."

Damien exploded at this latter statement.

"This is pure bullshit, I never touched her, I never wanted to, she was ugly and she stank. She's talking absolute bollocks."

David decided he had to probe a little.

"Why do you think she has made these allegations Damien?"

Damien blew up again,

"I don't fucking know. She may have been spaced out on crack, or the police have got her to lie."

Warming to this latter theme he continued,

"They probably offered her drugs to make up this story."

David moved on swiftly.

"Damien, she does corroborate, that is, support your account that there were two other males present in the flat when the murder took place. However, we cannot call her to say that because the Prosecution would discredit her in cross examination due to the fact she has given three different versions and then they would prejudice the jury by reminding her that she claimed you tried to rape her."

"I never did though, it's a pack of lies."

"I appreciate what you are saying Damien but please remember I have to point out difficulties in the evidence. Let's move on. You have had an opportunity of seeing all the papers now. Is there anything you would like to raise with us?"

"Yeah, what's my chances, what do you think's going to happen?"

David paused before answering, it was a question all clients asked and it was one of the most difficult to answer.

"Damien, none of us have a crystal ball. None of us know who will be on the jury, how they will be feeling on the day, how the witnesses will come across when they give evidence, how you will come across when you give evidence. It's impossible to judge these things accurately. We know there are difficulties in your case. There are difficulties with some of the evidence as I have explained, but rest assured, we are all determined to do our best for you."

In other words, David thought to himself, you have a snowball's chance in hell of being acquitted at the moment.

The conference came to an end and David received another lift from Charles Rooney to Woolwich Arsenal Station and made his way into Chambers. Tonight Chambers was hosting an Art evening. The wife of the Head of Chambers, Virginia Wontner, was an amateur painter and had inflicted a number of her "works of art" on Chambers. Now she had encouraged Chambers to sponsor some students of the art college she patronised (in all senses of the word), the Rankin School of Art. For the last two days Chambers had been receiving a number of works of art from the college which were being displayed on the walls and in the Conference rooms. Wine and nibbles were offered and a number of Solicitors invited to judge the art. At the end, the lucky student whose work was judged to be the "best" would receive a plaque from Chambers and a cheque for £500. There would also be the chance for the students to sell their works to anybody who took an interest.

David already had an idea of what was in store. There had been perceptible pleasure when Virginia Wontner's artwork had been moved from the walls of Chambers but there had been considerable concern when the College's works of Art had started to appear. Graham Martin had already sent a text to David to say,

"Watch out when you go into Chambers, you are likely to catch your suit on the scrap metal and other assorted shite passing itself off as art exhibits."

He returned to Chambers and felt Graham's text was understating the position. As he entered the Chambers the first sight he saw, just outside the Clerks' room, was a full size painting in red of naked dead bodies called, "Orgasm of Death." He made his way past the Clerks room and almost snagged his suit on what could only be described as lump of hammered metal called "Oneness." As he moved towards his room he saw what the "piece de resistance" was for him, two lumps of wood, joined by a curled piece of steel with two large nails hammered into the wood. It was simply called "Life's ending." He began to seriously miss Virginia's poorly painted landscapes.

A couple of hours later he was walking around with a glass of Claret in one hand and small plate of nibbles, trying to perform a balancing act as he manoeuvred around the various works of "art." Graham Martin had been unable to control his mirth and had to leave Chambers rapidly as one of the students was explaining his inspiration for, "Orgasm of Death." David had meanwhile joined Stephanie, a very attractive "mature" art student, aged about 30 who was explaining to him what had inspired her to create, "Oneness."

"I feel a bit of a fraud being here," she said to David.

She told him this as he sipped from his Claret whilst balancing a vol au vent on his plate. David turned to her and was impressed. Finally, he thought, some honesty, one of the students was going to admit this was a "con." She was going to admit she had picked up a scrap of metal in a local car dump and was trying to pass it off as art.

"You've probably noticed, as I'm sure that everyone has."

Here it comes, David thought, she is going to own up, the need to confess to lawyers never ceased to amaze him.

"The truth is "Oneness" isn't finished. I started it three months ago and just haven't been able to finish it. I felt the need to create a piece that summed up the hopelessness of material gain. The destruction of the soul from man's greed and man's incessant need to constantly improve monetarily at the cost of the Earth's limited resources."

Right, so no confession there then! Seemed to be the day for that..

"Really."

David was able to mutter, preventing the rising need to laugh and nodding at the delectable and, as far as he was concerned, deluded Stephanie.

"It looks finished to me, but then I'm not an expert in art, I only know what I like."

And this does not fall anywhere near that category, he thought to himself.

"Tell me, Stephanie, I'm interested in the reason why you associate "Oneness" with the "hopelessness of material gain"?

"Because, material gain is associated with greed and greed is selfishness and selfishness is a lonely state of "Oneness."

David smiled and thought to himself, I wonder what she will do if her "artwork" wins the prize and she makes a "material gain" of £500.

At that moment, Virginia walked across and said to both of them,

"David and Stephanie I see you've met."

Turning to David she added,

"Stephanie is one of our brightest new artists. The thought that goes into her artwork is phenomenal.

She is a perfectionist. I wish I had just 1% of her determination to make her pieces the ultimate work of art."

David smiled again, he was beginning to think this must be a dream. They were looking at a lump of battered metal and describing it as if it was the Mona Lisa.

His discomfort was made worse when Virginia added,

"And David here is one of the **Older** members of Chambers. An Experienced and much valued member of our Chambers who is an established Queen's Counsel."

He gave a slight smile at Virginia. "Experienced" and "much valued member" he could deal with but why the need to add "Older"? Also he thought, since when has Virginia been a member of "our Chambers."

Stephanie intervened before he had a chance to say anything.

"Oh, you're a lawyer, I assumed you were a guest."

David turned to her and gave his most practiced smile.

"Yes, Virginia's husband is our Head of Chambers."

Stephanie's smile showed from her demeanour that she was not interested in the hierarchical structure of Chambers.

"I've always wondered about your work. How can you possibly represent a person you know is guilty?"

Oh no, he thought, here it is, the usual dinner party question. He had no idea how many times he had been asked this question in this or similar forms. If he had a £1 for each time he could easily have retired by now. He had a few stock answers depending upon how annoying the questioner was. Stephanie, although deluded in his mind, was still attractive and so he chose the stock reply.

"The point is we don't know our clients are guilty. The Prosecution say they are, the client says he is innocent. It is no part of a lawyer's function to judge his client but to represent him. If he tells us he is guilty then we advise him to plead guilty but if he tells us he is innocent then we advise him about both the strengths and the weaknesses of the evidence against him and if he chooses to fight a case, we represent him to the best of our ability."

On other occasions he would sometimes answer,

"Easy, it's much easier to represent someone you think is guilty than someone you think is innocent. If guilty there is no stress when he is found guilty but it would be immensely stressful to see a person you thought was innocent convicted of a serious crime."

Stephanie looked at him quizzically, clearly not satisfied with his answer.

"Surely, it's human nature for you to judge your client. Really, you must know if he is guilty or innocent."

Again, he produced his practiced smile.

"I'm afraid it's not as simple as that Stephanie. Judging whether someone is telling the truth or not is not as easy as it appears on the television. Some clients even convince themselves they are innocent when they are guilty and some Prosecution witnesses are quite compelling witnesses even though they lie."

He was tempted to add, 'for example I don't know if you are being serious when you say this piece of trash is a work of art', but he decided nothing could be gained from such honesty.

Virginia was clearly not satisfied with being left out of this part of the conversation and had to add,

"Yes, well James, my husband, always tells me he does have difficulty with defence cases which is why he much prefers to Prosecute."

That is not the James Wontner QC I know, thought David, he had never seen any reluctance on the part of James "Want More" QC to conduct any brief and a positive keenness to be first in line for any defence work.

Virginia then moved on to the subject of holidays. She explained how she had truly enjoyed seeing Egyptian pieces of art "in situ" in the Cairo museum before those "frightful" rioters had broken in and stolen or damaged many items. Suddenly she remembered a conversation she had with David months before when he had expressed an interest in Ancient Egyptian history. She decided to mention it.

"David and I share a secret love ..."

David smiled at her and broke in to add, "Yes and it's not James."

He thought it time to inject a mild degree of humour but the look on both Stephanie's and Virginia's faces told him this was not the way to do it.

The conversation moved on with David rapidly losing interest. From Modern Art to Egyptian art to the Renaissance to holidays and finally the subject of health had been introduced into the conversation by someone. David, once again looking at the delectable but deluded Stephanie tried again to inject a modicum of humour by adding that he had joined a gym in order to get healthier but had been disappointed to find that he could not make any progress unless he actually attended. The dismissive expressions he met from both of them convinced him that further conversation was probably pointless and he started to look around the room. He noticed in the corner Wendy Pritchard was deep in conversation with the artist who had created "Orgasm of Death." He decided that Wendy was far more interesting than Stephanie and Virginia, and he excused himself by saying he had been interested in the inspiration behind "Orgasm of Death" and wanted to ask the artist about it. He smiled at both women, who barely looked at him as he moved away. Fortunately, he did not have to actually talk to the weird looking individual who was telling Wendy how he had been allowed to spend three days in a Morgue sketching dead bodies in order to paint his masterpiece, as James Wontner announced that the Judges had made their decisions about the art and the prize giving was about to begin. David moved slowly over to the table containing the bottles of Claret as he felt the decision might require a large sip of red wine.

The evening ended with a joint prize being awarded to both "Orgasm of Death" and "Oneness." The Head of Chambers gave a wonderful speech about the "excellent art" they had seen and how difficult the Judges' decision had been. He added that if anyone wanted to buy these works of art, he was sure the artists would listen to any reasonable offers that were made.

David smiled and clapped the winners and left as soon afterwards as he could. Only a couple of

Solicitors had turned up to this art extravaganza and they were the usual hangers on who never briefed Chambers but accepted every invite for a free drink and a nibble. He decided that if Virginia in her finite wisdom should ever suggest any other evenings of such stunning entertainment, he would be certain to have other plans that had been arranged months before.

CHAPTER 10.

PRO BONO IN THE COURT OF APPEAL.

The following Monday 6th August 2012, David received a call from Tony, his first Junior Clerk, to advise him that he had a hearing in the Court of Appeal the next day. He had not needed reminding because the date had been set a couple of months before but the Clerks were duty bound to tell everyone who was due in Court, which Court they were in and at what time.

"You are in Court 4 before Mr Justice Pollard and His Honour Judge Tanner who is sitting in the Court of Appeal tomorrow. You are first on at 10:00am."

David had been shaken by the news that he had another appearance in front of Tanner. He had avoided him for the best part of thirty years and now it seemed he was destined just to appear in front of him.

Tomorrow's case was a "pro bono" renewal of leave to appeal case. David hated the words "pro bono" as it simply meant he was working for free. The client had not got the money to pay for his representation and as he had already applied for leave to appeal and that application had been rejected, the renewal application was for free.

Further David hardly felt a great deal of sympathy for the client. The client was Mark Jenkins, a 53 year old man who had been convicted of four different sets of rape involving four young girls many years before. All four were his nieces, aged 12 and 13 at the time, although the rapes had taken place over a period of about ten years. The Prosecution case was that Mark Jenkins was one of five children. The other four had left home to get married and have children but Mark had chosen to remain at home and look after his widowed Mother. His siblings would take it in turns to visit their mother on different Saturdays so as not to overwhelm her. They would bring their children with them. Mark Jenkins stated that, in order to avoid tedium for the children, he allowed the older children to come into his bedroom to listen to his expensive sound system. He maintained that is all that happened.

His nieces had a different version of events. The first called Daphne stated that in 1990 when she was 12 he would invite her up to his room and rape her every Saturday, threatening that it would break her grandmother's heart if she said anything about their "little secret." This went on for over a year until she started menstruating and then he no longer invited her up to his room but invited her younger 12 year old female cousin, Rachel. Rachel said that when she got up to the room she was subjected to the same treatment for a further year until she started menstruating. In 2010, Mark's mother died and left the house to him which had caused friction in the family. It was shortly after that Daphne and Rachel decided to make allegations to the Police about what they had allegedly been subjected to 20 years before. The Police had done a thorough job of investigating the matter and spoken to other nieces who refused to cooperate or make any allegations against Mark. David had represented Mark at the trial of these allegations in late 2010 and a jury had acquitted Mark of some of the allegations of rape, been undecided on others and convicted him of indecently assaulting the girls. The Prosecution had decided to prosecute him again in relation to the rape allegations that the first jury had been undecided about. David had represented him at the second trial in 2011 which had been complicated by the fact that two other nieces had now come forward and made similar allegations against him when they were aged 12-13 in 1994-1995 and 1999-2000 respectively. The second trial had been almost impossible to conduct with so many allegations being made and Mark had been convicted and received a sentence of 16 years imprisonment. David had been concerned about certain legal rulings during the trial and had advised and drafted grounds of appeal for the Court of Appeal. These had been submitted on paper to a Single Judge in the Court of Appeal who had rejected the grounds in early 2012. Mark had decided to renew his application for leave in front of Court of Appeal and David had been asked to conduct it "pro bono."

David arrived at the Court of Appeal early to see Mark in the cells, only to discover that he had decided not to come to Court. Like a lot of prisoners, there was always a fear that if you attended Court you might go back to a different prison than the one you were brought from and have to start all over again in the prison system spending months trying to get the trusted jobs. The safest course was simply to waive your right to attend these hearings just as Mark had, but it did mean than David had no update information from Mark to bring to the attention of the Court.

At 10:00am he was seated in Court 4 when the Court was told to rise and Mr Justice Pollard came in to court first and smiled at David, His Honour Judge Tanner followed and gave David his usual grimace. David immediately decided that even the rarefied air of the Court of Appeal had not mellowed Tanner's disposition but he would keep smiling at both of them throughout the application.

David waited until his application was called on and then began by addressing their Lordships on the two points of appeal that he had. One was that the case should have been stopped as an abuse of process because many potential witnesses had died before the trials took place which prevented the defence from calling them. The mother and quite a few of Mark's siblings had died who attended the mother's house on the Saturday and they were no longer able to give evidence that they had heard nothing untoward from Mark's bedroom and that they never noticed any change in the girls demeanours when they came downstairs from the bedrooms, nor could they give evidence to suggest that there was no reluctance on the part of the girls to go upstairs with Mark each weekend. The other ground of appeal concerned the fact that the trial judge had allowed the jury to hear that Mark had a previous conviction for unlawful sexual intercourse with a girl when he and she were both 15.

David had ten pages of typed notes before him covering the issues in the case and detailing each ground of appeal. He had barely got through the first paragraph on page one of those notes when Mr Justice Pollard interrupted him,

"Mr Brant, we have read your Advice and the Grounds of Appeal and we are well aware of the facts and the issues in the case. We would probably benefit by your assisting us with why you say the Learned Judge was not in the best position to deal with the Abuse of process application. Stays for Abuse of Process as you know are exceptional courses and this Court will not readily interfere with a Trial Judge who from his reasoning has on the face of the papers properly considered all aspects of the application."

David smiled again, he had wondered how far he would get in his typed notes before there was such an interruption. He had guessed about halfway into paragraph one so he was a little surprised to find that he had almost finished the paragraph before the inevitable interruption. He fended the question off, pointing to the wealth of points he had in response, when His Honour Judge Tanner decided to intervene.

"Mr Brent..."

"It's Brant, My Lord."

Why does he deliberately mispronounce my name, was David's only thought.

"Yes, Mr Brant, surely your best point in the whole of this Appeal is not the Abuse of Process application but allowing the jury to hear about the very old previous conviction for unlawful sexual intercourse when your client was a young offender."

There it is, thought David, the trap! Many a young advocate falls into this trap in the Court of Appeal. He remembered his first appearance in the Court of Appeal almost thirty years ago when he was arguing an Appeal again Conviction. There had been three judges then as well and he had been surprised how quickly he had been interrupted in his submissions. First the Judge on his far right had asked questions and just when he felt he was answering them the judge from his far left came in with yet further questions. Just as he felt he was answering those the judge in the centre raised an issue he had never thought about and as he struggled to find an answer a lifeline had been thrown from his right with those same words,

"surely your best point is ....."

He had conceded that it was his best point only to be met with a response from his left,

"surely the answer to that is ...."

He had watched as the point he had conceded was his best, was destroyed in front of his eyes, leaving him, by his own admission, with weaker points. He was not going to fall for that again and he resented that His Honour Judge Tanner believed he, Queen's Counsel, with thirty years' experience at the Criminal Bar, would fall for such an obvious trap.

"My Lord, I accept there is a great deal of merit in the bad character issue for reasons that your Lordship points to and **for other reasons** I would like to develop in due course, however, it would be wrong for me to concede the obvious strength of the abuse of process issue."

He continued for another half hour, pushing all of his points and raising a few he thought of whilst on his feet. Eventually, both Mr Justice Pollard and His Honour Judge Tanner just let him get on with what he wanted to say and the interruptions ceased altogether.

He ended his submissions with his smile and the words,

"My Lords, those are my submissions" and then sat down.

Mr Justice Pollard again smiled at him and His Honour Judge Tanner gave his by now customary grimace. They turned to each other for a few moments and whispered for what was probably thirty seconds before Mr Justice Pollard gave the judgment of the Court.

It began with a short reciting of the facts and then went on to deal with a summary of the points David had raised, adding,

"We are impressed by the attractive way in which Mr Brant QC put his arguments."

That was it then, he knew now he had not won this one. Once the Court of Appeal starts praising you, it was almost inevitable that you had lost the case.

"However, we have no doubt that the trial Judge was in the best position to weigh the factors in favour of both a stay on the basis of Abuse of Process and whether the previous conviction should be admitted in the particular circumstances of this case."

David gave his best smile to them both, bowed and left the court. Although he had acted pro bono, at least he had enjoyed the intellectual challenge and the fact that His Honour Judge Tanner was now associated to a judgment that praised David's advocacy skills. It almost made up for all those bad references he had given throughout the years .... almost!

CHAPTER 11.

THE CHAMBERS EGM.

Thursday 9th August 2012 and David found himself once more on the way into Chambers for an ECM, an Extraordinary Chambers Meeting. Normally he contented himself with letting others run Chambers and he only appeared at the Annual Chambers Meeting held the first Thursday of October every year, really just to show he existed. However, an Extraordinary Chambers Meeting had been called by the Management Committee of Chambers formed by the Head of Chambers, the Treasurer and five annually elected Members of Chambers. It appeared that concern had been raised about John Winston and what he actually did for Chambers and why his salary was so high. Noticeably, the meeting coincided with when John took his customary three weeks off in August.

It was not a major surprise to anyone that these issues were being raised as they were discussed frequently in quiet corners of Chambers or in local hostelries around the area. Probably just about every Criminal set in the Temple were having similar conversations. Most Barristers thought their Senior Clerks were paid too much and did next to nothing for it. The Junior Members of Chambers rarely had any dealings with the Senior

Clerk so tended to be most vociferous about him, the middle rankers had more exposure but with the general downturn of criminal work, they were getting concerned how mortgages were going to be paid. The Senior end of Chambers tended to be more satisfied with the Senior Clerk because he dealt with their practices and tried to ensure the top end were happy because they were the most experienced and influential in Chambers and the most likely to keep him in a job.

James Wontner, headed the meeting and sat at the Head of the Table with other Members of the Management Committee on either side of him. Most of the tenants had crowded into the largest room in Chambers to hear what was going on but some of the Juniors had to stand outside the open door to the room because of a lack of space.

James Wontner made a customary opening speech, stating that this meeting had been called at the behest of the Management Committee of which he was a proud Member and happy that Chambers was democratically run so that such issues could be dealt with democratically. David immediately read the subtext which was simply that James Wontner believed, like Benjamin Franklin, that democracy was simply two wolves and a lamb voting on what to have for dinner. He made it subtly clear, he did not want a meeting, did not think one was necessary and that it had been called by a few hotheads on the Management Committee who had been recently elected. He went on, foolishly in David's opinion, to extol the virtues of John Winston, "a man I am proud to call my friend", "a man of the utmost integrity" and "a real asset, who is the heart of these Chambers."

David thought that John Winston was a lazy Senior Clerk who was not hungry and only did the bare minimum in Chambers. However, he did not want rid of him because there was an element of "better the Devil you know" and his experience of losing Senior Clerks in the past was a negative one. They had always been replaced by someone who appeared keen and hungry and a good candidate who as soon as they got the job showed that they were as lazy as their predecessor. He was firmly of the view that virtually all Clerks who became Senior Clerks, spent most of their time ensuring they kept their jobs rather than actually doing them.

One of the mid-range Juniors, Sean McConnell, spoke after James' eulogy. He had been in Chambers for about ten years from when he was a Pupil. David thought he was affable enough, although he was a bit of a firebrand and did often engage his mouth far in advance of his brain.

"John Winston is a lazy Clerk who is of no advantage to these Chambers."

Some of the Senior members did make noticeable disapproving grunts at this comment but noticeably, a few, mainly Junior Members, were nodding in agreement.

"The Criminal Bar has to change, we need to move on and do away with the whole concept of Clerks. We pay ludicrous wages to people with no qualifications who are incapable of doing the job we give them. In this day and age what company would pay £150,000 a year to an unqualified barrow boy ...."

There was more murmuring at that comment.

".... When we could get graduates from business schools or in marketing who would do the job for £30,000. It doesn't take a genius to realise ...."

He pointedly looked at the Head of Chambers when he made this comment.

"..... that we could employ five graduates to do John's job and they undoubtedly would do it better."

He continued in this vein for a while and clearly got some support from the more Junior end of Chambers and interestingly, some support from the Middle and Senior end of Chambers.

Others joined in with the spirited debate whilst David wondered how much of this John Winston would get to hear and how many previously assigned briefs may now be taken away from Junior tenants as a result of these robust comments.

James Wontner, valiantly fought a rear guard action on behalf of John Winston, describing how just the other day before he went on holiday, John was discussing what new work he had brought in for Members of Chambers and his plans for expanding the Chambers into the Regulatory and Disciplinary field where much higher fees were payable than those payable on Criminal legal aid.

Graham Martin decided to say a few words on the subject. He was no fan of either James Wontner or John Winston, and was still reeling from being forced to go to Northampton Crown Court on a "loss leader" for a firm that owed him large amounts of money and showed no interest in paying him or instructing him on a decent case.

"James, everyone here respects you as a Head of Chambers and I'm sure we all want you to continue to lead us through the difficult times ahead."

An interesting start thought David. The issue was about John Winston but Graham had made an implicit threat to James Wontner's position as Head of Chambers. Graham continued,

"However, you have already told us that you consider John Winston to be a friend and we all know how difficult it is to make reasoned logical judgments when you are a personal friend of the subject of those judgments."

James Wontner was about to intervene when Graham held up a hand and continued.

"Clearly there is a great deal of concern about Chambers, about Criminal work in general and about the constant reduction in fees. Sean has raised a few interesting points for discussion, though I doubt a chap as sensible as Sean is advocating we simply sack John and replace him tomorrow with five graduates who know nothing about a Criminal set of chambers. If we were to dismiss John simply like that, we would undoubtedly be in breach of Employment legislation and paying him for years to come. What we surely need to do is give John the chance to improve, **if he can**."

There was an interesting emphasis on those last three words.

"He has told James that there are areas of work he can direct Chambers towards and if he does I am sure we will all be happy with him and we may be able to afford one, or even more, of Sean's five graduates. I suggest we look at structuring John's employment and setting a few parameters. If he meets them, all well and good, if he doesn't, well, regrettably we may have to let him go. What do you think David?"

David was taken aback by being introduced into this discussion. James had clearly been the voice of self-interest, Sean had been the voice of a firebrand and Graham had been the apparent voice of reason with many people nodding at what he had to say. The truth was everyone in the room who had known John Winston for a few years knew he was no more capable of changing his working practices than Virginia Wontner was capable of painting a masterpiece. The apparently reasonable scheme that Graham had suggested in such a persuasive way was actually merely setting John Winston up to be fairly, as opposed to, unfairly dismissed.

David, who had not intended to say a word, had no choice but to respond to Graham's "kind" invitation. He selected the same smile he had used in the Court of Appeal and continued,

"Thank you Graham. I think there is a lot in what you suggest. We are facing difficult times. I recall thirty years ago as a young Pupil Barrister being told by a then Junior Member of my first Chambers, "don't come to the Criminal Bar, there's no future in it." Those words are undoubtedly more true now than they have ever been. There will be no Criminal Bar unless we change with the times and adopt work practices that truly gear us up for the future. It may be Sean's idea of graduates is the future for this profession, but I like to think that there is still a place for experienced Criminal Clerks who have dedicated their lives to the profession and know all the Solicitors out there. I think we should talk to John about the possibilities of new work and have regular meetings with him. However, I am against the idea that the solution is to simply sack him and I am against any idea of providing a set of hurdles for him that we know he will not be able to jump over. Graham, any conditions we set must be with a view to him succeeding, not with a view to him failing and consequently he must be able to deal with people he feels he can work closely with, who are not setting him up for a fall."

This met with general approval and David felt quite proud of his impromptu speech which he knew would get back to the clerks room, if it had not already. It would accurately demonstrate his true stance that he was not simply out to sack the Clerks but actually wanted to continue working with them, although he saw some better work practices as inevitable. It had the twofold advantage of being what he actually thought and might even be worth a Silk brief or two from John Winston!

The meeting ended shortly thereafter with a Committee being set up to look into new working conditions for the Clerks, particularly the Senior Clerk with a view to the future. David accepted a role on the committee, not because he wanted to, but simply to add some barrier to the loony suggestions of the some of the firebrands in Chambers.

CHAPTER 12.

DAY ONE, THE TRIAL COMMENCES.

David took a customary two weeks off in August (he had no Court work to conduct anyway) and had a thoroughly enjoyable two weeks in a private villa on the Western coast of Corfu, near the town of Arillas. It was a three bedroomed villa that he had stayed in before with his family when he was married. It was far too big for him but the owners had allowed him to have it for £1,000 a week. He could not afford such luxury at the moment but he decided he deserved a proper break away from London and his concerns about his practice. The Bank Manager would undoubtedly be a little concerned at the size of the cheque going through the account but so what, he had a Murder brief so at least the Bank Manager would know some money was on the way.

He enjoyed the glorious weather, the local red wine, Greek beer and cocktails, the swimming in his own pool and the sea and now he felt ready to face His Honour Judge Tanner and a jury in the Old Bailey. He had one more conference with Damien in Belmarsh which had achieved nothing in reality. Damien continued to maintain he was innocent of the crime and showed an increasing irritation when the Prosecution evidence was mentioned to him.

He had also seen the Defence's own Pathologist who had given his opinion that the blood in the hall did look like it was caused by an impact into an already injured body, although it was just possible that it had been caused in one of a number of different ways. David had decided there was no point in calling this Pathologist because under cross-examination by the Prosecution he would undoubtedly state the most likely cause of the blood stain in the hallway was that someone had hit an already wounded Usman. However, the information he had gained in the conference would be helpful cross examination material.

On Monday 10th September 2012, he awoke early, had a coffee and made his way to the Old Bailey, the Central Criminal Court, where he would be conducting the Murder trial. Somehow Damien's case had been transferred to Court One so Damien's case would be conducted in the same court room where Dr Crippin, the Yorkshire Ripper, Ruth Ellis and other infamous murderers had been tried.

David arrived early at 9am, signed in on the computer, got robed and went upstairs to the Bar Mess on the fifth floor for a cooked breakfast to start the day. He was just about to dunk a slice of lukewarm bacon (it was always lukewarm) into his freshly cooked fried egg when Joanna Glass QC appeared from his right with Timothy Arnold following closely behind.

"Enjoying your morning cholesterol David?"

David, put down his fork, annoyed at the interruption to his pre-trial ritual of a cooked breakfast.

"Joanna, Tim, how nice to see you both, are you going to join me in a spot of breakfast before the case starts?"

Joanna responded immediately,

"Starts David? Is your client seriously going to trouble a jury with this defence? There is still time for him to get some credit for a plea and a plea will certainly help his chances of parole in 15 years or so."

"Joanna, surely you are not going to subject me to robing room tactics before I've even had chance to finish my breakfast? Damien Clarke is an innocent man, if the Police had properly investigated this case they would have caught the real culprits by now. I had hoped you were coming over to say the C.P.S. had finally seen sense and were dropping the case against young Damien."

Joanna smiled at the banter,

"Sorry David, there's a good reason why they are called the Crown *Persecution* Service. Anyway we'll let you finish your breakfast and hopefully we can chat about the case when you've finished."

David finished his rapidly cooling breakfast and then went over to Joanna and Timothy to discuss preliminary matters involving the case. At 9:30am Charlotte Williams arrived, unfashionably early for her and fifteen minutes later David and Charlotte were in the cells with Damien to have the final Conference before the trial commenced.

Damien was looking better than David had ever seen him. He had shaved for Court and someone had brought a suit, shirt and tie for him to wear, which made him look smarter than normal and had the added advantage of hiding most of his tattoos.

"Are you ready for the trial Damien?"

David asked the obvious question even though in reality Damien had no choice but to be ready for the trial.

"Yeah I am, I just want to get it over with now."

"I understand."

David replied pretending to have some empathy but failing miserably as he could have no real idea how anyone felt facing a life sentence for such a serious crime as Murder.

The Conference was relatively short as all the work had been done by now, all the possible instructions taken and David was fully prepared for trial. This was in reality a "hand holding" exercise, merely designed to make Damien feel more at ease, if that was possible and to go through the essential pre-trial check list. David explained that the Clerk of the Court would tell Damien that he had a right to challenge jurors. However, in fact he had no such right as the challenge had to be made for "cause" and as they knew nothing about the jurors, nor could they, they had no "cause" to challenge them, save in the unlikely event that Damien or one of them knew one of the jurors and that never happened in practice.

At 10:15am Charlotte and David left the cells and made their way to Court One in the old part of the Central Criminal Court.

David walked into Court 1 and took his position in Counsel's benches situated to the left of where the Judge sits. He recalled how the Court had been designed over a hundred years ago when trials were shorter and how the design was unlike modern courts as the witness box was opposite Counsel's benches and situated next to the jury box which is directly opposite Counsel's benches. It has the effect that the jury can see Counsel face on, but only see the witnesses from the side.

At 10:35am His Honour Judge Tanner came into Court, sporting his usual grim expression and David wondered for a moment if he could ever recall him smiling. He amused himself with the thought that His Honour Judge Tanner only ever smiled at the end of a week when he added up the number of years imprisonment he had handed down that week.

He was awoken from his daydream by His Honour Judge Tanner calling out his name.

"Mr Brant are we ready for a jury to be sworn in this case?"

David was so taken aback at the correct use of his name, that he paused longer than he intended before replying that they were.

The jury panel was brought into Court from which twelve jurors would be selected.

The Clerk of the Court read out the name of each one who then came into the jury box to be sworn.

David heard the names which meant nothing to him until he heard the name, "Mary Jones." He immediately looked up and saw his cleaner Mary walking into the Jury Box. In all the hundreds of trials he had conducted throughout his career he had never once come across someone he knew on a jury. Now of all the people he knew who could sit on a jury, it had to be Mary Jones who was called to sit on this case. He knew she had told him she needed two weeks off from cleaning but had never dreamt it was so she could sit on a jury. His thoughts immediately travelled to that Tuesday morning when she walked in on him and saw him naked on his bed. He felt a reddening of his cheeks which was made worse when he saw that Mary recognised him and was pointing him out to the juror next to her. He had no idea what she was saying but he instinctively thought it would be a reference to his manhood and he now felt that his cheeks must be the colour of beetroot.

Once the swearing in process began he waited until Mary rose to take the oath and then he got to his feet.

"We challenge this juror for cause."

His Honour Judge Tanner, smiling at the juror, immediately riposted,

"Why Mr Brant, what conceivable reason could you have for challenging this good lady?"

All eyes turned towards David now as though he was some school bully unfairly attacking a young girl with pigtails. David was not sure which was more galling, being made to look like the school bully or witnessing His Honour Judge Turner's attempt at charm.

"I know this lady, she is employed by me as my cleaner and it would not be appropriate for her to sit on this case."

The Judge immediately saw there was no alternative but to accede to the request and with an apology released her from the Jury.

His Honour Judge Tanner could not resist a little jibe,

"Thank you Mr Brant and no doubt you will tell us if any more of your domestic staff appear on a Jury."

Not to be outdone, David replied,

"Thank you My Lord, there is no fear of that, a Barrister's income unlike that of her majesty's Judiciary, does not stretch to hiring more than a part-time cleaner."

Mary looked at David and smiled. David knew she would probably be selected for some other Jury and would no doubt regale members of his Jury with stories about the size of his manhood when she met them in the Jury canteen. Why oh why did he not have a lock on his bedroom door?

CHAPTER 13.

DAY ONE, THE PROSECUTION OPENING.

Having sworn in the Jury, His Honour Judge Tanner gave them a few words of warning about not being influenced by newspaper articles, not to do any personal research on the internet and to report any approaches made to them about the case. Joanna Glass QC then rose to her feet and facing the jury she opened the case for the Crown.

"Thank you my Lord, Ladies and Gentlemen, I appear on behalf of the Prosecution together with my Learned Friend Mr Arnold. My Learned friends Mr Brant, Queen's Counsel and Ms Williams represent the Defendant, Damien Clarke.

The Defendant, Damien Clarke, is charged with the murder of Usman Hussain. Mr Usman Hussain was 52 years of age on the day he died, which was the 4th February 2012, a Saturday. It is the Prosecution's case that the Defendant stabbed Mr Hussain repeatedly causing wounds to his arms, chest and neck, a number of which could have been independently fatal. Then within a few hours of the killing the defendant presented himself at a police station, claiming that he had witnessed a knife attack on Usman Hussain by two assailants whilst he was in Mr Hussain's flat. It is the Prosecution case that the Defendant has invented the two assailants in an attempt to cover up his own responsibility for the killing.

Ladies and gentlemen there are a number of documents I am going to ask the Usher to give you. There is a Jury Bundle and what we call a Graphics Bundle. The Jury Bundle contains; the Indictment, which is simply another word for the charge sheet, a plan of the area where Mr Hussain lived, a plan of Mr Hussain's flat showing where the body was found as well as bloodstains and footprints and a series of photographs. The Graphics Bundle contains diagrams showing where the wounds were inflicted on Mr Hussain's body. These are in a computer graphic form to save you from having to look at photographs of the deceased."

The documents were handed out by the Court Usher and Joanna Glass QC continued.

"Let me deal with the evidence in a little more detail now. At about 7am on Saturday 4th February 2012, Police and Fire Services were called out in response to a fire alarm sounding at Cambridge Gardens, Woolwich, London. Smoke was coming from the front door of flat number six. Firemen forced open the front door of the first floor flat. Inside they found the dead body of a man later identified as Usman Hussain. It was covered in a duvet lying on a bed in the main bedroom. Paramedics who arrived at 7-15am thought he had possibly been dead for a couple of hours. A Pathologist later examined him and described his injuries. He had twelve different stab wounds and cuts to his chest, neck, arms and hands. Some of those to the arms and hands were "defence wounds" where Mr Hussain had undoubtedly tried to defend himself from his assailant. He measured the wounds and determined that the knife used to cause them was somewhere in the region of between 2 and 2.5cm in width and 12-13cm in length. He was shown a knife recovered from Mr Hussain's kitchen and stated that it could have been the Murder weapon. One of the injuries had been inflicted with severe force because it had fractured Mr Hussain's breast bone and was then deflected through the rib cage into the heart.

A fire had caused damage in the flat and soot and debris covered the floor. The fire had mostly burnt out although in some places it was still smouldering. The deceased was pronounced dead at the scene and the flat was treated as a crime scene. A Murder investigation began immediately.

At 14:00 that same day the Defendant presented himself at the front desk of Woolwich Police Station, wearing, probably appropriately, a T shirt with the words "Mindless Behaviour" emblazoned across the front."

David looked towards the jury at this moment to see how they reacted to this poor attempt at humour when hearing the details of someone's death. None of them showed the slightest emotion.

"He appeared distressed and was saying, "Why him, why did it have to be him." He was asked questions by Police and he told them about his movements on the Friday. He explained that he had met an ex-girlfriend called Jenny and spent most of the day with her until they had a falling out. You will hear from Jenny Jones about this incident and you will have to determine whether that incident has any bearing upon what happened later."

David had no doubt the Prosecution would be making a great deal about this incident if allowed. Joanna Glass QC continued,

"Mr Clarke stated that he left Jenny at about 11:30 pm and then made his way to Mr Hussains' flat. He went there to smoke Crack Cocaine with him.

Now, I need to add at this stage, you will be aware that Crack Cocaine is an illegal drug. You may have your own views about people who possess it and people who smoke it but, please, we are not dealing with the offence of possessing or smoking cocaine, we are dealing with the offence of Murder."

Again David looked towards the Jury, Joanna was doing an excellent job of appearing fair whilst emphasising that Damien was a user of an illegal drug, a Crack addict.

"Mr Clarke told the police that he was buzzed into Mr Hussain's flat where he claimed two other men and a woman called "Babs" or "Babe" were present. One of those men sounded Arabian and one sounded Scottish to him. He told the police that Mr Hussain was very worried about his flat mate, Gillian Banks. She stayed in the second bedroom in the flat and was expected back by that time. You will hear from her that she had attended a Magistrates Court that day and been remanded in custody and that was the reason why she did not return that night.

According to Mr Clarke all of them in the flat were smoking Crack Cocaine and when they ran out of it, they all pooled their money so that Mr Hussain, who knew where to get supplies, could go out and purchase more.

Mr Clarke said that Mr Hussain left the flat and he, feeling tired, fell asleep in an armchair. He awoke to find the other two men trying to rape the girl Babs or Babes. He claimed he stayed in the armchair and then noticed Usman return to the room and remonstrate with the men. The Scottish man then went to the kitchen picked up a kitchen knife and repeatedly stabbed Mr Hussain killing him. In the confusion, Babs or Babes left the flat. The two men threatened Mr Clarke and made him carry out some elementary cleaning in the front room, clean the knife and wrap the body of Mr Hussain into a duvet and take him into the bedroom.

Shortly after this Mr Clarke claims he saw an opportunity to escape and he ran to his mother's house. There he showered and washed his blood stained clothing before attending the police station to give his version of events.

Ladies and Gentlemen I have described it as he described it to the police. The police were unhappy with his contradictory and disjointed account. It had emerged randomly and in broken sentences. He was arrested on suspicion of Murder and later on 5th February 2012 at 10:00 am he was charged with Murder, once cautioned he said "I didn't kill him."

Meanwhile the Police continued to investigate the case.

Ladies and gentleman you will hear about that continuing investigation and a number of important matters that arose. Matters that make it clear that Mr Clarke's version of events simply cannot be true.

Firstly, according to him he went to Mr Hussein's flat at about 11:30pm, he then left, escaping from the two men and rushed to his Mother's flat. You will see from the plans provided that both properties are just under a mile apart. It would have taken a maximum of fifteen minutes to walk between the flats. You will hear from Mr Clarke's sister, Christine that she let him into their mother's flat at about 7:30am. We know the Fire Brigade and Police were called to the flats at just before 7:00am, 6:57am to be precise. Where was Mr Clarke during that half hour period, disposing of items of clothes and **trainers** perhaps?

Secondly, his other sister, Karen Clarke heard him arrive home at 5am that day and leave again at 6am. How does that evidence fit in with his account? Did he leave after killing Mr Hussain and then panicking, returned to set fire to the flat to destroy the evidence?

Thirdly, the victim's flat was examined by Scenes of Crime experts. Blood staining was found mainly in the living room which is probably where Mr Hussain was first attacked. However, some bloodstains were found in the hallway which was consistent with force being applied to someone who was already bleeding. That blood was Mr Hussain's and the Prosecution suggest it could only be caused by the assault continuing into the hallway, probably as a bleeding Mr Hussain retreated from his assailant. That is wholly inconsistent with Mr Clarke's account.

Fourthly, someone set fire to the flat after the Murder, this must have been the murderer. Noticeably, Mr Clarke had a burn injury to his hand. He stated this was caused from smoking

Crack Cocaine. However, a Doctor who saw him gives his opinion that it was an injury that was consistent with the type experienced by people who start a fire.

Fifthly, as a result of the fire, soot staining covered all the rooms in the premises. The fire started in the living room and there is evidence to suggest that the fire was started in two separate areas. A number of similar shoe prints in blood were photographed at the flat. They have been noted to display a particular pattern, a pattern containing a star and although the exact size cannot be discovered, all are in the range which would include Mr Clarke's shoe size. Significantly these footprints were in the blood of the deceased but below the soot level. No other blood stained shoe marks with a different tread pattern were apparent in the flat below the soot layer. A number of prints on the top of the soot layer have been identified as being made by members of the emergency services. The presence of one set of shoe prints in the blood below the soot layer suggests there was only one person in the flat after Mr Hussain was killed and before the fire was set and that person was the killer of Mr Hussain.

The Prosecution say that man was Damien Clarke, the Defendant."

CHAPTER 14.

DAY ONE, THE FIRST WITNESSES, THE NEIGHBOURS.

David had to admit that Joanna Glass QC had done an excellent job. She had the jury eating out of her hand and he noted quite a few were taking notes about her five points, her route to conviction. The trouble was they were good points and in reality he had difficulty dealing with most of them at the moment. It was close to lunchtime when Joanna finished her opening and His Honour Judge Tanner, no doubt keen to get a good seat at lunch, rose early until 2-05pm to allow all parties to have lunch. He reminded the Jury they had not heard any evidence yet and must keep an open mind and then sent them off for lunch.

David and Charlotte went upstairs by lift to the Bar Mess, both saying nothing about the trial just in case they were overheard. Joanna and Timothy joined behind and once they reached the Bar Mess David could not resist making the comment,

"Excellent opening Joanna, I'm just grateful your evidence isn't as strong as your speech."

Joanna, just smiled at him and said,

"Actually, the evidence is a lot stronger, I just didn't want to open it all in case the Jury wondered what they were doing here."

After the usual banter they sat apart at lunch so both teams could discuss the Witnesses that were to be called that afternoon. Having consumed Monday's Shepherd's Pie, Charlotte made her views of the opening known.

"We haven't got a chance in this case."

David was slightly taken aback at the complete lack of optimism of his Junior and so he made the obvious retort.

"Steady on Charlotte, we haven't actually heard how the evidence plays out yet."

David had prepared the entire cross examination of the first Witnesses to be called, namely the neighbours, the Fire Brigade representative and the Police who had initially attended the scene. As was customary in his preparation he had yet to prepare any cross examination of the Pathologist, the cell site expert or the Officer in the Case, (or the "OIC" for short, who is the Senior Officer who has control of all the papers and is in charge of the investigation) as he liked to see how the evidence came out before dealing with the experts or OIC. He noted that Charlotte, who was undoubtedly too busy, had not provided a single note to assist his cross examination.

"Charlotte, I've prepared all the cross examination notes in relation to the first few Witnesses. I've yet to prepare any in relation to the Pathologist or the OIC, could you put your mind to it and prepare some notes for me?"

Charlotte's reply was expected.

"Surely David, you don't need any help in this case, it's so straight forward."

Oh well, he thought, it was worth a try.

After lunch the Prosecution called the first witnesses in the case, the neighbours.

Joanna Glass QC announced to the Court that the first Prosecution Witness was Mr Leonard Feeley. A few minutes later Mr Feeley walked into Court and went into the Witness Box to the left hand side of the Jury. David noticed that he was probably in his early sixties. He was quite gaunt and did not look well. Mr Feely was sworn and then answered questions asked by Joanna Glass. He described the flats and pointed out their location on the agreed plans of the area. A diagram was produced of his floor and he pointed out that he resided in flat eight which was directly opposite flat number six where Mr Hussain lived. He mentioned that he had lived in the flats for the last few years with his wife. He knew Mr Hussain by sight but had not exchanged many words with him. It was more of a nodding acquaintance. He thought the man was in his late fifties or early sixties and was surprised to hear the agreed evidence that the man was fifty two years of age.

He had noticed the large number of visitors to the flat who came at all times of the day and night and how sometimes the noise from the flat would be very loud. He had often heard people from outside the block of flats shout up asking Mr Hussain to buzz them in or to throw down keys to them. He knew that a girl lived at the flat but he did not know her name and he had never spoken to her. She was often seen taking different men back to the flat and he had wondered what her occupation was.

He recalled the early morning of 4th February because just before 7am he had heard a smoke alarm go off. He thought it was from number six and when he went outside his flat to look, he had seen smoke pouring out from under the door of number six. He now thought the smoke alarm he had heard was from the communal hallway. He had not been aware that the smoke alarms in flat number six had been disconnected and he was not aware that crack cocaine was regularly smoked in that flat, but it did not surprise him when he recalled how the visitors to that flat appeared.

He had not heard any particularly loud sounds coming from the flat the night before and had not seen anyone visit or leave the flat the night before or during the early hours of Saturday.

Once he had seen the smoke he had gone back to his flat and called the fire brigade and the police, he and his wife had then got dressed and left the property before the fire brigade or police arrived in case the fire spread to their flat.

Joanna Glass QC sat down after her examination in chief of Mr Feeley. Nothing new had resulted from her questioning and David rose just to ask a few questions and set the scene for the existence of the two men and the woman in the flat.

"Mr Feeley, you've told us that there were many visitors to this flat."

"That's right."

"Can you tell us now how many different people you saw visit the flat, would it be the same people over and over again, or different people?"

"I didn't really study the people who visited. I thought it better not to, as you never know what might happen."

"Quite understandable Mr Feeley. Perhaps I can ask you to assist with another question. The people who visited were presumably a mixture of individuals, males and females from different places."

"I don't know where they came from."

"I'm not suggesting that you did Mr Feeley, but would it be fair to say you saw males and females visiting the property?"

"Yes I did."

"Did you ever hear any names used. For example did you hear one of the females referred to as "Babs" or "Babes"?"

"Yes I do remember one blonde girl who visited regularly and I remember Mr Hussain calling her, I think it was Babes."

"Thank you. Did you notice people with Arabian accents ever visit the flat."

"A number of people came with different accents, English, Irish, Scottish, Caribbean, Arabian, you name it."

"So Mr Feeley, you recall amongst the visitors there was a girl called Babes, Scottish and Arabian men amongst others."

"Yes I do."

"Thank you Mr Feeley."

David sat down at least having accomplished that someone called Babes, an Arabian man and a Scottish man had visited the flat at some time. It went a small way to establishing that there may be some truth in Damien's account.

The Prosecution next referred the Jury to the transcript of Mr Feeley's 999 call which was logged at 6:57am on 4th February 2012.

Graham Storey was called next by the Prosecution. He was 69 years of age, retired and ex-army. He gave a similar version of events to that given by Mr Feeley about the number and types of visitors to Mr Hussain's flat and the loud noise that emanated from it. He gave evidence that he had taken to wearing ear plugs at night to avoid the noise. He was referred to a plan of the flats and pointed out that he resided alone at number five which was next to Mr Hussain's flat.

He recalled the night of 3rd February 2012 when just before midnight he had heard someone shout up to Mr Hussain's flat asking to be let in. He recalled that he had gone to sleep without putting any ear plugs in as the noise was not so bad that night. However, he had been woken in the early hours of the morning by loud noises coming from the flat. He thought this was at about 3 or 4am but he could not be sure. He recalled hearing Mr Hussain's voice and that of a girl and one man. He had put in his ear plugs and gone back to sleep and heard no more until he was awoken just after 7am by firemen knocking on his door.

David rose to his feet to cross examine this witness. There were certain matters of concern in the evidence which made him wonder just how much Mr Storey had heard but he did not want to look like he was attacking a seemingly independent witness.

"Mr Storey, you witnessed many people visit Mr Hussain's flat over the years?"

"Yes, Sir."

David smiled at the polite response, sadly lacking in most witnesses in court these days.

"Can you tell me this, did you ever discover the names of anyone who visited Mr Hussain's flat?"

"No, Sir."

"Did you hear the name Babs or Babes being used to describe a female visitor to the flat?"

"No, Sir."

"Can you recall now if anyone with an Arabian accent ever visited the flat?"

"No, Sir."

"Anyone with a Scottish accent?"

"No, Sir."

David realised this was going to be as slow and painful as pulling teeth, with Mr Storey replying mainly with two syllables.

"Let me take you to the night of 3rd February 2012. Did you see anyone visit Mr Hussain's flat?"

"No, Sir."

David was now determined to get more than a two syllable answer to his questions.

"Mr Storey, at just before midnight you heard a man shout up to Mr Hussain's flat asking to be let in. Do you recall what the man actually said?"

"No, Sir."

Clearly David needed to try a different tack.

"What time would you normally go to bed on a Friday night?"

"Sorry?"

Another two syllable answer.

"What time would you normally go to bed on a Friday night?"

"About midnight, Sir"

David had managed to get five syllables out of Mr Storey, over double his best so far, progress was being made in this cross examination.

"What time did you go to bed on this Friday that we are dealing with?"

"Midnight"

Back to two syllables.

"You have told us you normally wear earplugs because of the noise. Why did you not put them in that night?"

"I was tired Sir. I was in bed when I heard the noise but then as it was quiet I just drifted off."

David felt that he had made tremendous progress. The witness was finally communicating with him.

"You next recall waking to hear voices coming from next door in Mr Hussain's flat?"

"Yes, Sir."

"You cannot recall the exact time, it may have been 3-4am, presumably it may have been earlier or later than those times?"

"Yes, Sir."

"Can you recall now, how many voices you heard coming from that flat?"

"No, Sir."

Mr Storey was back to the two syllable answers but at least the answers themselves were not hurting his case.

"Could it be you heard as many as five people talking in that flat?"

"I don't recall that many voices. I remember hearing Mr Hussain's voice, a voice of a girl and a male voice. I don't remember any more Sir."

That was annoying, David had thought he was getting somewhere.

"But you have told us a moment ago that you do not remember how many voices were coming from the flat, so it could have been more than three voices you heard?"

"Yes, Sir"

Good, back on track.

"And indeed, there could have been persons in the flat whose voices you did not hear?"

Joanna looked like she was going to rise to her feet to object to this speculative question but she chose not to.

"I suppose so, Sir."

David thanked Mr Storey and sat down. Joanna then got to her feet to re-examine.

"Mr Storey, you have told us you awoke at about 3-4am and heard voices from Mr Hussain's flat?"

"Yes, Madam."

"You have been asked by my Learned Friend just how many voices you heard."

"Yes Madam."

"You told us you heard Mr Hussain's voice, a woman's voice and another man's voice?"

"Yes, Madam."

"Do you recall any other voices coming from that flat that night other than the three you have mentioned?"

"No, Madam."

It was certainly not the most difficult piece of re-examination that Joanna had ever conducted, but she was clearly very satisfied with the answers.

Joanna next called another neighbour called Annabelle Lyons who was a sole occupant of flat number seven, directly opposite Mr Hussain's flat. She walked into Court wearing a ladies business suit and was immaculately presented.

She had not heard any noises coming from that flat on the night of 3rd February 2012 nor did she recall seeing or hearing any visitors going to that flat. She stated she went to sleep at about 11pm and was woken by a loud scream coming from Mr Hussain's flat at about 4-30am. She knew it was that time because she glanced at her bedside clock which had an illuminated face. She was sure that the voice was a male one.

Joanna looked at Ms Lyons' witness statement and asked her if her memory might have been clearer at the time she made that statement, months before. Ms Lyons looked at her as though her evidence was being criticised and simply replied.

"No, my recollection is as good now as it was that day."

Joanna had simply wanted to remind her what she said about the scream in her Witness Statement but in view of the witnesses' answer, she simply sat down.

David rose to his feet. It did not really matter to Damien's case who was screaming. It could have been Babs/Babes subjected to a rape attack by the two men or Mr Hussain after being stabbed or some other incident altogether that night. What did matter was the timing as if the screaming was as a result of the rape or the murder, 4-30am did not tie in with Damien's times but might tie in with Damien's sister Karen's witness statement that stated he first came home at 5am.

"Ms Lyons, you would be aware from your position opposite Mr Hussain's flat that he had many visitors to his flat at all times of the day and night?"

"I did see many visitors in the evenings and night time although I work during the day so I was not around to see any visitors then."

"Presumably you would see visitors in the day on Saturdays and Sundays?"

"Yes, I did."

"There would often be loud noises coming from his flat at all times of the day and night?"

"I do recall being woken a number of times by loud noises coming from the flat. In fact I complained to the supervisor, Mr Davies, about the noise on a number of occasions."

David was taken aback at that answer as nowhere in the papers was there any reference to a flat Supervisor.

"Sorry, we've never heard of Mr Davies before. Where does he live?"

"He lives on the ground floor of the flats, flat number 1."

"Do you know if he was there on the night of the 3rd February to 4th February this year?"

"Yes, I recall on 4th February 2012 when I left my flat because of the fire, he was downstairs talking to a policeman."

"Thank you Ms Lyons, that's very helpful. Now can you just assist me with the morning of the 4th February 2012. You awoke at 4:30am when you heard a scream?"

"Yes."

"You have told us you are sure it was a male's voice?"

"Yes."

"Could it have been a female's voice?"

"No."

"Are you sure?"

"Yes, absolutely."

"The only reason I ask is that you made a Witness Statement to the Police on 6th February 2012. You stated, and I quote, "It sounded like a female voice but it could have been a male voice, I cannot be sure." Do you remember saying that now, you can certainly see a copy of your statement if you wish?"

Ms Lyons asked for a copy of her statement and saw the part mentioned.

"I was sure it was a male voice, but clearly when the statement was taken from me I thought it may have been a female voice. I'm not sure at all now."

"Thank you, you have also told us that you were sure it was 4-30am because you looked at your bedside clock?"

"Yes."

"Obviously you had just woken up, possibly from a deep sleep, it is possible that you made a mistake about the time as well?"

Ms Lyons was now confused. She had not recalled her statement and not wanting to be caught out again simply said,

"I'm not sure."

David smiled at her and said thank you and sat down. It was the furthest he was going to get with this Witness. What was more important was the fact that she had mentioned a Flat Supervisor who was actually present on the night and spoke to the police on 4th February 2012 and yet there was not a single reference to him in the prosecution papers, or the Unused Material.

The Prosecution's final Witness for the day was Alexander McDonald. He lived in flat number 2 directly beneath Mr Hussain's flat. He was 77 years of age and lived on his own. He was aware of visitors to Mr Hussain's flat and the noises that came from there which sometimes woke him up. He did not recall any noises on 3rd February, nor did he recall seeing or hearing anyone visiting Mr Hussain's flat. He had gone to sleep at 10pm that night because he was not feeling very well. He was awoken at about 2am on 4th February when he heard loud noises coming from the flat above him. He had put the light on and checked his bedside clock which is why he was aware of the time. He was falling back to sleep when he had heard a scream. It annoyed him but did not concern him unduly because he had heard louder screams from there in the past. He believed the man above his flat lived with a young girl and they were always arguing and the noise often travelled through the floor to him.

David did not consider this evidence particularly important. A scream at 2am could surely not have anything to do with the Murder although it was important to establish that there were often screams coming from the flat so those that Ms Lyons had heard may have had nothing to do with the case. He began by asking the usual questions about Babs/Babe and the Scottish man and the Arabian man. Mr McDonald had not been able to help but it did not really matter as David just wanted to keep reminding the Jury that it was Damien's case those three had been present at the time of the Murder. He asked Mr McDonald if he could be sure that the time was 2am and Mr McDonald was adamant it was. He then asked,

"Did you hear any further screams at all, later in the morning say at around 4-30am?"

"No, the only scream I heard was at 2am."

"Thank you Mr MacDonald, I've no further questions."

The first day came to a close at 4:20pm. No major in-roads had been made into the Prosecution case but then again at least the Prosecution case had not got any stronger. David took Charlotte down to the cells to see Damien just to discuss the Prosecution Opening and the Witnesses. He also asked Charlotte to make sure her firm take a statement from Robert Davies just in case he could assist in some way. You never know, he thought to himself.

CHAPTER 15.

DAY TWO, THE EVIDENCE OF THE EX GIRLFRIEND AND THE ARSON EXPERT.

Day two of the trial was delayed due to the fact that the Prosecution had witness difficulties. They had wanted to call Gillian Banks, Usman Hussain's flat mate but she had not turned up to Court and was not answering her phone. Other witnesses had been lined up to give evidence but there were problems with the trains so the case was adjourned for half an hour. David had arrived early that morning because he knew the Prosecution was calling the fire officer Mr Wardle and he had arranged for the Forensic scientist Helen Forster to be there early so that he could ask her a few questions about arson, seats of fire and accelerants. Now he had extra time on his hands and David took Charlotte to the Bar Mess to have his third cup of coffee of the morning.

"Do we really need Gillian Banks?"

Charlotte asked in a manner in which suggested she could see no possible reason for having Gillian Banks anywhere near a courtroom.

David was tempted to answer, if you had any input into preparing this case you would know why I want her, but he decided it was time to be diplomatic.

"I think we do Charlotte. We need to keep hammering the idea that the Scotsman and the Arabian man exist. Gillian Banks was not there the night that Usman died but she was there other nights. She lived there and may well have known who the Scotsman and the Arabian man were."

They were called back into Court at 11-00am and a Witness Summons was issued to bring Gillian Banks to Court, when the Police found her. Joanna then announced that they were proposing to call Jenny Jones as their next witness. David pointed out that the Defence objected to parts of her evidence.

"My Lord, we do not mind that she gives evidence that they had a falling out that day and that text messages were sent to her and the location where they were sent from. However, we do object to her giving evidence that there was an attempted rape. It can have no conceivable relevance to the case, amounts to "bad character" evidence, and there is no formal application by the Prosecution relating to it and it is of course by its nature, highly prejudicial."

Joanna rose to her feet in response to this objection, smiled at His Honour Judge Tanner and told him how essential this evidence was.

"My Lord, this evidence is an important part of the Prosecution case. We do not accept that it is "bad Character" requiring a formal application. Indeed it is part and parcel of the night's activities, occurring as it did just a few hours before the Murder. We are not seeking to establish that there was an attempted rape, merely that such an allegation was made. The Jury will hear of the Defendant's claim that the Arabian man and the Scotsman were attempting to rape the girl Babs/Babe. In deciding how credible that account is, they should be able to consider the fact that just a few hours before someone was making a similar allegation against him."

His Honour Judge Tanner had defended people for most of his career at the Bar. Now he was a Judge he was, perhaps ironically, considered to be one of the most Prosecution minded. David had no doubts which way he would rule. To be fair he thought a few more defence minded judges would rule in favour of admitting this evidence.

His Honour Judge Tanner ruled that whether the evidence was evidence of bad character or not it was important explanatory evidence and should be presented before the jury. He would warn them that it was the fact of the allegation that was important and they were not to involve themselves in collateral litigation in deciding whether there was an attempted rape, but to concentrate on the fact that this was a murder trial and the issue they were to concentrate on was whether the Defendant murdered Usman Hussain.

The Jury had been absent from Court whilst this point of law was decided, and were brought back in. An explanation was made that Witnesses had been delayed on the way to Court but the Prosecution could now proceed.

Jenny Jones was called to the stand. She was a young girl of about 25 years. She was dressed in jeans and a T shirt, sporting a gold Giraffe motif on the front. She had clearly made an effort for the Court, although it was slightly offset by the home-made tattoos which could just be made out underneath her sleeves. David could not make them out from where he was, although one looked like it began with a capital 'D' and he wondered if it read "Damien."

Joanna began by asking her a few background questions about knowing Damien, having been in a relationship with him, the fact, although not the detail, of how they broke up and how they kept in touch and would see each other quite regularly after they split.

The questioning then moved on to 3rd February 2012. She stated that they had arranged the meeting the day before. They met at about 12pm and went to a local pub, the Prince Rupert Pub for a few drinks. She had not counted how many drinks they had had but they were both drinking cider all day. After a few hours they left and bought some cans of strong lager from a local off licence. She recalled that they roamed the streets together for a few hours drinking. They also shared a couple of Cannabis joints that Damien rolled for them in a small park area. Sometime in the evening they visited another pub called the Queen Mary. She could not recall what time they left that pub or how much they had to drink but she accepted they were both drunk when they left.

Joanna then moved on to the important part of Jenny's evidence.

"Ms Jones, can you recall where you went after you left the Queen Mary public house with Mr Clarke?"

"I remember going home afterwards, although I can't remember actually getting home."

"Were you on your own or was anyone with you?"

"I was on my own, I'd had a falling out with Damien."

"What was the falling out about?"

"I can't really remember."

Joanna Glass QC realised that she was going to have difficulties with Jenny who was now showing a reluctance to say much about Damien, so she decided to ask questions of Jenny that would allow her to put her Witness Statement to her which contained the allegation of attempted rape.

"You made a Statement about this nearer the time. Would your recollection of this matter have been significantly better at that time than it is today?"

"I don't think so. I was drunk I don't really have a good recollection of what happened. I made a statement to Police, but I wasn't really sure what had happened."

"Surely your recollection would have been significantly better when you made your statement than it is now?"

David rose to his feet. This was not unlike the American movies and he rarely objected to questions unless they were really inappropriate as he thought objecting usually caused a Jury to think that you have something to hide and don't want them to hear important evidence. Here the Prosecution were desperate to get Jenny's allegation of attempted rape before the Jury.

"I do object to this line of questioning, Ms Jones has given her answer and it appears my Learned Friend is now trying to cross examine her own witness."

His Honour Judge Tanner looked at him solemnly.

"Mr Brant surely most people would remember matters more clearly when they had just occurred?"

"Not necessarily My Lord, in any event the question is a leading one and contrary to this witness's own evidence."

He looked down at his notes,

"Ms Jones said, "I don't think so. I was drunk I don't really have a good recollection of what happened."

His Honour Judge Tanner conceded the point and told Joanna to move on.

Joanna knew the allegation of attempted rape was important and might cast a light on what happened in the flat that night. She was not going to abandon the allegation that easily. She smiled at his Lordship and said,

"Very well my Lord, I will move on. Ms Jones, you provided your phone to police the following day. This was a phone that had messages on it from a number of people including Mr Clarke?"

"Yes."

"I believe you are aware that phone was analysed and a text was recovered that Mr Clarke sent to you."

"Yes."

"The text was sent at 23-17 and read, "You fucking bitch you led me on again." We will hear Members of the Jury that his phone was cell sited in the vicinity of Mr Hussain's flat at Cambridge Gardens.

Do you recall that text Ms Jones?"

"I remember something like it."

"Can you tell us what he was referring to?"

"We both got pissed, he tried it on, but I weren't interested and told him I wasn't. I then went home and he sent that text. I just ignored it."

Joanna decided to change tactics,

"What was the state of your clothes when you got home?"

"I remember my blouse got torn but I can't remember how."

"Were any other items of clothes torn?"

"I don't think so."

Joanna could see that she was getting nowhere with Jenny, so she made one last effort,

"Do you recall what Mr Clarke did or said before your blouse got torn?"

David looked up at this. It was a nice juxtaposition of questioning suggesting by implication that Damien had torn the blouse. He need not have concerned himself as Jenny did his job for him when she replied.

"No, I don't even know when my blouse was torn, don't even remember if it was before or after I left Damien."

Joanna made a final effort.

"Do you recall if anyone else was around when you left Mr Clarke, a passer-by for example?"

David was tempted to object but Jenny seemed to be fending these questions off without any assistance.

"No I don't remember anyone."

Joanna paused for a few moments, showing the jury her complete disbelief in what this Witness had just said by her icy stare at Jenny. She then turned to His Honour Judge Tanner and said,

"Thank you my Lord, I have no further questions of this Witness"

Without any further questions to the Witness or even a Thank You, she sat down.

David's opinion was that the secret of good advocacy is not asking questions, anyone can ask questions, the secret is asking the right ones and knowing when not to ask a question. Jenny's evidence had not hurt Damien. She had not mentioned the attempted rape or accused him of tearing her clothes and had made no mention of Damien running off after the passer-by had shouted. It would be the height of bad advocacy to deal with any of those matters now as Jenny might change her version of events or at least it would permit Joanna to re-examine on these issues and have a further attempt at getting Jenny's original statement before the jury. He decided to ask one or two anodyne questions that covered nothing of importance and then sat down.

The final Witness before lunch was Thomas Wardle, the fire fighter who had attended Usman Hussain's flat. He gave his evidence, relying on notes that he had taken at the time. He described visiting the flat, gave a brief description of the interior of the flat and then a description of the condition of the flat. He described the soot layer in the flat and how the smoke alarms had all been disconnected before the fire.

David was not surprised by this evidence, Damien had explained that Usman disconnected the smoke alarms for fear that the smoking of crack cocaine might set them off.

Mr Wardle continued to describe the various rooms in the flat and what was discovered there. He then moved on to describe the living room and the burning he had discovered. He checked to see if there were any accelerants, ignitable liquids used to start the fire. He could find no trace. From his observations he concluded that there were two seats of fire in the living room, one started on the sofa, the other on a carpet by the window. It followed that as there were two seats of fire, it was not accidental.

David could see the Jury liked Mr Wardle. He was dressed smartly in his fireman's outfit, came across as perfectly honest and perfectly efficient. Consequently, he was one of the worse types of Witness to cross examine. David knew that whether the fire was started deliberately did not really matter as far as Damien's defence was concerned. After all the two men who killed Usman could have set fire to the flat. However, there was the evidence of Doctor Monkton yet to deal with. Doctor Monkton said the injury to Damien's hand could have been caused accidentally when he set fire to the flat. If David could persuade the jury that the fire was accidental then the evidence of the Doctor would be neutralised before he had even given it.

David had dealt with many arson cases throughout his career so knew a large amount about deliberate arson, seats of fire and accelerants, he also had the advantage of discussing matters with Helen Forster who was sitting behind him now, ready to assist by giving him notes should he need them. He had explained to her as he did with every expert witness that if she sent a note it must be in such a style that he could readily understand it and cross examine upon it. This was not as patronising an advice as it might sound. He recalled years ago cross examining a computer expert on a difficult area about the cache memory of a computer. His own expert sitting behind him had tugged at his gown and sent him a note. David had paused, asked the Judge for a minute to read and digest the note expecting it to be a useful expose of the defects in the Prosecution expert's evidence. He had opened the note to discover the word "Bollocks." He never wanted to be in that position again.

"Mr Wardle I want you to help us in relation to whether the fire was deliberate or not."

This was not really a question but simply a statement to the Jury about what his questioning was aimed at.

"No doubt you have attended many hundreds of fires throughout your career?"

"Yes Sir."

"Have you any idea how many?"

"No Sir, I've never made a count, but I have been in the Fire Service for 25 years and I attend a number of fires every week so it's probably in the thousands now."

"Mr Wardle, I accept that you are very experienced officer who has investigated a great many fires."

David thought it never hurt to praise a witness especially if you are about to try and get him to discredit his own evidence.

"Obviously, fires can be caused accidentally or deliberately?"

"Of course Sir."

"It is sometimes difficult to tell whether a particular fire is accidental or deliberate?"

"Sometimes, Sir."

"Of course, if someone has poured an accelerant all over a property, for example petrol or something similar and then set fire to it. The detection of that accelerant assists you to determine that the fire was deliberate."

"Yes Sir, although not always, for example if the fire was in an area where petrol was stored."

"Yes, thank you Mr Wardle. In this case you looked for traces of an accelerant and did not find any?"

"That's right Sir."

"Trying to detect an accelerant requires a scientific investigation?"

"Yes Sir"

"You used a Hydrocarbon Gas Detector (GasTec). It is used to detect parts per million levels of hydrocarbons and other flammable materials. It works on the phenomenon of what is called flame ionisation. Hydrocarbons drawn into a hydrogen flame burning inside the instrument produce an electrical effect which can be detected and amplified by suitable electronic circuits?"

"That's right Sir"

David was really only quoting back parts of the Witnesses' own statement which had not been dealt with in front of the Jury. It had the desired effect of making him look like he knew a lot about accelerants.

"In this case having used such scientific equipment you obtained no positive readings which would suggest an ignitable liquid was involved in the areas surveyed."

"Again, that's right Sir."

"It is fair to say in your experience, most people who are going to deliberately start a fire try to obtain an accelerant?"

"If one is available, Sir."

"Yes and to be fair, in most houses or flats there is usually something that could act as an accelerant such as white spirit?"

"Yes, Sir."

"In any event, in this case there is no evidence of an accelerant being used."

"That's right Sir."

"Let me ask you about the seats of fire. You concluded there were two seats of fire, both in the living room?"

"Yes Sir, one on the sofa, one on the carpet near the curtains."

"Mr Wardle, having looked at the plan you drew, the areas you identified as being the seats are in fact very close together?"

"Yes Sir"

"I take it that in this case it would be impossible to say which started first."

"Sometimes that is possible, but not in this case."

"It is feasible that the fire on the sofa started first, then the fire on the carpet?"

"Yes Sir."

"In this case the internal doors to the flat were all open and this would have provided a lot of ventilation for the fire?"

"Yes Sir."

"It is also possible that once the sofa caught fire, burning material from the sofa could have been detached at some time and landed elsewhere in the living room."

"That is possible Sir."

"You could not discover an accelerant near the carpet area but did you discover any other debris?"

"There was a lot of debris all around, I could not say what it came from."

"It is possible that burning debris from the sofa floated down onto the carpet and started a secondary fire there?"

"That's possible Sir."

"In other words, there could have been one seat of fire on the sofa which spread and caused a separate fire elsewhere?"

"That is possible Sir."

"Mr Wardle, you will be aware of the difference between a fire that flames and a fire that smoulders?"

"Yes, Sir."

"A smouldering fire may be caused by a carelessly discarded cigarette, for example on a sofa?"

"Yes, Sir."

"In this case you are not able to assist whether the fire on the sofa was a smouldering fire or not?"

"No, Sir"

"A smouldering fire, would smoulder for some time before taking hold and producing flames?"

"Yes, Sir."

"The process could take between 30 minutes and a few hours depending on the material the sofa was made from and the amount of the ventilation?"

"Yes, Sir."

"So, to summarise in this case. There were no accelerants that would suggest the fire was deliberate?"

"No, Sir"

"There could have been one seat of fire on the sofa that spread to the carpet in the living room."

"Yes Sir."

"That fire on the sofa could have been a smouldering fire, caused by a carelessly discarded cigarette?"

"Yes, Sir."

"In other words the fire in this flat could have started accidentally?"

"Yes, Sir."

"Thank you Mr Wardle, you have been very helpful."

David sat down, thoroughly satisfied that this cross examination had gone well. Joanna decided not to bother re-examining in the circumstances and the case was adjourned for lunch. David decided that he did not need to call Helen Forster and then allow her to be cross examined by the Prosecution to the effect the fire was deliberate, so he would thank her and tell her she was no longer needed.

It had been a good morning for Damien.

CHAPTER 16.

DAY TWO, THE SISTERS' EVIDENCE.

The afternoon was less helpful to Damien as his sisters were being called to give evidence. They had no reason to lie about him and their evidence did cause difficulties about his whereabouts in the early hours of 4th February 2012. Damien had given instructions that he went to Usman Hussain's flat just before midnight and had not left until after the Murder. He could not recall the time he left but he was adamant he had gone straight to his Mother's flat and had not returned to Usman's flat.

Karen Clarke was called first. She was older than Damien and David knew from Damien that she was aged 35 although she looked considerably older. Life had clearly not been kind to her although she had made an effort for court putting on a clean white dress with a green top. David could not make out any home-made tattoos which was a feature he had been getting used to.

She came into court with a handkerchief in her hands. She reached the Witness Box and saw Damien in the Dock to her right and dabbed at her eyes. She took the oath on the Bible, gave her name and started to answer Joanna's questions.

The questions were clearly designed to settle her down and were at first simply innocuous ones about her background, where she lived, how long Damien had lived with the family and matters like that. Joanna knew she was an important witness for the Prosecution because of her evidence of timings which would cause considerable problems to Damien's defence. It was therefore important to treat her politely and to extract her evidence slowly, ensuring that she did not change anything through some misguided concept that "blood was thicker than water."

Having obtained the basics, Joanna moved on to 3rd February 2012. Karen had got up to go to work at 7-00am. She worked in Woolwich in a dry cleaners which opened at 8-00am to catch people going to work so she had to leave the flat at 7-45 every morning. She had not seen Damien as he was not in employment and never got up early.

Joanna then moved on to Saturday 4th February 2012.

"Ms Clarke, I want to ask you about the events of 4th February 2012. You will recall that day because it is the day your brother, Damien Clarke was arrested for Murder."

Joanna thought it did not hurt to remind the Jury that was what the case was about.

Karen Clarke's demeanour noticeably changed, she began dabbing at her eyes again with the handkerchief and then blurted out,

"Damien is no Murderer, he's got into trouble in the past like most young boys, but he is no Murderer."

Joanna immediately regretted reminding Karen about the murder charge and moved on rapidly.

"Ms Clarke, I am sure we all understand how difficult this is for you. I don't have a large number of questions for you, but please just wait for the question and answer that."

"I'm sorry", said Karen dabbing more at her eyes than before.

"That's alright and perfectly understandable. Now I want to ask you about the early hours of Saturday 4th February 2012. Do you remember anything in particular happening in the early hours?"

"I remember that I got up at about 7-00am and got ready for work and left at just before 8am as we open later on Saturdays."

"Do you remember anything happening before you got up?"

"I remember hearing noises during the night, sounding like someone coming into the flat and later a noise sounding like someone was leaving the flat."

"Do you recall what time this was?"

"I can't recall the exact time. I looked at my clock and remember it was past 5 when I first heard the noise of someone coming in and it was near to 6 when I heard someone going out."

"Was that before or after 6am?"

"I remember it was before 6am"

"Can you recall how long it was between hearing someone coming in and someone going out?"

"Not really, I think I went back to sleep."

"It must have been less than an hour based upon what you have told us?"

"Yes."

"Do you know who it was coming into the flat and leaving at that time?"

"No."

Joanna was slightly taken aback at this answer so tried a different tack.

"Do you recall what time you went to bed on the Friday night?"

"It would have been about 11pm."

"Who was in the house when you went to bed?"

"My Mother and my Sister, Christine."

"Did they go to bed before or after you?"

"We all went at about the same time."

"Where was your Brother, Damien?"

"He was out."

"So who did you think it was coming in at about 5 in the morning and leaving at about 6?"

Although what Karen "thought" was irrelevant and inadmissible, David did not object as the answer to the question was obvious.

"I thought it was probably Damien because he is always coming in late."

Having got the answers she wanted, Joanna sat down.

David smiled at Karen who smiled back at him.

"Ms Clarke, I am going to ask you some questions on behalf of your brother Damien, who I represent together with Ms Williams who sits behind me."

He thought it would make it easier for her to answer his questions if she knew he was representing her brother, and he noted that she kept smiling when he said this.

"Ms Clarke, you never saw your brother on Friday 3rd February?"

"No, I didn't. He wasn't up when I went to work and he didn't come home before I went to bed."

"Did you see him on the Saturday at any time?"

"No, I know he came back to the flat because my Sister told me she saw him, but I was getting ready for work when he came back and I didn't see him before I left. I came back home in the afternoon and he had gone out again. I didn't see him again until I visited him in Prison."

That was probably more information than the Jury needed but David was not unduly concerned.

"So you never saw him at all on the Saturday?"

"No, I never did."

"It follows you never saw him between 5am and 6am?"

"No I didn't."

"You cannot recall the time differences between hearing the noises of someone apparently coming in and someone apparently leaving?"

"No."

"You fell back to sleep and weren't really looking at your clock when you heard these noises?"

"No I wasn't."

"So it could be the distance in time was much less than an hour?"

"Yes it could have been."

"Sometime after 5am and sometime before 6am could in fact have been a matter of minutes?"

"I thought it was longer but I'm not really sure."

"Yes, that's understandable."

Joanna looked up at this, but before she could object to a blatant comment, David moved on.

"The noises you heard sounded like someone coming in and someone leaving?"

"Yes."

"Presumably it was the same noise?"

"I don't understand."

"I'm sorry, I'm just suggesting that the noise of someone opening a door is the same whether they are entering or leaving a property?"

"Yes, I suppose so."

"It follows, the noises you heard could be someone leaving the house sometime between 5 and 6am and then coming back a few minutes later between 5 and 6am?"

"I suppose so."

"Yes, thank you very much."

David smiled at Karen and sat down.

Joanna felt that the evidence could not be left in this parlous state leaving an impression that it was either Karen's Mother or Sister who left the house.

"Ms Clarke, do your Mother or Sister ever get up between 5 and 6 in the morning and leave the property?"

She received an answer she certainly was not expecting and certainly did not want.

"Sometimes my Mother cannot sleep and does get up early to let the Cat out or in."

"Do you know whether she did on this occasion?"

"I don't know, you will have to ask her."

Joanna gave up on the questioning and passed a note to her Junior to ensure that a Statement be taken from the Mother.

The next Witness was Karen's and Damien's younger sister Christine. Unlike her Sister, she had made no effort to impress the Court. She was wearing a pair of scruffy jeans and a scruffy top. She carried with her an air of open contempt for the Court and its proceedings. She took an Affirmation and then smiled at Damien. As soon as Joanna rose to her feet she scowled at her. Joanna knew this was not going to be easy. Again she tried the approach of asking innocuous questions but received monosyllabic answers in reply. Eventually she moved on to deal with the events of Saturday 4th February 2012.

"Ms Clarke, do you recall Saturday 4th February 2012?"

"Yeah."

"Do you recall what time you got up that day?"

"Nope."

"Do you recall whether you saw your brother Damien or not?"

"Yeah."

"When did you see him?"

"This is stupid. I told the Police all of this. I shouldn't be here!"

His Honour Judge Tanner had shown remarkable patience up to now but turned upon her.

"Ms Clarke, I assure you that this is not stupid. These are serious proceedings and you will not be assisting anybody, including your Brother if you have an attitude like that. Ms Glass QC has a job to do and has to ask you a number of questions. Your time in the Witness box will be much shorter if you simply answer those questions."

Christine Clarke looked at him with an expression that was clearly contemptuous but her expression soon changed when she thought about the consequences. Like her Brother she was no stranger to the Criminal Justice system and had spent some time in Prison for a street robbery. She did not want to return so she said "Sorry" and turned back to Joanna.

"Ms Clarke, I will ask you again, when did you see your brother on that Saturday morning?"

"It was about 7-30am. I'd got up to get a glass of water and then I heard a knock on the door. I went and undid the lock and let Damien in."

"What was his condition?"

"What do you mean?"

"What did he look like?"

"He just looked normal."

"Did you notice anything about his clothes?"

"No."

"Do you recall what he was wearing?"

"Not particularly, just his ordinary clothes."

"How did he appear?"

"I don't know what you mean."

"Did he appear as if he had been running or walking?"

"He just looked normal to me. He wasn't out of breath."

Joanna decided that was enough effort for one day and sat down.

David stood and tried the same technique as he had with Karen, smiling at her he said,

"Ms Clarke, I'm going to ask you some questions on behalf of your Brother, Damien who I represent."

It did not seem to have any effect as the scowl she directed at David was the same as the one she had directed at Joanna. Clearly she disliked all lawyers, even the ones representing her brother.

"Ms Clarke, you say you saw your brother at about 7-30 am on Saturday 4th February 2012."

"Yeah."

"Are you sure it was about 7-30am, may it have been earlier?"

"It may have been but not much because I was getting up."

"Damien did not appear out of breath to you but you could not tell whether he had been running or had walked to the flat?"

"No."

"You've been asked about Damien's clothes. You did not notice anything in particular about them?"

"No."

"They were not saturated in blood for example?"

"No."

"Can you help me on this point? Did you get up earlier that morning?"

"No, I got up just before Damien came in at 7-30 am."

"Damien possessed a key didn't he?"

"Yeah we all had our own keys."

"However, he knocked on the door at 7-30 am?"

"Yeah."

"You had to undo the lock to let him in?"

"Yeah."

"So the door was locked from the inside?"

"Yeah it was, that's why I had to let him in."

"So someone had put the lock on the door from the inside?"

"Yeah, the bolt was on so I had to undo it."

"Thank you Ms Clarke."

David was quite content with this piece of cross examination. Damien had not told him he could not get into the house but now it started to make sense. Someone had locked the door from the inside. Damien could not have come into the property at 5am and left at 6am and put the bolt on the inside of the door. Someone else had bolted the door from the inside before 7-30 am and it was likely to be the person who left the property and then came back into the property sometime between 5 and 6am and that was not Damien. The only problem was that the 7-30am timing did not fit with Damien's evidence that he went straight there from Usman's flat after the Murder. The Fire Brigade had been called just before 7am and it took 15 minutes to get from Hussain's flat to Damien's flat. There were 15 minutes unaccounted for and in reality probably more.

The rest of the afternoon was taken up with Timothy Arnold reading to the Jury statements of witnesses the defence did not require to attend Court.

Again the afternoon had gone well for Damien. If David could keep this up, Damien might even have a chance.

CHAPTER 17.

DAYS THREE AND FOUR, THE EXPERT EVIDENCE.

David arrived at the Bailey at 9:30am on the Wednesday. He knew from experience that Charlotte would not be there for another half hour but he could not face the lukewarm bacon again that week so he settled for a hot coffee. Joanna joined him a few minutes later to mention that the Police had still not located Gillian Banks and were now concerned that they may not be able to. Joanna asked if David would object to her reading Gillian Banks' statement to the Jury but he was not feeling in a charitable mood and thought that Gillian Banks might have some evidence that may assist Damien and wanted the opportunity to ask her questions, so he declined the offer.

The day in Court was taken up with the Prosecution calling a number of Witnesses to deal with what was found in the flat and to deal with the searches of Damien's Mother's flat. The Prosecution spent some time dealing with where the bloodstains were found, the condition of the flat when the fire fighters and paramedics arrived as well as the position of Usman Hussain's body. David asked a few questions but did not cover any major areas as none of the witnesses were that important to the Defence case. They were more "continuity" Witnesses demonstrating what was found, and where, so that the experts could be called the following day to say what the relevance of this evidence was. As David did not have much questioning and the Prosecution ran out of Witnesses the case was adjourned early.

David spent Wednesday night preparing his cross examination of the Experts. Charlotte had not provided any notes to help him although she was providing him each night with a verbatim note of the evidence that was given in court.

On Thursday the Prosecution's first Witness was the Pathologist Dr Alistair Forsyth. David had not even required him to attend Court as he had no challenges to the evidence and agreed that it could simply be read rather than be dealt with in great gory detail before the Jury. However, Joanna had decided that she wanted the Pathologist to give evidence for two reasons; firstly it saved Tim or her reading out a long and complex statement and secondly because a Jury was more likely to concentrate on the evidence if they heard Dr Forsyth live in court, rather than hear his Statement being read out.

Dr Alistair Forsyth entered the Witness Box and swore on the Bible. It gave David a slight degree of amusement that a man of Science who saw what man could inflict upon his fellow man in a myriad of horrific ways, still believed in God. The truth was that David did as well but his Faith had been shaken severely on a number of occasions in his life.

Joanna started by asking Dr Forsyth what his qualifications were. He listed them all, and added where he had gone to University and his experience since then. He listed his Degrees, Diplomas and Fellowships in such a way that no one could doubt he was an Expert before he had answered even one question about the case. He moved on to discuss his instructions and his knowledge that his duty was to the Court and not to the party that paid him.

Joanna took him through his report in some detail although she did not cover every part with him as some of the content, such as the weight of the dead man's organs, was clearly irrelevant to any issue the Jury had to decide. He dealt with the fact that Usman Hussain was clearly dead before the fire or fires had been lit because there was no evidence of burns or inhalation of fire fumes. He went into great detail about the injuries caused, listed all stab wounds and cuts and showed where these were caused on the body graphic that was in the Jury bundle. He also stated that he had noticed that he had seen significant traces of dried blood around Mr Hussain's nose and mouth when he carried out the post mortem. Clearly Joanna had spoken to him before he gave his evidence because he gave far more detail than had appeared in his report. There was nothing wrong with her speaking to an expert about his evidence and David was not surprised that she had taken this elementary step.

Dr Forsyth went into detail about defence wounds, stating the obvious that people who are assaulted with knives and who have time to react, use their arms and hands to ward off blows and so that defence wounds are often found on the arms and hands. He also dealt with less obvious evidence such as how easy a knife can penetrate flesh and how little force is actually needed to cause a serious wound. However, he pointed out that severe force must have been used here because of the injuries to the breastbone and ribs. He gave his estimate of the size of the knife from his measurements of the wounds but pointed out this must be an estimate as tissues compress and therefore a knife with a relatively short blade can leave a deep wound that is significantly deeper than the length of the blade. Of the twelve wounds, he concluded that four were potentially fatal. The positioning of the injuries and the measurement of them suggested the same knife was used to cause them all and that they were consistent with one person wielding the knife. He was shown a knife that was recovered from the Usman Hussain's kitchen. It was clean and had no traces of blood or tissue upon it but he concluded that it was of the right size to cause the injuries that he had seen here and could be the murder Weapon.

David had not asked for him and had no real questions to ask, but he thought he would try a few of the staple questions he used when he cross examined pathologists

"Dr Forsyth can you assist me, what is Locard's principle?"

Dr Forsyth looked at him as if he was an idiot for asking such a basic question.

"Locard's **Exchange** principle is based upon the works of Dr Edmond Locard. He was an important pioneer in forensic scientist and was even nicknamed the "Sherlock Holmes of France." He formulated a basic principle known as "Locard's Exchange principle." Stated simply it is the principle that, "Every contact leaves a trace.""

"Thank you Dr Forsyth, I stand corrected, "Locard's Exchange Principle" is that "Every contact leaves a trace." Put simply, it means that if a person grabs another person, one would expect some trace to be left. It could be DNA from blood, sweat, saliva, hair or fibres from clothing?"

"Yes it could, although it is right that Forensic science has come a long way since Dr Locard died in, I believe, 1967."

"Actually it was 1966 but I am sure we need not quibble. Nevertheless the basic principle still stands?"

"Yes it does."

"Were you aware that in this case no such material was found on Mr Hussain that came from Mr Clarke?"

"I understand that is the case."

"Thank you Dr Forsyth, that is all I ask."

David sat down, it was not a great point because he was aware from checking the Unused that no such material had been found from anyone else either, but he saw no reason to raise this and assumed that Joanna had not read the Unused in any great detail. When she did not re-examine Dr Forsyth he realised he was right.

Dr Forsyth left the witness box at 12:45pm, as there were no other witnesses available. His Honour Judge Tanner gave the jury an extended lunch hour and as he had another matter to deal with at 2pm he adjourned the case until 2-30pm.

As they had 1 hour 45 minutes David invited Charlotte out for lunch. They removed their court robes and made their way down to the ground floor by lift. He decided to take Charlotte to Carluccios in Smithfield as it was only five minutes' walk away. Charlotte ordered a Fritto Misto and David the Bistecca Di Bue Con Patate. They both agreed to share a bottle of Pinot Grigio, Serra Di Pago, Veneto, described on the menu, "as fresh and fruity produced by a leading cantina in Veneto." David did not normally drink wine at lunch, but he decided to make an exception today as he knew that the afternoon ahead was not going to be a difficult one. The Prosecution had only been able to line up the Cell Site expert as again they were having Witness difficulties and His Honour Judge Tanner had already stated he had to rise at 4pm for a "Judicial Meeting."

The case resumed at 2-45pm as the Judge's 2pm case finished later than he had anticipated. Joanna immediately called the expert, George Rollins to explain the Cell Site evidence in this case.

David had not come across George Rollins before but noted that he was quite a short man, wearing a thick tweed jacket and a red bow tie. He explained that he had worked as a Cell Site engineer and an Expert Witness since 2006 and had completed in excess of one hundred and fifty Cell Site Reports and given evidence in more than fifty trials. He had twenty years' experience of working in the radio communication and mobile telecommunications industries. He held a HNC in electronic engineering and had held senior engineering roles within the Ministry of Defence. He stated that these roles gave him an in-depth knowledge of how mobile networks operate and how the mobile handset communicates with the network.

Joanna asked him to explain the background to Cell Site evidence and he did. He explained that all his surveys were carried out using the NEMO measurement system, which uses a standard handset loaded with special software to enable network measurements to be made and logged onto the handset's internal memory.

He gave a detailed history of how mobile phones worked, explaining that they were radio transceivers that operated by communicating with base stations, or Cell Sites by using radio signals. These Cell Sites were located on different structures such as buildings, masts or even fake trees. The calls were then routed from the Cell Site to a network operator for processing and onward to its destination which could be another mobile or landline. Records were kept for the billing of these calls which indicated who the call was to and how long the call lasted. The records also showed which Cell Site was used by the phone and from which direction. Most masts operated in three separate directions each of 120 degrees. Consequently if you drew a circle around each mast and divided it into three, you could tell which individual section, or Cell, a call came from. It was not exact as the Cells would slightly overlap. He pointed out that the range of any cell varied considerably. In a dense urban area the range could be 200-500 metres, in an urban area the range could be 0.5 to 1 kilometres, in a suburban area it could be 1.5 to 3 kilometres and in a rural area it could be 3-5 kilometres and in some instances longer.

He went on to point out that a mobile phone would try to use the Cell that gave the strongest signal and that this was often the closest Cell. However, he had to point out that this was not always the case and a more distant cell might be used if there was congestion from too many phones trying to use the Cell Site, or a Cell was blocked, by, for example, tall buildings.

David had heard this type of evidence before so was not taking a note. He noticed however, that two male members of the Jury were busy scribbling away as Mr Rollins gave his evidence.

Having got Mr Rollins to give enough background information, she moved on to the relevant evidence in this case.

"Mr Rollins, you have obtained the Call Data for three phones in this case."

"That's right Madam."

"I want to ask you about four calls or text messages."

She turned to the Jury and with her most charming smile said,

"Ladies and Gentlemen, you have this evidence in your Jury bundles if you would like to follow it."

The Jury turned to the right pages in their bundles.

"Mr Rollins, the first call was made on 3rd February 2012 at 11:37am. It was made by Mr Clarke's phone to a phone belonging to his ex-girlfriend, Jenny Jones."

Joanna's emphasis on the "ex" made it clear she was trying to suggest that they may be far closer than either was claiming.

"Mr Rollins, can you tell us where Mr Clarke's phone was cell sited to at that time?"

"Yes it was cell sited in the area of the mast serving Woolwich High Street."

"Thank you, I now want to move on to a text message sent from Mr Clarke's phone to Ms Jones' phone almost exactly twelve hours later at 23:17. We know from an analysis of Mr Clarke's phone that message read, "You fucking bitch you led me on again." Where was the phone cell sited to at that stage?"

"It was cell sited to a mast in the vicinity of Cambridge Gardens where I understand Mr Hussain, the deceased, died."

"Thank you, I now want to ask you about a phone call made from Mr Clarke's phone to a phone registered to a Mr Christopher White at 5:21am on 4th February. Where was that cell sited to?"

"It was cell sited to a mast in the region of Thamesmead Way in Woolwich, which I believe is where the defendant's accommodation is situated."

"Yes, that's his mother's address. So he was using his phone at his mother's accommodation at 5:21am?"

David jumped to his feet,

"My Lord, my Learned Friend knows she cannot make a statement like that. She should ask relevant questions. As she knows Cell Site evidence only tells us which phone made a call and the vicinity it was in, not who made the call or where the phone actually was."

His Honour Judge Tanner had to accept David's intervention was correct but decided to add rather unhelpfully,

"No doubt we will hear in due course who made this particular call and where he was."

Joanna continued with her charming smile and David, rather uncharitably, wondered if she practiced it for hours in front of a mirror. Joanna continued,

"Thank you my Lord. Mr Rollins I will ask you about a fourth call. At 12-32 on 4th February, Mr Clarke's phone called Mr White's phone again at 12-32. Where was the phone cell sited to?"

"In the vicinity of Thamesmead Way in Woolwich."

Joanna could not resist adding.

"Where Mr Brant's client told the police he was at that time. Yes thank you, I have no further questions."

Joanna sat down believing correctly that she had persuaded some members of the j#ury that Damien

Clarke was in his Mother's flat at 5:21am. In other words it must have been him who entered the flat at about 5am and left around 6am.

David gathered his papers together and turned towards Mr Rollins.

"Mr Rollins, you have told us that a mobile phone will try to use the closest mast but sometimes will use one further away if the signal is blocked by a building or other structure?"

"That's correct Sir"

"Further, the mast may have a great number of mobile phones using it, "congestion" as you say and a phone may have to use a mast further away?"

"Again that's right sir."

"You made tests to see which masts were useable at these locations?"

"I did Sir."

"We are dealing with four calls and in fact four different masts are we not?"

"We are Sir."

"Even though two of the calls were said to be in the vicinity of Mr Clarke's flat?"

"That's not uncommon Sir."

"What day and time did you conduct your tests?"

"I think it was a Friday, Sir, after 2pm"

"Obviously there is more likely to be "congestion" at 2pm on a Friday than at 5am on a Saturday."

"I would think so."

"Did you not think to use your equipment at the time and day that the relevant calls were made?"

"No Sir, I did not think it would make that much difference."

"It could though."

"It could."

"For example, you have provided a map of the relevant Cell Sites in this case. The Cell Sites that you say served Mr Hussain's flat and Mr Clarke's Mother's address are only 0.5 kilometres away from each other?"

"I haven't measured it."

David produced Mr Rollins' own map which had a scale on it and he produced a ruler for Mr Rollins. Mr Rollins measured the position of the two Cell Masts and stated,

"They are just less than one half kilometre apart."

"Using the ruler again Mr Rollins, could you confirm that Mr Hussain's flat and Mr Clarke's mother's flat are less than a mile apart, less than 1500 metres?"

Mr Rollins measured again and confirmed that was the case.

"Mr Rollins it is feasible is it not, that due to the close proximity of the masts and the buildings in this case, taking into account possible congestion when you conducted the tests, that in fact the 5:21am call was not in the vicinity of Mr Clarke's flat but in the vicinity of Mr Hussains?"

"I suppose that is possible."

David was a little surprised at the answer as the Defence had commissioned their own Cell Site expert who said this was unlikely. Having obtained this answer he decided it would be wrong to press it and, thanking Mr Rollins, he sat down.

Joanna acknowledged to anyone who was interested in listening, that she had never really understood the nuances of Cell Site evidence. Nevertheless, she was an excellent advocate and was not going to leave the case there. She decided to cover this topic in re-examination.

"Mr Rollins, in answer to my Learned Friend, Mr Brant's questioning, that it is possible that the 5:21am call was in the vicinity of Mr Hussain's flat rather than the Defendant's?"

"That's right Madam."

"However, does that concession change your opinion in any way?"

"No, it is **possible** that the call was made from the vicinity of Mr Hussain's flat but in view of the number of tests I conducted I consider it far more likely that the call was made from the vicinity of the Defendant's flat."

Joanna, put the charming smile back in place and thanked Mr Rollins and as it was now near to 4pm the case ended for the day because His Honour Judge Tanner had to go off for his "Judicial Meeting." David knew from experience that this could be anything from a lecture, a meeting of Judges or simply a meeting with a friend who happened to be a Judge! David recalled how he was once in a Crown Court in Kent when a Judge had adjourned a case for a few days to go on a "Course." He had later discovered the "Course" in question was the Cheltenham Racecourse!

David was not bothered about having a slightly early day. He thought about the evidence that had been given and that although it was not a great day for Damien it had not been as bad as he thought it might be. Damien was still in with a chance.

CHAPTER 18.

DAY FIVE AND MORE EXPERTS.

Friday arrived and still the Police could not find Gillian Banks. The Prosecution had lined up a number of Expert Witnesses and David had spent most of Thursday night working on lines of cross examination. He had taken a break in Chambers at 7-30pm and shared a bottle of Claret with Wendy Pritchard in El Vinos. She had asked him how the Case was going and he had told her, truthfully that he thought it had gone quite well for Damien so far, but he was not looking forward to calling Damien to the Witness Box as he thought Joanna Glass QC would tear him to shreds, chew him up and spit him out and never once drop her charming smile.

The first witness the Prosecution called that day was Dr Roger Allbright, an expert on blood staining. He began by outlining his experience which was very detailed. He was a Bachelor of Science and a Doctor of Philosophy. He obtained a First Class Honours in Biology from the University of Nottingham and for his Doctorate researched blood groups and body fluids. He had worked in Forensic Science specialising in blood staining for the last twenty years.

Joanna took him through his evidence of where the blood staining was found. He produced a large A3 chart for the Jury which contained diagrams of the flat with where the bloodstains were found with arrows pointing to small photographs of the actual blood stains. David looked at the diagrams and was impressed at the amount of effort that had gone into producing them, he realised that Dr Allbright would not be an easy Witness to deal with.

Dr Allbright began by taking the Jury to the living room and pointing out where the major concentrations of blood had been found after the soot had been removed by the application of liquid latex which was allowed to dry and was then removed, picking the soot up with it. Joanna then asked him to deal with the different types of bloodstains and where they were found.

"Dr Allbright, can you assist us now with where the bloodstains were found in the flat, what types of bloodstain they were and how they were caused?

"Yes, certainly. When an injury results in bleeding it is possible that objects at the scene and the persons involved in the assault will become bloodstained. Such bloodstaining can arise in a number of ways. For example, blood may drip from the wound onto a surface. In this case for example we can see that there are areas of the carpet where blood appears to have dripped and pooled when Mr Hussain was wounded and probably lying in a prostrate position. Blood may also be spattered as a result of forceful impact into an object already wet with blood. We see bloodstains like this on the walls of the living room and on a coffee table. Blood may also be projected from an object such as a knife that is covered in blood and swung through the air. We see blood spots of this nature on the walls in the living room. Blood may also be smeared onto a surface through direct contact with a wet blood stained surface. We see such smears again on the walls of the living room.

The nature and patterning of staining on a surface can therefore be an indicator of the manner in which the blood has been deposited. This in turn may provide information which allows for an interpretation of what occurred."

Joanna went on to ask him about all the bloodstains that were found in the living room taking the Jury to photographs of the relevant areas coupled with the diagrams produced by Dr Allbright. She then moved on to the hallway.

"Dr Allbright, let's move away from the living room to the hallway. Can you help us here with the bloodstains that were found and their cause."

"Yes, as you will see from the diagram of the hallway a number of bloodstains were found in this area. There were bloodstains caused by dripping but there were also spattered bloodstains that can be seen in the photographs. The Drip bloodstaining could be when an already bleeding Mr Hussain walked in the hallway or was carried. The "spattered bloodstains" would have been caused by force being applied to areas of Mr Hussain that were already wet with blood."

"Thank you Dr Allbright, can I ask you to move to other areas where bloodstaining was found, the types and how you consider these were caused"

"Yes, as can be seen from the diagrams further bloodstains were found in the main bedroom where the body of Mr Hussain was discovered. Drip bloodstains were found in the bedroom between the door and the bed and a large amount of blood was found on both sides of a duvet that was found on the bed."

"Are you able to assist as to a cause of this bloodstaining?   "

"Again, the Drip bloodstaining could be when an already bleeding Mr Hussain walked into the bedroom or was carried. The blood on the duvet looks like blood soaked through from one side to the other side of the duvet. As I understand it, Mr Hussain's body was found on the bed wrapped in the duvet. The amount of blood on the duvet does suggest that it was wrapped round him and the blood soaked in from his wounds and then soaked through to the other side."

"From the bloodstains you have seen in the various rooms, are you able to assist with what happened?"

"Any situation like this is chaotic and bloodstaining can be caused in a number of ways, however, it is clear that as most of the bloodstaining was in the living room, that was where the major assault took place. However, the blood spattering in the hallway does suggest that there was at least one forceful blow to Mr Hussain in the hallway. Mr Hussain then walked, more likely staggered or was carried to the bedroom and at some stage was wrapped in a duvet which he bled into."

Joanna concentrated a little more on the hallway, spending some time reminding the Jury of the photographs of that area. She then sat down quite content that David would be unable to deal with this telling point, that showed that Damien's account of all the blows taking place in the living room simply was not true.

David knew that this Witness would be challenging. He was clearly very intelligent, very experienced and capable of explaining to a Jury in simple terms the basics of bloodstaining. This was not an expert who would be destroyed by a simple line of questioning such as the one the great Norman Birkett KC had asked of an expert engineer who was giving evidence about a car fire in a murder case. The opening question was, "What is the coefficient of the expansion of brass?" The Witness eventually admitted he did not know and was discredited by a question that actually had nothing to do with any issue in the case. David knew that more would be required here to make any headway with this witness.

"Dr Allbright, I want to ask you a number of questions about the bloodstaining found in this case."

"Yes Sir."

"I want to ask you about an answer you gave my Learned Friend. You said, 'Any situation like this is chaotic and bloodstaining can be caused in a number of ways'?"

"Yes Sir"

"It follows from that comment that many different actions may cause blood staining?"

"That is right."

"Further, possible patterns of blood may be confused. Blood staining deposited in one action can be altered by a subsequent action if it involves direct contact?"

"That is right. I am giving an interpretation of what I have seen but I readily concede that blood staining can be caused in different ways."

"Yes, thank you. You have dealt with a number of bloodstains found in this property. I want to deal with what you have referred to as "spattered blood." Correct me if I am wrong, but I understand that what you are referring to are aerial blood droplets which can result from forceful contact with an already blood stained surface such as skin or clothing?"

"That is right, aerial blood droplets cause arrays of tiny spots, 'spatter patterns'. These are evidentially significant because it takes some force to break liquid blood into droplets and send those flying through the air. Generally you require more force to generate finer blood spots than larger spots ......"

David was a little concerned that Dr Allbright was giving the Jury a little bit too much information that might not help Damien's case so he interrupted.

"Yes, thank you Dr Allbright but I want to deal with some specific matters if you can"

"Of course."

"Aerial blood droplets can also be caused in other ways as well as forceful impact into an object already wet with blood?"

"That is right, small blood spots can also be created by someone coughing or exhaling blood from their mouth or nose. Usually this differs from the bloodstains I described because the distribution of blood from exhaled blood can often appear diluted, or have a pale centre because of air bubbles trapped before they dried. Sometimes the spots discernibly "bead" together."

"However, it is right that those features are not always present and it is not always possible to discriminate between what you refer to as "spattered blood", forceful impacts into an area already wet with blood and exhaled blood from someone who is bleeding, coughing or sneezing blood."

"That is right but I ought to add that exhaled blood droplets tend to be impeded more by air resistance and generally do not travel more than a metre."

"Yes, thank you again Dr Allbright. I want to ask you in particular about what you describe as "spattered" blood in the hallway."

"Yes, there were small areas of spattered blood in the hallway."

"And they were just a few feet, less than a metre away from the living room."

"I believe that is correct."

"We know from the post mortem in this case that Mr Hussain did have traces of blood around his nose and mouth. So in fact a possible cause of those droplets could be Mr Hussain exhaling blood when he was near the door of the living room?"

"Yes, that is possible."

"It also follows that if exhaled blood meets more wind resistance than spattered blood, then spattered blood can travel further?"

"Yes that is right."
"So another possible cause of what you describe as spattered blood in the hallway is that force was

applied to an already bleeding Mr Hussain when he was further back in the living room but still near the doorway to the hallway?"

"Again that is possible."

"Another possible cause of spattered blood is where blood drips from a height into blood that is already pooled on the ground. The resulting effect can be to cause aerial droplets of blood?"

"That is a possibility."

"In this case we know there were areas of blood in the hallway that you have described as "dripped blood"?"

"Again that is right."

"Near to those areas of dripped blood you found what you have referred to as spattered blood?"

"Yes."

The areas of "spattered blood" could have been caused by blood dripping from Mr Hussain's body into blood that has already pooled on the floor and then spattered?"

"That is a possibility but unlikely in my opinion because the spattered blood was found at a higher level than I would expect to find if it had resulted from dripping."

"Nevertheless, it is a possibility."

"I cannot discount it entirely, no."

"Thank you, I want to move onto the blood stained duvet. We know that was wrapped around the body of Mr Hussain?"

"Yes it was."

"Of course we do not know when it was wrapped around him?"

"No that is impossible to say."

"It could be that Mr Hussain was stabbed in the living room and then the duvet wrapped around his dead or dying body."

"That is possible."

"His body could have been then carried in the duvet from the living room to the bedroom dripping blood as he was taken."

"That is possible, which is why I referred to the blood dripping being as a result of him walking, staggering or being carried."

"Yes, Thank You. It is also possible that in his dying breath he exhaled blood in the hallway causing what you suggest was the spattered blood."

"Again, that is possible."

"Indeed it is possible he was already dead and the carrying caused air to be expelled from his lungs spattering the blood."

"Again that is possible but I would think less likely as the force from the lungs would be less than a cough or sneeze."

"Nevertheless it is possible."

"Yes it is."

"It follows that there are a number of possible reasons why what you called "spattered blood" was found in the hallway rather than just force being used on the already bleeding Mr Hussain."

"Yes that is right."

"Thank you very much Dr Allbright you have been very helpful."

Joanna looked at David with renewed respect. She thought this evidence was water tight. She may have to rethink her own case. She did decide to re-examine to try and reduce the damage to her case.

"Dr Allbright you have been asked about a number of possibilities in this case. Are you able to give a definitive opinion how the blood spattering in the hallway occurred?"

"In my opinion it is more likely that it occurred as a result of a forceful blow to Mr Hussain in the hallway. However, I cannot exclude the matters raised by Defence Counsel as being possible causes."

With that he was excused and as lunch time was approaching the case was adjourned until 2:05pm for the next expert to give evidence.

David had a working lunch in the Bar Mess settling for a prawn sandwich and a tin of ginger beer rather than the Friday battered fish the look of which did not appeal to him. Charlotte joined him in the queue and congratulated him on his cross examination even apparently showing a belated interest in the case by asking him how he was going to deal with the Footprints expert. He told her he had a few ideas but needed to work a little more over lunch. She told him that she had asked Tim Arnold if she could see the Exhibits in the case. She had seen Damien's trainers which had been seized on his arrest and which she noted were Adidas trainers and not "Star 'D' Sprints." She had noted that his trainers were size 8 and had a zig zag pattern on the sole and not a Star pattern. Having consumed the sandwich he moved to the Bar Mess library and started looking at Geoffrey Turnton's evidence for about the fifth time, now armed with this extra nugget of information.

At 2:05 pm Geoffrey Turnton appeared in Court, he was a short man appearing almost weighed down by the plans, diagrams and photographs he was carrying. David noted how he was about thirty years of age and was wearing far more relaxed clothing than some of the experts who had given evidence, sporting a white T shirt and tie. The tie obviously looked like an after-thought, no doubt forced upon him by some well-meaning female friend.

He began his evidence with the usual details about his qualifications and experience. He held a Bachelor of Science Degree with Honours in Natural Science (Biology and Chemistry) from Brunel University, London and a Master of Science Degree in Environmental Technology from Queen Mary College, London. He had been a Forensic Scientist since 2007 and had conducted a large number of investigations using shoe sizes.

Joanna asked him a number of questions about shoeprints generally just to get the jury used to his evidence. He covered the number of shoeprints found originally, how these were compared with shoeprints taken from the shoes worn by the police officers, paramedics and firemen who attended the fire so that any prints that matched could be eliminated from the enquiry. Having done this he concentrated on the prints that were found in the blood but under the soot layer as these must have been created before the fire had taken hold but after Mr Hussain was stabbed and therefore were likely to be shoeprints from the perpetrator of the assault or someone who was present at the scene.

He listed how the prints had been found, how most could not be seen with the naked eye, but how with the use of chemicals and photography he had managed to take a series of photographs.

Joanna then moved on to where the shoeprints had actually been discovered.

"Mr Turnton, you have produced diagrams for the Jury showing where all of these prints were found.

I would like you to look at the shoeprints found in the living room."

"Yes, certainly, I found six blood stained shoeprints in the living room in the areas shown on the plan of that room. Noticeably most were by the sofa near to the door although two were near the curtain."

"Can you help as to the patterns, if any, on these prints?"

"Yes, in fact twelve prints were found throughout the flat, six in the living room or lounge, two in the kitchen area next to the lounge, two in the hallway and two in the main bedroom where the body was found. Of those, ten prints all contained the same type of pattern. A star or a part of a star design. The only ones that had no such pattern were the two prints found near the curtains in the living room. Those prints were too smudged to discern any pattern or tread."

"Does that mean they had no pattern or tread, or that none could be seen?"

"None could be seen."

"Thank you, so it follows that they could have had a star pattern or a completely different pattern, we simply do not know?"

"That's right."

"Did you discover the type of trainer that made such a pattern?"

"Yes, I checked with the National data base and the only trainer that makes such a print is known as the "Star 'D' Sprints.""

"Were you able to discover the size of the trainers that made these prints?"

"I was able to determine a range of sizes but not the exact size. The reason for this is manufacturers of the Star 'D' Sprints use the same size of sole on a range of trainers. It makes them easier to mass produce. The Police obtained a number of pairs of "Star 'D' Sprint" shoes and I was able to determine that the range was somewhere between 7.5 - 9.5."

"Ladies and gentleman of the Jury, you will hear agreed evidence that Mr Clarke's shoe size was 8, right in the middle of the range we are dealing with. Yes, Thank You Mr Turnton, will you wait there, my Learned Friend will probably have some questions of you."

David had expected a far more ranging examination in chief by Joanna and was slightly taken aback at the speed with which this had been conducted. He looked towards Joanna and then rose to his feet to ask his first question.

"Mr Turnton you told us you have been a Forensic Scientist since 2007 and have conducted a large number of investigations into shoe sizes?"

"That's right Sir."

"No doubt in that time you have discovered the average shoe size of a male in this country?"

"Yes I believe it is size 9."

"The trainers that left these patterns, the Star 'D' Sprints were in the range 7.5-9.5, so that would include the shoe sizes of a significant amount of the UK male population?"

"Yes it would."

"Can you also assist me on this, it was not possible to narrow the shoe size down to less than this range 7.5-9.5?"

"No it wasn't"

"Were there any distinguishing marks on the trainers apart from the Star?"

"I'm sorry, I don't understand."

"Sorry, let me make it clearer. All the shoeprints that had a pattern clearly came from the same type of trainer?"

"That's right."

"However, can you say whether it was the same trainer that made all ten of these marks?"

"No, I'm sorry, I didn't understand the question. No there are no clear distinguishing marks in the pictures, such as scuffs or tears or other marks that can be made out. Therefore I cannot say they were made by the same trainer."

"Thank you. So it follows that those ten prints could have been made by one or more than one person wearing a similar style of trainer in the range of 7.5 – 9.5?"

"That is correct. One or two of the images are better than others and could narrow that down to demonstrate that the same trainers made two or more marks but I am unable to say how many trainers made these marks."

"Were you able to discover how many pairs of this style of trainers were made for the UK market?"

"I was not able to obtain exact information but I am aware from the National database that in excess of 100,000 pairs of these trainers were destined for the UK market."

"And in theory, any one of those pairs could have made these marks."

"Any within the range 7.5 - 9.5, which would have been the majority of them."

"Also, I am sure you would concede, that sometimes markets are flooded with counterfeit trainers?"

"Yes, that is right."

"Are you able to assist with any possible figures how many counterfeit trainers with a Star 'D' Sprint might be on the UK market?"

"No, by the nature of counterfeit goods, there won't be any records."

"So, the numbers of pairs of trainers in the UK that could have made the marks you found in this case could be in excess of 100,000?"

"Yes, I suppose so."

"Can you assist me with the shoe sizes of the trainers that were supplied by the Police in this case?"

Geoffrey Turnton shuffled through some of his papers and then said,

"Yes, they supplied me with sizes 7, 7.5, 8.5, 9, 9.5 and 11"

"So you never tested the prints against sizes 8, 10 or 10.5?"

"No"

"Presumably from your findings size 7 was too small?"

"Yes"

"Size 11 was too big?"

"Yes"

"However, can you rule out size 10 and 10.5 when you in fact never had such trainers to measure against the prints you found."

"No I suppose not, I made an educated guess?"

"Often a dangerous thing!"

"It can be. I would have to concede that the prints could have been from size 10 and 10.5 trainers but I think it unlikely because the sole on size 11 trainers was a much bigger pattern."

"Nevertheless it could be, increasing the number of trainers in the UK that could have left these prints?"

"Yes, that is possible."

"I want to move on to the shoeprints that made no discernible marks. These of course could have been made by "Star 'D' Sprints" or by a wholly different trainer or shoe altogether?"

"Yes that is right"

"Of course you have only looked at shoeprints that were made in the blood?"

"Yes."

"You did not look for other prints that might have been made that were not left in blood?"

"No."

"It follows, that from your investigations you cannot say how many persons were in the flat after the murder took place and before the fire took place. It could have been one person it could have been two or **three** or even more."

"That is right, I cannot tell the number, I can only report that I only found traces of one style of trainer."

"You have told us that you were able to compare the prints you found with Star 'D' Sprint trainers supplied by the Police?"

"Yes, that is correct."

"You did not compare them with any trainers belonging to Damien Clarke?"

"No, none were produced for me to compare."

David turned to His Honour Judge Tanner,

"My Lord, I have asked that the Prosecution produce Exhibit GM 27, trainers belonging to Mr Clarke and which were taken from him on his arrest."

The trainers were produced and David asked that they be shown to the Witness.

"Mr Turnton, these were the only trainers found belonging to Mr Clarke when he was arrested and his property searched. You will notice that they are not Star 'D' Sprint trainers, they are in fact Adidas trainers?"

"That's correct."

"You will also notice that they do not have a star print on the sole. The print is a zig zag print?"

"That's right."

"These trainers could not have made the ten prints you mention where a discernible print could be made out?"

"No that is right."

"We will also hear agreed evidence that no traces of blood were found on these trainers. Yes, Thank You, Mr Turnton that is all I ask."

Again Joanna rose to see if she could repair any of this damage to her Witness but his answers to her re-examination did not add anything to the case and so she eventually gave up and thanked him for his evidence.

The rest of the day was spent with the Prosecution reading a number of Witness Statements from Witnesses who were not required by the Defence and then in reading a number of "Admissions", agreed facts between the parties, dealing with the time of "999" calls, the attendance of Police at the flat and other matters that the parties had decided did not require any Witnesses to give the evidence.

Again David felt the case had gone well. Too well in many ways. He was beginning to feel that there was a real chance of an acquittal. A feeling he recognised from the many cases he had conducted where real progress is made during the Prosecution case. However, he also knew that the case could go horribly wrong once the Defence case commenced.

CHAPTER 19.

DRINKS WITH THE HEAD OF CHAMBERS.

David took a rest from the case on Friday night. It had been an intensive week and he felt that he was entitled to a break. He returned from the Bailey at 5pm and went into Chambers. The Clerks appeared pre-occupied dealing with Monday's diary and were not communicative. He went to the Silk's room where James Wontner was working on his Fraud case.

"Hello David, how's the Bailey going?"

"Hi James, its actually going very well at the moment but of course we are still dealing with the Prosecution case. There's plenty of time for my little hero to bury himself when he gives evidence."

James smiled, it was the same banter they had practised together over the years that David had been in Chambers. It was generally felt at the Criminal Bar that the best time for a Defendant was always during the Prosecution case because points could always be made in his favour at that stage. The worse time was when a client gave evidence as then the Prosecution had the opportunity to score points against him.

"David, do you fancy a glass of Claret or two. I think it's time we Senior chaps have a chat about pressing Chambers matters."

David readily agreed, he was more interested in a, "glass of Claret or two" than Chambers matters but it always helped to find out what was going on.

They walked out of Chambers, turned into Middle Temple Lane and then through Fountain Court towards Daly's Wine Bar. James Wontner preferred it to El Vinos and David was not really bothered where he consumed his House Claret. It would all taste the same to him after the second glass.

They managed to find a table outside and James ordered the House Claret and a few nibbles. They poured the first glass and consumed a healthy amount before James moved on to his reason for the meeting.

"David, you are a Senior and respected Member of Chambers."

Ok thought David, the soft sell, what does he want?

"We have a few hotheads in Chambers who seem hell bent on destroying the structure and sacking John. They seem to forget that without John there wouldn't be a Chambers. We are all busy and we owe it to John."

It never ceased to amaze David how many Heads of Chambers came out with this nonsense. Because the Clerk kept them fed with work they automatically assumed everyone else was busy or they wilfully buried their heads in the Chambers sand refusing to look around and see that other people were struggling.

"James, I agree we have a few hotheads but I tend to think that is no bad thing if they are being constructive rather than destructive. I don't agree with sacking John, I think he is important to Chambers although I don't agree that he is as important to Chambers as you seem to think. It is wholly wrong to think that everyone in Chambers is busy and it is wholly wrong to think that everyone who is busy owes it to John. Quite a few people have their own practice and are actively out there drumming up work without any assistance from John. Others, who are not as able at attracting work are struggling at the moment with the legal aid cuts and the in-roads into the Bar's work by Solicitor Advocates. In order to survive I really do believe that we all need to adapt to rapidly changing times. I tend to think John is, or at least could be, a very good Senior Clerk. However, I think he tends to be complacent, he is not as hungry as he once was and he needs to be encouraged to work harder than he is at the moment."

"You surprise me David. I'm busy, you are busy. I know from John that he got you the Murder brief that you are conducting at the moment. I know

John works very hard for Chambers doing a lot of work behind the scenes that no one hears about."

All right then, it's a wilful burying of his head in the sand, thought David.

"James, we have both been around a long time. We both know that just because a Clerk **claims** he was the one who got a brief into Chambers does not mean that he did. John obviously has to keep his Head of Chambers busy and rightly so, there are few other perks from being a Head of Chambers and a lot of disadvantages. However, he does not keep everyone else busy. The Murder case I am conducting is the first new brief I have had in months. I became used to months of John saying "there is no Silk work out there" every time I asked him was there any work. I'm not alone in that. I know there are Members of Chambers struggling to pay their mortgages, there is at least one member who is talking of selling his house and another who is talking of entering into a voluntary arrangement because he cannot pay his tax. Now of course this cannot all be put at John's door, Members of Chambers cannot sit back and say, "I'm a Barrister therefore I deserve a Brief", but I do believe John could and should do more and certainly take up less time drinking with other Clerks and more time out there with Solicitors."

Clearly David's stance was not expected by James who had anticipated a like mind and ally in a fellow

Silk. He sipped at his claret and moved uncomfortably in his seat.

"Well David, do you have a solution?"

"No, I cannot pretend to have the answer. If I did, I would bottle it and sell it to every Criminal Chambers out there because I suspect our problems are repeated in virtually every set. However, I do have some ideas and once the new Chambers Committee sits I propose to put them forward. Put simply, I think there should be more accountability. One of the problems with John is he needs to be more accountable. He needs to have a Diary of where he is going and who he is seeing. It's all very well to tell us he is out with Solicitors but we need to know there is a structure behind his working practices. We need to know that he is targeting the right Solicitors and not just having drinks with the same people over and over again who are simply friends of his and have no intention of sending us any more work. I suggest he keeps a Diary and enters every appointment in it. It may be annoying at first for him, but ultimately it will protect him when people ask where is he, is he out drinking again or playing golf? He needs to be able to say I was out with X, we discussed Y and my follow up will be Z."

From James' expression it was clear that he did not agree with a word that David said. He had seen a potential ally, but no longer. He simply wanted Chambers to carry on as it was. John Winston was good to him, ensured he was kept busy in work and he did not want to see any threats to that by introducing practices that might lead to John leaving or being sacked. He rapidly moved on to other subjects discussing David's holiday in Corfu, places he had visited on the island in the past and the scenes that Virginia had painted there. They shared another bottle of the House Claret but then both parted agreeing to discuss Chambers' problems again in the near future and look toward solutions. David knew from the conversation that James had no interest in any solutions he might propose but there was no reason to be anything other than polite.

CHAPTER 20.

DAY SIX, THE BURN INJURY.

David put the case out of his mind on Saturday and relaxed. On Sunday, he started working on his cross examination of the Officer in the Case and preparing his final speech. He viewed cross examination of the Officer in the Case as highly important because it allowed him to refer to useful areas of the Unused Material without having to call Witnesses and allow the Prosecution to score points against the Defence. In relation to his Final Speech, although the case was far from finished, he found it saved time during a case if he made notes as he went along. Now he was able to add to his notes having reviewed the evidence heard, and could assess the direction that Damien's case was taking. He curled up in his favourite armchair, settled for a cup of tea rather than anything alcoholic and started to re-read the Unused Material to see if there was anything that was helpful and admissible in the case. By the evening he had completed both his notes for cross examination of Detective Sergeant Monkton and had a draft of his Speech. He knew from experience that he would re-write the draft a number of times before he delivered it but at least he had a format now. He was surprised to find how late in the evening it was when he finished. He opened his favourite bottle of Rioja Reserva and had a couple of glasses of wine before turning in.

On Monday he attended Court at 09:30 to discover that yet again there was no trace of Gillian Banks.

After a brief conference with Damien in the cells, he entered Court just before 10:30am to be greeted by a beaming Joanna.

"Hello, David, did you have a good weekend?"

"Thank you Joanna, very relaxing, managed to forget all about this case."

Of course he had worked almost solidly on the case on Sunday but he preferred to give the air that there was nothing to worry about and that the case did not need any further preparation. Joanna, who had also been working solidly on the case on Sunday preparing her cross-examination of Damien and her final speech, adopted the same approach.

"Yes, it's so nice to be able to put these cases out of your minds between 4-00pm on a Friday and 10-30am on a Monday."

Joanna told him that the Police had tried to locate Gillian Banks over the weekend but had been unable to. However, they had a fresh lead and would make one last effort that day to locate her. Joanna warned that if they failed she would apply to His Honour Judge Tanner to read her statement to the Jury. David told her that he would oppose such an application but he knew that it was likely that the Judge would rule in favour of reading her statement which would mean David had no opportunity of testing her evidence or discovering whether she knew of any Arabian or Scottish visitors to the flat.

Shortly after this brief conversation His Honour Judge Tanner came into Court. He seemed even grumpier than normal which suggested that he had either not enjoyed his weekend at all, or had enjoyed it too much and was not looking forward to another day of this case.

Joanna called Dr Adrian Monkton to give evidence.

"Dr Monkton, I take it you are not related to the Officer in the Case, Detective Sergeant Monkton."

This slight attempt at humour mildly amused Dr Monkton who smiled at her and replied,

"I don't believe so."

Joanna then moved on to ask him about his arrival at the police station on 5th February 2012 when Damien had been arrested.

"I was called to the Police Station to see a suspect who was in custody. I saw him in the early hours of the morning at about 1am. He had been interviewed by Police by then but after the interview he had complained about an injury to his right hand. I arrived and examined his hand and found a superficial burn to the palm. It was not a serious injury and was easily treated with ointment and a non-adherent gauze and I then prescribed a mild analgesic for the pain."

Having established the background, Joanna moved on to the potential causes of this type of injury.

"Dr Monkton you are described as a Forensic Medical Examiner, an FME for short. Can you assist us and inform us what an FME is?

"Certainly, the term FME or Forensic Medical examiner has been in use for about 20 years now. The title used to be Police Surgeon which was slightly misleading as the persons undertaking the role were generally, neither surgeons nor working for the Police so the new term was adopted. A Forensic Medical Examiner is basically a Doctor who is instructed to provide healthcare and a medical assessment to either those in custody at a Police Station or to Witnesses and victims of crime. There are about one hundred FMEs in the London area, many of whom are GPs and all of whom are independent from the Police. Our function is to provide medical care or to make forensic assessments in an impartial, objective and independent manner."

"Thank you Dr Monkton. Can you confirm how long you have been providing such services?"

"Yes, I was first instructed in this type of work about fifteen years ago. On average I conduct 3 twelve hour shifts a week in this area visiting

Detainees and victims of crime at various Police Stations in the London area."

"In that time you must have seen a great number of Detainees?"

"I've never counted but it would number in the thousands."

"No doubt you have seen numerous injuries in that time?"

"Yes, all manner of injuries which occurred when crimes were being committed, during the course of arrests and sometimes injuries inflicted at Police Stations through self-harm."

"I want to deal with the injury you saw to the Defendant in this case. You have described it as a superficial burn to the palm of the hand?"

"Yes."

"Did the defendant tell you how he said this was caused?"

"Yes, he told me it had been caused through an accidental burn when he was smoking crack cocaine."

"Did you have any opinion about this, based upon your experience?"

"In my time as a Doctor I have seen the types of injuries received from smoking crack cocaine. The typical injury you find would be multiple blackened hyperkeratotic lesions, that is a growth, a thickening of the skin, of the palmar aspects of the fingers and palm. These involve mostly the dominant hand and are caused by the heat of the glass cocaine pipe. The injury I saw did not look like these but looked more like the injuries I have seen from those who have been involved in committing acts of arson and have burnt themselves by direct contact with a flame."

"Could the Defendant have caused this injury to himself by smoking crack cocaine?"

"It is a possibility, that he could have directly applied the flame to the palm of his hand but I would have thought that was extremely unlikely in this case and the most likely cause of this injury was direct contact with a flame."

"Yes, thank you Dr Monkton, that's all I ask."

Joanna sat down content that another part of Damien's defence case had been damaged and that as the defence had not served any expert defence report in relation to this injury, David would not be able to make any headway with Dr Monkton.

David smiled at Joanna before starting his cross examination. The best policy appeared to him to be complete openness in relation to this. Damien had lied to the good Doctor so David may as well make that point as soon as possible.

"Dr Monkton, as you have told us, you are considerably experienced in your area and have seen many injuries to those in police custody?"

"That is right."

David was tempted to add, "a few caused by the Police" but decided there was no advantage.

"You have seen many crack cocaine injuries and you concluded the injury you saw was not caused by smoking crack cocaine."

"I could not say it was not caused that way, I just consider it was most unlikely to have been caused in that way."

"Yes, thank you. Your conclusion is that this injury was more likely to have been caused by direct contact with a flame."

"Yes that is right."

"The type of injury that could be caused by someone setting a fire and accidentally burning themselves."

"Yes."

"It could of course be caused in other ways as well."

"It could be caused in other ways."

"It could presumably be caused by someone deliberately placing a flame under his hand."

"It could be."

"When you saw Damien Clarke in the early hours of that morning were you aware that he had smoked crack cocaine in the early hours of the day before?"

"I was informed that was the case."

"Were you aware that he had been drinking most of the day before he smoked crack cocaine?"

"I was not told that."

"You were aware that he had been interviewed for a number of hours before seeing you."

"I was aware of that."

"Did he appear exhausted to you."

"He was clearly tired, I'm not sure about exhausted."

"Let me assist you Doctor. It is accepted that Damien Clarke lied to you. He had not received the injury from smoking crack cocaine. It is his case that he received that injury because one of the perpetrators of this murder held his hand over an open flame. You accept that the injury to his hand could have been caused in that way?"

"As I have said it could have been caused in that way."

"Yes thank you."

David sat down, satisfied that, as far as he possibly could, he had limited the damage of pointing out that his client was willing to lie if he thought it was in his interests.

The next Witness called was Dr Wakeley, the Doctor who had seen Damien at Queen Elizabeth hospital a few days after his arrest. He gave evidence that Damien had been complaining that his injury had become infected. Joanna asked a few questions about the incident.

"Dr Wakeley, you treated the Defendant?"

"Yes, I removed his dressing, checked the injury, which was infected. I cleaned it, redressed the wound and prescribed antibiotics."

"Did the Defendant say anything to you about the injury?"

"Yes, I asked him how it had occurred and he told me that someone had held his hand over a naked flame."

"Did you form any opinion about that?"

"Yes, the injury was a few days old by then but I considered it quite feasible that it could have been caused in that way."

David did not think he could improve on these answers so he did not ask any questions.

His Honour Judge Tanner decided that this was an opportunity to make a point.

"Mr Brant, did you ask for this Witness to attend Court?"

"We did My Lord."

"You have not asked any questions. I'm sure the Doctor has far better things to do than attend here if no questions were to be asked. There is also the question of Wasted Costs."

David smiled at him.

"My Lord, the Witness was required to attend Court by the defence because we had a few questions to ask him. However, the questioning of Dr Monkton followed by my Learned Friend's helpful questioning of Dr Wakeley has rendered any questioning redundant."

His Honour Judge Tanner knew that there was little he could do in the circumstances so he satisfied himself with making a gesture.

"I shall say no more about this Witness, but I shall keep an eye on the Witnesses who are called in this case and if I see any examples of a Witnesses' time being wasted I shall consider making a Wasted Costs Order and Counsel should be fully aware of that."

CHAPTER 21.

DAY SEVEN, THE FINAL PROSECUTION WITNESSES.

The case ended early on Monday because of a lack of witnesses and David returned home to the Barbican where he looked again at his notes for the cross examination of the officer and added a few notes to his final speech.

On the Tuesday morning he was surprised to see that Charlotte was at Court before he arrived at 9-30am. He was worried for a moment that something serious had happened.

"Hello David, I thought you were never going to arrive."

He smiled at this attempt at irony and reposted.

"Hello Charlotte, what's happened, have the clocks gone forward and I missed it?"

"Funny! No the reason I'm here at this ungodly hour is that there has been a development in the case. Firstly I was told when I arrived that the Police have found Gillian Banks and they are providing a "taxi" service to get her here this morning to give evidence. However, that's not the reason I came this early. I had a call last night...."

He immediately thought to himself, Charlotte takes work calls at night?

"... Charles Rooney has managed to contact Robert Davies, the Cambridge Garden Supervisor. He has spoken to him on the phone and he has some interesting information about other users of Hussain's flat including an aggressive Scotsman. Charles has got him to go into the office today to take a witness statement which we will have tomorrow."

"That's excellent news Charlotte although it's likely we will be calling Damien tomorrow and I'd like to know what Robert Davies says as soon as possible. Can you contact your firm and ask them to send a draft copy of his witness statement by email as soon as they have it."

"No problem David, I will call them now."

Joanna informed him in the absence of the jury that Gillian Banks had been discovered and was being brought here by a police car. She was expected to be there by 11-00am. The Prosecution was not asking for an adjournment because they had a friend of Mr Clarke's, namely Christopher White, to give evidence.

The jury was brought into Court and then Christopher White was called in. He had apparently gone to the same School of Dentistry as Damien because he was missing a few teeth in the front and he was sporting similar homemade tattoos on his arms and neck. David immediately wondered how much biro ink was used in Damien's neighbourhood.

Christopher gave his name, told the Court he was unemployed and was then asked by Joanna about how long he had known Damien.

"I've known Omen all of my life, we grew up on the same estate."

"Omen?"

"Yeah we saw a very old horror film a few years ago called, "The Omen". There was someone in it called Damien, so we gave Damien the nickname "Omen" and it stuck."

David noted this particular piece of information with concern. He had not heard that Damien had a nickname and there had been no mention of this fact in Christopher White's statement to the police nor even in an interview that was conducted with him by Police and which had been served in the Unused Material. No one else had referred to Damien by this nickname including Damien. It was slightly concerning because he had read in a piece of Unused Material served late on the Friday before the weekend that a witness had been told by someone that the killer was called "Omen." David had thought of somehow trying to use this piece of information to cross examine DS Monkton as he had assumed "Omen" was the Arabian friend of Usman Hussain. He had not made the obvious connection between "Damien" and "Omen". He rapidly decided to abandon that particular line of enquiry. He was relieved that this piece of Unused had only been served on Friday and not earlier in the trial as he might have cross examined witnesses about "Omen" being the killer and conceded a terrible own goal.

Christopher continued with his evidence outlining that he knew Damien smoked crack cocaine and he used to smoke it with him. He knew Usman Hussain and had visited his flat a few times and smoked there but he claimed he did not smoke anymore and had not visited Mr Hussain's flat for some months. He certainly had not visited it the night he was killed.

Joanna asked him how well he knew Usman Hussain.

"I didn't know him that well. I visited his flat maybe every couple of weeks for a year or so but as I said I hadn't been there for months and I hadn't seen him around."

"What sort of person was he?"

"He came across as someone very quiet. A passive person."

David was quite surprised at the use of the word "passive" by Christopher, he imagined from Christopher's appearance and demeanour that he did not know anyone who could be described as passive. Clearly there were some hidden depths here.

"You say you smoked crack cocaine there."

"Some months ago, but I gave it up, it was killing me. I was in a constant daze and I knew if I kept on I would die soon."

"Did you see where Mr Hussain got the crack cocaine from?"

"No, I don't think he was a dealer in crack but he was a user. He was also a "runner." He knew all the dealers in Woolwich and if you gave him some cash he'd be able to get crack for you within 30 minutes."

"As far as you were aware, did he have any enemies?"

"I was not aware of him having any enemies. As I said he was very passive, very quiet. I can't imagine anyone wanting to hurt him."

Joanna moved on to the early hours of 4th February 2012.

"Mr White, we know from the evidence we have heard in this case that at 05:21 on 4th February 2012 you received a phone call from the Defendant."

"Yeah, the Police took my phone and they haven't given it back yet."

"I am sure when the case is over the phone will be returned to you. That call lasted 2 minutes and 10 seconds."

"I don't know, I can't remember."

"That's alright Mr White, we know it lasted that time from the phone records. We also know that the Defendant's phone was cell sited to the vicinity of Cambridge Gardens."

David quickly jumped up,

"We know nothing of the sort. This Witness cannot assist us with where Mr Clark's phone was when the call was made and it is disputed that the phone was at Cambridge Gardens at that stage. The Prosecution's own Witness, Mr Rollins, conceded that it was possible that this call was made in the vicinity of Mr Hussain's flat."

Joanna decided to concede the point by saying,

"My Learned Friend is correct, Mr Rollins did concede that was a **possibility.** I will move on. Mr White do you recall receiving a call at 05-21 on 4th December 2012 from the Defendant?"

"I remember receiving a call from him that day but I thought it was about midday. I don't recall any phone call before that time."

"Mr White we know that your phone received a call from the Defendant's phone at 05-21 and there was a 2 minute 10 second conversation. Did anyone else have access to your phone?"

"No it was just me. It was the only phone I had at the time. I've had to get a new one since the Police took it."

"You cannot recall any conversation at 05-21?"

"No."

"Did you receive a voicemail from the Defendant that morning?"

"Not that I recall. He may have phoned but I can't remember the conversation. I would have been up most of the night and trying to sleep then, so I have no idea if he called at that time or what he said if he did."

Joanna decided to move on, she noted the look of scepticism on the faces of the Jury who seemed to disbelieve this evidence and she wondered if they were wondering whether Christopher White was lying in order to protect his friend who may have just been confessing to Murder during this phone call.

"We also know from the evidence that the Defendant phoned you again at 12:32 for 1 minute 12 seconds. I think it is agreed that this call was from the Defendant and the phone was at his mother's address. Do you recall that call?"

"I remember him phoning me about lunch time to say he had witnessed a Murder. He told me it was Usman Hussain who had died and he had been threatened by the Murderers. He asked me if I thought he should go to the Police and I told him I thought he should go."

"How did he sound when he made this call?"

"He sounded scared, frightened. I've known him a long time, he's no angel but I know he couldn't commit no Murder."

"Obviously Mr White, that is a matter for the Ladies and Gentlemen of the Jury. Thank you, I have no further questions."

Joanna sat down trying to convey with her expression that she did not believe a word of what she had just heard but as Christopher was her own Witness she could not cross examine him.

David expected this Witness to be friendly to Damien so he felt he could risk a few questions.

"Mr White, I am going to ask you questions on behalf of Mr Clarke who I represent along with my Learned Friend Ms Williams who sits behind me."

Having established that he was on the side of Damien Clarke, he continued.

"Mr White, as you told us, you have known Mr Clarke all your life?"

"That's right."

"You have explained that he is "no angel." Indeed the Jury will hear that he has a few criminal convictions."

"Yeah I know he has."

David was aware that the Prosecution were going to be able to prove Damien's previous convictions in the circumstances of this case and so he thought it strategically better if he mentioned their existence first.

"However, you have known him as a person and you know something about his character."

"Yeah I've known him since we were kids. I see him regularly to speak to. He's a good man in the community."

David thought that Christopher was going too far with that comment so he quickly moved to the point he wanted to make.

"You made a statement to the Police in this case."

"Yes I did."

"In fact, you were actually arrested by the Police and interviewed weren't you?"

"Yeah I was."

"You were interviewed by DS Monkton, the Officer in this Case?"

"Yeah I was, he's the one who took my phone and hasn't given it back."

"Do you recall what you were arrested for?"

"Yeah they came to my house at about 5am and said I was arrested on suspicion of Murder. I told them they were having a laugh, I hadn't murdered anyone."

"You were then interviewed at the Police Station."

"Yeah."

"You must have been concerned. Woken up early in your home, arrested on suspicion of Murder, taken to a Police Station, kept in a cell then interviewed in relation to a Murder?"

"Yeah I was, I didn't know what they were going to do."

"You were obviously concerned that they might charge you with Murder even though you had done nothing wrong?"

"I was."

"Nevertheless, even though you were naturally concerned about yourself, you were at one stage asked this question by DS Monkton about Damien Clarke. You were asked whether Damien had ever been violent in such a way that he'd be capable of killing anyone. Your answer was, "No way, Damien could never kill anyone, never.""

"Yeah that's right. It's stupid to think he'd kill Usman, he had no reason to."

"Yes thank you Mr White, I've no further questions."

David sat down trying to put an expression on his face that he believed every word of Christopher White's evidence.

Joanna did not bother to re-examine as she thought, undoubtedly rightly, that Christopher White would just try and help Damien even more. She moved onto her next witness, Gillian Banks.

Gillian came into Court with a beaming smile on her face. She was aged about 35 although looked about 45. She had clearly been quite good looking earlier in her life but drugs, alcohol and living as a Prostitute had taken a toll on her. Nevertheless, she had made an effort to dress for Court and clearly had spent a night in the cells that had allowed her some time to recover a little from the effects of her lifestyle.

Joanna began her questioning by asking Gillian about when she used to live in Cambridge Gardens. Gillian volunteered that she had moved out after the Murder as the Tenancy was not in her name and she had no right to stay there and in fact did not want to. She stated she had not known the Police were looking for her to give evidence in this case until they arrested her in Woolwich late on Monday night when she had been "working". She had been in custody since 8pm and had been brought to Court by two Policemen.

Joanna showed her plans of the flat and she indicated where the bedroom that she stayed in was. It was established that she was not there the night of the Murder because of a "mix up" relating to a Court appointment and the fact that she was remanded in custody when she arrived late at Court on the Friday.

Gillian told the Court how she first met Usman. He had picked her up one night in 2008 when she was working. They had sex which he paid for and then he had invited her back to his flat because he told her he could get her some crack cocaine. She returned with him to the flat and then accepted his offer to stay in the spare room. They had not been in a relationship but occasionally they had sexual intercourse. She did not pay him any rent but would buy the odd thing for the flat.

She explained that she used to have a key to the flat but lost it and he put a spare key to the flat under the mat outside the entrance. She had no idea if anyone else knew about the key. Often she would buzz him from the entry button downstairs and he would let her in. She knew he cared about her because he would wait up for her and be concerned if she did not come home.

Joanna decided to concentrate a little more on their relationship.

"You have told us you knew Mr Hussain quite well and indeed on occasions you had a sexual relationship with him. Was your relationship with him always a good one?"

"My relationship with Usman was quite good, most of the time. We both had a drug problem and when he smoked crack he could turn into a bit of a monster. We often had shouting matches when we both smoked. I know the neighbours complained a bit. He could get on peoples' nerves and when he smoked, he was a bloody pain in the arse, excuse my French. But he was harmless, he wouldn't hurt a fly."

Joanna then decided to move on to Gillian's relationship with Damien.

"You know the defendant in this case, Damien Clarke?"

Gillian smiled at this question and said,

"Yes I know him. I've known him for about two years since he first started visiting Usman."

Looking towards Damien, she said

"He's a nice person. I know he liked me because he made his feelings plain. He had a soft spot for me."

"What was his relationship with Mr Hussain like?"

"They were friendly, I think they liked each other."

"Did other people visit the flat?"

"Yes, Usman had lots of visitors."

Joanna thought she would ask the question before David did.

"Do you remember anyone called Babs or Babe visiting the flat."

Gillian's expression changed noticeable to a scowl.

"I remember a girl called Babe. I don't know why Usman let her come to the flat. She just used him. She flirted with him all the time and he used to provide her with weed, crack and drinks and she never gave him anything. She used to lead him on and then refuse to do anything when he asked her for sex. She was like that with all the men who visited the flat. I remember her leading Damien on once. She flirted with him outrageously in front of me and then when he showed he was interested she said "No." I could see he was really hurt."

David looked up at this evidence as this did not appear anywhere in Gillian's Statement. It was rather a double-edged statement, it could be useful to Damien's defence, perhaps showing that Babe had led the two men on that night and then refused their attention so they forced themselves on her, killing Usman when he tried to intervene. However, it might also provide the prosecution with a motive for Damien killing Usman. Annoyed with her flirting again he might have tried to rape her and killed Usman when he intervened. David would have to tread carefully.

Joanna decided there was an opportunity here to strengthen her case so she asked a few more questions.

"How did the Defendant react to this rejection?"

David was tempted to intervene at this question as he had no notice of what the Witness was going to say. However, the Witness did not seem to be against Damien and an objection might look to the Jury that Damien had something to hide so he stayed silent. He could hear noises from behind him as Charlotte was clearly getting concerned but he merely turned round and smiled to her to indicate he was in charge of the situation. He just wished he was!

"Oh like anyone would, you could see he was annoyed and he shouted at her but he never did anything. They just carried on smoking."

David tried not to show that he had visibly relaxed at this evidence of Damien's relative calmness when he was smoking crack-cocaine!

Joanna moved on and asked the next questions that she knew David would ask.

"Do you ever recall an Arabian gentleman visiting the flat?"

"Usman had many visitors, all types of Nationalities."

"Did a Scottish man ever visit the flat?"

"Yes, as I've said, he had many visitors, lots of Nationalities, I never got to know the names of most of them."

Joanna decided that she would not ask any more questions that might help the defence and she sat down.

David decided from what he had heard that Gillian Banks was a bit of a loose cannon and so he chose to ask just a few questions about the many visitors and not deal with any controversial questions.

"Ms Banks, I want to ask you a little background detail...."

Gillian's reaction was not what he expected.

"Oh here it comes. Yes I work as a Prostitute, yes I've got a drug problem, yes I've got a criminal record."

"I'm sorry Ms Banks, I assure you I do not want to know anything about **your** background. I want to deal with the visitors to yours and Mr Hussain's flat.
Your relationship with Usman was a good one?"

"We had our ups and downs but generally it was a good one."

"As you've told us in your own words, he could become a bit of a "monster" when he smoked crack cocaine?"

"Not a monster, but he did get aggressive."

"Did he get aggressive with visitors to the flat."

"He wouldn't hurt anyone but he would scream and shout at times."

"You have told us that you know someone called Babe?"

Again her demeanour changed just at the mention of the name.

"Yes, I know her."

"Would it be fair to say, you don't like her?"

"I don't like her, I never did because of the way she uses people."

Gillian never appreciated the irony behind her comment.

"You have been asked about a Scottish man and an Arabian man. Did you ever see the three of them together in the flat?"

"I may have done, I can't recall, there were so many people who visited the flat."

"Babe would flirt with men when she was there?"

"Yes she would, always leading them on."

"You have told us that this happened to Damien in your presence?"

"Yes it did."

"He got annoyed and shouted at her but did not do anything else?"

"That's right."

"Did you ever see anyone else react violently to her?"

"I remember a man slapped her once but I can't remember who it was. Usman told him to leave and he did and I never saw him again."

David decided to leave it there. He was aware from an entry in the most recent Crime Report compiled by the Police and served the Friday before that there was an allegation by an informant that Gillian Banks had once been involved in a fight with Babe when Babe had discussed moving into the flat with Usman. However, he could see no possible reason for introducing this piece of information to the Jury and so he asked no further questions.

The rest of the morning was taken up with "housekeeping" matters. Tim Arnold read out further Admissions that had been agreed between the Parties and then read further Statements from Witnesses who were not required to give evidence by either side. This included a Statement recently taken from Damien's Mother. She had spoken to Police and a Witness Statement taken from her. It simply said she could not recall what time she got up on 4th February. She could not recall getting up at between 5 and 6 am but sometimes she could not sleep and would get up and look for her Cat. The case was adjourned at Lunchtime with only one further Prosecution Witness available, DS Monkton, the "Officer in the Case."

David had a sandwich for lunch and then did some further work on his cross examination of the Officer in the Bar Mess library. He noted Charlotte also had a working lunch although hers had nothing to do with this case. She was preparing a completely different case for the following week.

CHAPTER 22.

DAYS SEVEN AND EIGHT, THE OFFICER IN THE CASE.

At 2:05pm Detective Sergeant George Monkton went into the Witness Box to give his evidence. He had been a Police Officer for twenty five years. He had considerable experience as an Officer and had seen many changes in the Police Force, most of which he thought were for the worse. He had given evidence in many cases and thought himself an expert at dealing with a Barrister's cross examination. David knew he would not be an easy Witness and that he would take every chance to make the case stronger against Damien.

Joanna asked him about his experience in the Police Force, and had him explain the function of an, "Officer in the case", namely that he was in charge of the case, collated all the papers and submitted them to the Crown Prosecution Service. She asked him a few questions about the Investigation and she then turned to the Interviews of Damien that took the rest of the afternoon to read to the Jury. The case was adjourned at 4:15pm with the Officer's Evidence part heard until the next day.

On Wednesday, Court commenced at 10:30am and Joanna continued to ask questions of DS Monkton, completing the remaining Interviews and then turning to Damien's previous convictions.

"Officer, we have heard in this case that the Defendant has a number of previous convictions. We heard this when Mr Brant cross examined the Witness Christopher White."

DS Monkton smiled, almost salivating at the prospect of telling the jury the full prejudicial detail of the previous convictions.

"That's right Madam."

"Can you assist us with some of the detail?"

"Certainly Madam."

The pleasure in his voice was there to be witnessed by all in Court. He knew this was the opportunity to put before the Jury the full details of Damien's criminal record. If the Jury needed to be swayed back towards the Prosecution case this was his opportunity. He began with Damien's first minor convictions and then moved on to the more serious ones.

"Then in 2008 he was convicted at Woolwich Magistrates Court of possessing an offensive weapon in a public place. The facts of that matter are that he was stopped by Police Officers in the Woolwich Dockyard area late at night. He was found to be carrying a flick knife. He received a Community sentence for that offence.

In 2010 he was convicted of wounding at Woolwich Crown Court. The facts of that matter are that he was seen by Police Officers in Woolwich High street late at night. He was involved in a confrontation with another man and was seen to forcefully plunge a knife into the body of the other male. He received a sentence of 30 months Imprisonment and was released after serving half that sentence in November 2011."

He did not say it directly but he tried to convey the impression that if Damien had received a sentence of an appropriate length, the current offence would not have been committed.

Satisfied that the Jury now had the impression that Damien was a knife wielding thug, Joanna thanked DS Monkton and sat down.

David looked at DS Monkton and saw the smugness on his face. He was not going to let any clever Barrister obtain an acquittal through questioning him and he was confident he could answer any question asked of him and add as much prejudicial material as he could in his answers.

"Officer, you have told us you are the Officer in the Case, having control of all the Used and Unused Material and also you are in charge of the Investigation. You are able to answer questions about the Investigation that took place in this case?"

"I hope I can Sir,"

DS Monkton thought it right to introduce a degree of modesty and deference at his stage.

"Thank you I am sure you will be able to assist."

The two of them were both smiling at each other as if they were friends but in reality each was trying to assess the other and see whether there would be a weakness they could exploit.

"DS Monkton, you would agree that as an Investigating Officer it is your duty to investigate not only the case against a Defendant but also to investigate matters that might be in his favour."

"That's right, Sir."

"Did you do that in this case?"

"Most certainly Sir. We investigated the case in order to see what the evidence was against the Defendant as well as if there was anything in his favour."

He could not resist adding,

"However, all the evidence pointed towards him committing the murder."

David reacted to this statement,

"Officer, try to confine yourself to answering my questions and not giving us your opinion."

His Honour Judge Tanner could not resist interrupting at this stage,

"Mr Brant, it appears you are trying to have your cake and eat it, you asked the question that elicited that answer."

David thought this might be the time to elicit a degree of humour.

"With respect my Lord, I have never seen any reason to have a cake unless you are going to eat it."

The effect was somewhat destroyed by Tim Arnold who looking at David's bulky frame could not resist a sotto voce,

"We can see that!"

There were a few laughs from the Jury box and David felt a reddening of his face which he hoped was not noticed by anyone in Court. He decided to move swiftly on.

"DS Monkton I will raise this now so that you can deal with it, your investigation was wholly inadequate and solely concentrated on the case against Mr Clarke rather than an investigation into anything that might be in his favour?"

"That's ridiculous Sir and I totally refute that and resent the suggestion that I did not do my job properly. The problem was that all the evidence pointed to your Client."

David noticed that this looked like a practiced response, probably something the Jury did not notice, he would have to move to specifics to prevent the Officer giving any more prejudicial opinions against Damien.

"Officer, what is an Anniversary Enquiry?"

"It's a standard investigatory technique in Murders and other serious investigations. A week, month, or even a few months after an incident we send out officers into the area the incident took place and they ask questions of people in the area to try and find witnesses."

"Was one carried out in this case?"

"Oh yes, exactly a week after the Murder, Officers went to the area of Mr Usman's flat to ask questions about the incident."

David looked down at the piece of paper in his hands that he had taken from the Unused Material and which was headed, "Results of Anniversary Enquiry."

"What was the result of that enquiry?"

"I understand it was negative. About 120 questionnaires were handed out to passers-by but none could assist the enquiry."

David looked down at the form in front of him again.

"Can you help us as to the type of questions that were asked on the questionnaire?"

"I'm not sure exactly. It would have been questions about the investigation."

"Let me assist Officer, here is a copy of the questionnaire handed out."

David gave a copy to the Court Usher to give to the Officer. He also provided copies for His Honour Judge Tanner and Joanna.

"You will note, Officer, that the questions asked begin with basic ones about whether the individual was in the area in the early hours of 4th February?"

"That's correct, Sir."

"There is then just one question asked about the incident, "Did you see a young white male leave the flats at Cambridge Gardens in the early hours of the morning. If you did, can you say what time this was?"

"That's right, Sir. If people had come back answering that they had seen him leave late in the morning, that may have assisted your client. However, no one did!"

"The problem officer is that it was your duty to investigate any matters that might assist Mr Clarke. You should have asked whether anyone saw anyone answering Babs/Babe's description leave the flat and whether two men answering the description of the Scottish man and Arabic man were seen to leave the flat that morning."

"I didn't set the questionnaire Sir."

"No but you were in charge of the Investigation weren't you officer?"

"I was and I am Sir."

"Did you check to see whether there was any evidence that the Arabian gentleman and the Scottish gentleman visited the flat that night?"

"We did but we did not find any credible evidence that they did."

"Did you discover that the female called Babs or Babe did exist?"

"We did Sir, we found her and took a Statement from her that was served on the Defence. We did decide she was not a credible witness so we did not rely on her as she changed her account several times."

"Nevertheless she does exist?"

"She does Sir and you can call her if you wish."

"Thank you DS Monkton. Does the name "Robert Davies" mean anything to you?"

"No Sir."

"He is the Flat Supervisor at Cambridge Gardens. Do you know if any Police Officer has taken a Statement from him?"

"I don't believe so Sir."

"Thank you Officer, let's look at a few other ways in which this investigation was carried out. The reality is that from within 30 minutes of Mr Clarke giving you his account of what happened you decided that you had your man and were not going to investigate any other possible suspect?"

"I dispute that Sir."

"Within 30 minutes of him giving his version to you, you arrested him on suspicion of committing the Murder."

"That's right Sir, but that was because the account he gave was contradictory, disjointed and quite frankly didn't add up."

"Officer, please tell us what happened just before he was arrested on suspicion of committing Murder?"

"He just gave his account Sir."

David picked up an Unused Witness Statement from Police Officer Angela Walters.

"It's right isn't it Officer that a female officer, Angela Walters came in to the interviewing room and gave you both a cup of tea and biscuits?"

DS Monkton could not resist a smug reply.

"I can't recall when tea and biscuits arrived, Sir. I was concentrating on other matters."

The emphasis on the Sir was made with as much contempt as he could muster. He did not like Defence Barristers, he had seen too many good jobs end in acquittals because of clever Defence Barristers. He noted happily, that some members of the Jury smiled at his comment.

"Let me assist Officer, PC Walters also brought you a document, it was a list of previous convictions of Damien Clarke."

The smirk was quickly removed from DS Monkton's face, he had forgotten that this Statement was in the Unused.

"Here you were Officer with a man present at the scene of the Murder and with a previous conviction for possessing an offensive weapon, a knife, and more importantly a conviction for wounding with a knife. You decided then and there you had your man, you were not going to look any further were you?"

The Officer was distinctly uncomfortable now and spoke more quietly,

"I dispute that Sir."

"It's right that you stopped the tape of the interview when the tea and biscuits arrived. Why was that?"

"I thought we could both do with a rest Sir."

"Or was it so you could say something to Mr Clarke that was not recorded."

"I dispute that Sir."

"It is of course right that you had a conversation that was not recorded?"

"We obviously spoke Sir, but not about what he had said, nor about anything that was relevant to the investigation."

David looked down at the transcript of Damien's police interview.

"Officer, when the tape started again you arrested and cautioned Mr Clarke on suspicion of Murder. You also told him that he could have free legal advice if he wanted and you added, "..but I understand you don't want a Solicitor." Had you discussed with him whether he needed a Solicitor?"

"I had told him I was going to arrest him on suspicion of Murder and that he could have a Solicitor present and that he would not have to pay. He said he was happy to continue and did not want a Solicitor present."

"Did you tell him the arrest and interview were, "more of a formality"?"

"Certainly not Sir, I would never say that."

"Did you try to discourage him from having a Solicitor present by telling him he would have to wait a long time for one?"

"No I did not Sir. I told him he could have a Solicitor present, I never mentioned anything about him having to wait for one. He said he did not want one."

"Wasn't it you who told him, he would not need one?"

"No Sir."

"Let us look at the reason you say you arrested Mr Clarke on suspicion of Murder. You say his account was, "contradictory, disjointed and quite frankly didn't add up". That's what you told us a few moments ago."

"Yes Sir."

"We've seen his account, it's been read out to the Jury. In what way do you say it's contradictory?"

DS Monkton was struggling now and beginning to forget the answers he had prepared.

"I can't recall specifics now but I recall it was contradictory at the time. During the course of thirty minutes he contradicted himself many times."

"We have heard his account read out to us, can you give us just one example of where he contradicted himself in that account?"

"Not at the moment."

"Very well, let's look at your next concern. You say his account was "disjointed". Again we have a verbatim record of what was said, taken from the tape recording of your interview with him. How do you say it was disjointed?"

DS Monkton eager to recover responded quickly,

"The manner in which he gave his account was disjointed. He would start, stop, go back on himself, say he remembered something new ...."

"Officer, surely you are not suggesting that all witnesses who tell the truth give perfect accounts straight away?"

"No."

"I suggest most honest Witnesses will stop, start, go back on themselves and remember something new when they try to give an account?"

"This was different."

"Can you give us an example?"

"Not a specific example, no."

"In reality Officer, you learnt he had previous convictions for possessing a knife and wounding and you decided you had your man."

"I dispute that."

DS Monkton was clearly looking uncomfortable and HHJ Tanner decided to intervene.

"Mr Brant, where is this line of questioning taking us? I will direct the Jury the Officer's opinion of your client's guilt or innocence is irrelevant. The issue is simply whether the Jury is sure your client is Guilty on all the evidence they will hear. I cannot see how this line of questioning will assist them."

David was quite happy that the Judge had made this interruption as it allowed him to make a short speech in front of the Jury pointing out the relevance of his cross- examination just in case it was not apparent to anyone.

"My Lord I had hoped the relevance was clear, that is my fault for not making it clear in the course of my cross-examination. As the Jury has heard from the Interview read out, it is Mr Clarke's case that he did not commit the Murder but that it was committed by two other men. It is his case that the Police have made no adequate investigation into that possibility thereby cutting off a potential and important part of his Defence. It is his case that they should have investigated those two men before the trail went cold. Nevertheless, I had actually asked most of the questions I wanted to about this matter and I am ready to move on."

"Good, Mr Brant, well let's move on."

David turned back to DS Monkton and continued where he had left off when interrupted.

"Officer, I was dealing with the moment you discovered that Mr Clarke had previous convictions. You have given us details about those convictions. I want to ask you a little more about them."

"Yes, Sir."

DS Monkton had managed to gain his composure during the Judge's intervention and his confidence had returned. However, His Honour Judge Tanner's was looking distinctly uncomfortable wondering whether to interrupt again. David Brant had said he was moving on but in fact was concentrating on the same issue. He decided to let it run for a short time.

"DS Monkton, the version of the facts that you gave us in relation to those convictions came from the Prosecution papers in those cases?"

"Yes Sir."

"Have you independently verified the facts of those convictions?"

"I've checked the Prosecution papers and the Memorandum of Conviction from the Courts."

"Did you discover that from your investigation that the flick knife was in fact broken and would not "flick" anymore?"

"No Sir"

"Did you also discover that he pleaded Guilty to the offence?"

"Yes Sir"

"Did you not think it important to tell the Jury that he in fact pleaded Guilty to all his previous convictions?"

"I wasn't asked that by Prosecution Counsel."

Good, thought David, he's trying to blame Joanna, she won't appreciate that.

"Did you also discover that the basis of his plea, accepted by the Prosecution, was that he had found the knife that very night when he was stopped. He had not had it long when the Police stopped him and he had not decided what to do with it?"

"No Sir"

"That might explain the relatively light sentence."

"It might Sir."

Noticeably Detective Sergeant Monkton was trying to give the impression that it did not.

"In relation to the wounding charge, that was also a plea of Guilty wasn't it?"

"Yes Sir."

"Again did you discover his basis of plea?"

"No Sir."

"Just so the Jury understand, when a person pleads Guilty they often put forward their version of events in a written document called a "Basis of Plea." It is then for the Prosecution to accept or reject their account. If the Prosecution accepts it then usually that is the basis that the Court will sentence on?"

"I understand that's right Sir."

"Thank you Officer, in relation to the wounding case a Basis of Plea was again put before the Court and the Prosecution accepted it."

"I was not aware of that Sir, but I will take your word."

"Don't take my word Officer, let me show you a copy of the Basis of Plea signed by both the Prosecution and Defence Barristers who appeared in that case."

David produced copies for the Officer, His Honour Judge Tanner and Joanna which he had obtained from the Solicitor's files.

"You will see that the Basis of Plea to the wounding was that Mr Clarke had received threats from a Mr Williams, a man with many previous convictions for violence. Mr Clarke had taken the knife with him as a form of protection in case he came across him. They did meet in the street and Mr Williams threatened him again. Mr Clarke had produced the knife to frighten Mr Williams, there was no forceful plunge of the knife into his body but there was a struggle and the man received a single shallow wound. Mr Clarke accepted that he should not have had the knife and he pleaded Guilty to injuring the other man."

"I hadn't seen that document before Sir."

"Yes Officer, so we can see. Might I suggest that you haven't investigated Mr Clarke's previous convictions properly, just as you haven't investigated this Murder case properly?"

David sat down before his comment disguised as a question could be answered or objected to.

Joanna decided to re-examine on the two previous convictions but was unable to obtain any further information from the Officer who had clearly only been interested in the original Prosecution version of events and not the Basis of the Plea. After he was released she closed the case for the Prosecution at 12:05.

Now the Prosecution had closed its case David's options were threefold. Make a submission to the Judge that there was No Case for the Defence to Answer, arguing that there was insufficient evidence upon which a properly directed Jury could convict and therefore seeking that the Judge to direct the Jury to acquit at this stage. Or he could call evidence in support of the Defence case or, finally, he could announce that he was calling no evidence and move on to closing speeches.

In reality he knew there was only one option. There was clearly evidence from which a Jury could convict Damien of Murder. Damien admitted his presence at the time of the Murder, he had admitted that he had cleaned the knife which was used to kill Usman, the confusing evidence about when he went to his Mother's home, the injury to his hand that was arguably consistent with setting fire to the property to destroy forensic evidence, the evidence of the Cell Siting of where he was at 5:21am, the evidence of one set of footprints in the flat immediately after the Murder, Damien's washing of his clothes when he got home and of course the fact that he had previous convictions for possessing and using a knife. No Judge was going to throw this case out. He could of course advise Damien not to give evidence in his Defence and move on to speeches but he knew that His Honour Judge Tanner would direct the Jury that they could draw an "adverse inference" against Damien and David considered this was a case where the Jury would be likely to do so! Accordingly there was only one option left and that was to call Damien to give evidence in the Witness Box. He decided that he needed one final conference with Damien and so he addressed His Honour Judge Tanner.

"My Lord, the time has been reached for the Defence case. Your Lordship will be aware of the difficulties there are in arranging conferences during a case in this building and I ask that we adjourn until 2:05pm to enable us to have a conference with Mr Clarke at this stage."

His Honour Judge Tanner knew the difficulties all too well for Defendants who were in custody. Often Defendants were not brought to Court until after 10-00am. Somehow the vans from Belmarsh prison, despite coming to the Bailey almost daily, frequently got lost and had sometimes found themselves on the way to Essex until prisoners pointed out they were going in the wrong direction. When a Defendant did arrive Counsel had to book a slot to see him which meant morning conferences were very short. It would then take Counsel at least 5 minutes to be checked in and searched. Further, Cells would not allow anyone to see the Defendants at Lunchtime before 13:45 and again it would take 5 minutes to get through security. In the evening when the case finished at 4:15pm the prison vans wanted to leave at 4:30pm and so again time was limited. The Judge would have felt obliged to agree to what, in the circumstances, was a reasonable request. In any event it gave him an extra hour to start preparing his Summing-up for the Jury.

"Mr Brant, I understand there are important decisions to be taken at this stage of the case and the conference facilities in this Court are limited, if you tell me you need between now and 2:05pm I will give you that time."

"My Lord, I anticipate we will need about an hour, that will take us up until the lunch hour which is why I have suggested that we adjourn until 2:05pm."

His Honour Judge Tanner agreed and the case was duly adjourned.

CHAPTER 23.

DAY EIGHT, THE DEFENDANT'S EVIDENCE IN CHIEF.

David and Charlotte took the lift to the lower ground floor where the Cells were situated. He felt that his cross-examination of the Officer had gone well. Charlotte was unconvinced.

"Why did you ask him such open questions about his use of the words "contradictory" and "disjointed", it was a bit risky wasn't it?"

Great, he thought, the job is difficult enough without being second-guessed by a Junior who has not contributed at all to the preparation of the trial. Still he had to be polite, he did not want any bad feedback going to Charles Rooney.

"Charlotte, I have read all the papers including the Unused Material."

He did not mean it as a dig at her but he realised it came across in that way, so he added quickly.

"As I am sure you noted, there are no contradictions in the tape recording of the Interview with Damien. Also his account does not come across in a disjointed fashion. I thought it was reasonably safe to cross-examine on those issues."

The reality was he had not been sure it was right to ask the questions even when he was asking them, he was just grateful that DS Monkton had not provided better answers.

After the usual security checks and searches they were both allowed into the cells to see Damien.

He was already in one of the conference room sipping from a plastic cup of coffee. David smiled at him and said,

"Hello Damien, how are you feeling? Are you ready to give evidence?"

Damien stopped sipping from his steaming hot cup.

"I'm not sure Mr Brant. Do I have to give evidence?"

It was a conversation they had already had but clearly Damien was nervous and wanted to see if there was a way he could avoid the Witness Box.

"No Damien, as I've told you, you don't **have** to give evidence. No one can force you. However, if you do not, both the Prosecution and the Judge will tell the Jury that they can hold it against you that you did not give your account from the witness box. The Prosecutor will tell the Jury the only reason you have not given evidence is because your account is not true and you know it wouldn't stand up to being tested under cross-examination. What we have to consider is whether we have done enough to obtain an acquittal at this stage. We may have done, the case has gone well so far but in my opinion the Jury will want to hear from you. This is your opportunity to put your version across and if you do not, there will be no second opportunity. You could be convicted of Murder and spend years thinking, "Why didn't I give evidence?" but then it will be too late."

In reality David would much prefer not to call clients to give evidence if he could because frequently they did make the Prosecution case stronger against themselves. Nevertheless he thought in this case the Jury would want to hear from Damien. They might convict when they had heard from him but he thought they almost certainly would convict him if they did not.

Damien considered his options and the information that Robert Davies, the flat supervisor at Cambridge Gardens had made a Statement and recalled seeing a Scottish man, a Lebanese man and a woman visiting Usman Hussain's flat on the night of 3rd February 2012. He was available to give evidence the following day.

Damien decided to heed David's advice and to give evidence that afternoon.

At 2:05pm the case resumed and David informed the Court that he would be calling Damien to give evidence. He was entitled to make an Opening Speech because he was calling a Witness to the facts of the case as well as Damien but he decided not to make one. He was not a great fan of making

Opening Speeches for the Defence at this stage, telling a Jury what evidence he was about to call only to find that the evidence did not come out that way. He also thought making an Opening Speech at this stage gave the Prosecution too much advance notice and too much time to prepare for what was coming.

David told the Court he was going to call Damien Clarke as a Witness and invited Damien to come out of the Dock and walk to the Witness Box. Damien made the short walk moving from the right of the Jury box where the Dock was situated, walking in front of the Jury to the Witness Box on their right. He would have looked like any other Witness in the case if it were not for the fact that he was followed by a burly Prison Guard who sat behind him in order to ensure he did not try to escape!

Damien was wearing the same suit he had worn every day with a clean white shirt and a blue flowery tie that his Mother and Sisters had taken to Belmarsh prison for him. He would have looked neat and tidy but for the fact that he had the top button of his shirt undone and his tie was pulled too tightly ruining the knot. It did not assist that his homemade spider tattoo was showing through the open collar.

David looked across at Joanna who was smiling. He knew what she was thinking. Her case had been damaged in cross-examination, she would soon have the opportunity to use her formidable skills to try and ruin Damien's case.

After Damien had sworn an Oath on the New Testament, to tell the truth, David asked him some background questions. How old was he, where had he been brought up, what was his education and work experience? He asked him about his previous convictions, emphasising the fact he had always pleaded Guilty when he was guilty, and had always therefore been truthful to the Court. He took him through the circumstances of the previous convictions, reading out the Basis of plea to the Jury. He then moved on to his crack cocaine smoking. Damien stated he smoked for recreational purposes and was not addicted. (David had not been able to get him to agree that crack cocaine was one of the most addictive drugs and no one smoked it recreationally). He talked of his Family life, the Father he had never known, his Mother with whom he had been close, and his Sisters for whom he had a strong affection, but with whom he was not always on good terms. He spoke of his relationship with his ex-girlfriend Jenny, how often he saw her even after they split-up and how she constantly flirted with him. He then spoke of Usman Hussain, how he had met him, how he had thought he was a nice man who would not hurt anyone, although he would get verbally aggressive when he smoked crack cocaine. He spoke of Gillian Banks who he liked and how he believed she liked him.

It took almost an hour to get Damien to cover these topics. At first he had been slow to respond to questions, clearly nervous. He had been quiet so that David had frequently asked him to speak up so that everyone could hear him in the Court room. As time had gone on Damien became more relaxed and answered the questions without frequent pauses and he spoke loudly enough for everyone to hear. It was partly why David had asked him so many questions about his past, so that he would be more relaxed and confident giving his evidence when the difficult questions were asked.

Having exhausted the sanitised version of Damien's personal history, David decided it was time to move on to the facts of the case.

"Mr Clarke, I want to ask you questions now about your movements on 3rd February 2012. We have heard evidence from Jenny Jones that you met her at about 12pm. Indeed we have seen evidence that you phoned her at 11:37am that morning?"

"I did, we'd arranged to meet up in Woolwich and I was just checking that she was still on for it."

"We heard that you spent the day drinking together."

"Yeah it was nothing special. Just an ordinary day."

"We have heard that you went to a public house called "The Prince Rupert" and had a few drinks there?"

"Yeah we did."

"Ms Jones stated that you drank throughout the day and shared a couple of Cannabis joints, did you?"

"Yeah we did, it was no big deal."

"Do you have any idea how much you drank that day?"

"It was a lot, but I wasn't counting."

"Were either of you drunk?"

"Jenny was, I was merry."

David wanted to deal quickly with their disagreement.

"We have heard that there came a time when you separated and at 23:17 and you sent a text to her that said, "You fucking bitch you led me on again." What was that all about?"

"It was just a silly thing really, we both drank too much. I wanted to get back with her and I thought she wanted the same because she flirted with me all day. Then when I asked her she said "No", and I felt hurt. I regret sending it, I was just drunk at the time."

David noticed Joanna busily scribbling notes in her notebook and underling them when this was said.

"We have heard that a call was made from the vicinity of Mr Hussain's flat?"

"Yeah, I had decided when I left Jenny that I would go to Usman's, as I fancied a smoke and I knew he could always get some."

"Do you recall what time you arrived, approximately?"

"Not really. I wasn't wearing a watch and I wasn't watching the time. It would have been a few minutes after my text to Jenny."

"So just before midnight?"

"Yeah, something like that."

"Was anyone else there when you arrived at Mr Hussain's flat?"

"Yeah there were three people there. There were two males and a girl. I'd seen the girl before, she was called Babs or Babe. I hadn't seen the men before but clearly Usman knew them."

"When had you seen the girl before?

"I'd seen her at Usman's on a couple of occasions. I didn't know her well."

"Mr Clarke we have heard that you were interviewed by Police and you told them you had never seen the girl before, why was that?"

David thought it better to deal with this when he was questioning rather than let Joanna deal with in cross examination.

"Yeah, I was in a state of shock when I was interviewed. I made a few mistakes because I was still feeling the effects of a day's drinking and the night's smoking crack cocaine."

"How much crack did you smoke that night?"

"I don't know but it was a lot. I remember we ran out of crack and we all put some money in and Usman went and got some more from one of his suppliers. I remember I was tired and I fell asleep in the armchair."

"Do you recall what awoke you?"

"Yeah it was Babs or Babe trying to scream."

"Why was she trying to scream?"

"I woke up and could see her on the sofa. They'd got some of her clothes off, the Scotsman was holding her down with his hand over her mouth and the Arab guy was between her legs trying to rape her?"

"What did you do?"

"Nothing, I was just shocked, I was out of it, I didn't move."

"What happened next?"

I remember Usman coming in and shouting at them, telling them to leave her alone. I remember him shouting more at the Arab because the Scotsman let go almost immediately and walked off towards the Kitchen area. I then saw him return and he was carrying a kitchen knife",

"Did you see where he got the knife from?"

"I didn't see him pick it up but I presume he got it from a drawer or something."

"What happened then?"

"Usman was holding the Arab with both his hands, the Scotsman just stabbed him in the chest. It was all so quick. Usman let out a scream, he let go of the Arab and put his hands up to defend himself but the Scotsman just kept stabbing. It was horrible."

"Did you do anything?"

"No, it was all over so quick. Usman collapsed onto the floor then the Scotsman turned to me. I saw his look, it was frightening. I thought I'm a goner, I'm next."

David, thinking of Damien's Interview statement said, "Where was the Arabian man at this stage?"

"I can't remember."

"What about Babs or Babe?"

"I can't remember, I was just shocked by it all."

"Did she remain in the flat?"

"No, I remember her leaving, but it is a bit of a blur."

"What happened to the two men?"

"I remember the Scotsman came up to me, told me to get out of the chair and go and get the Duvet from Usman's bedroom. I did that and he told me to wrap Usman's body in it."

"Did you do that?"

"Yeah. Then he told me to move the body to the bedroom, which I did. He kept pointing the knife at me and I believed he was going to stab me. He then put the knife down and told me to take it and wash it which I did. They both confronted me and told me if I said anything about what happened they would kill me. The Scotsman grabbed my hand and lit his lighter under it burning my hand. I thought they were going to kill me anyway. A few moments later I saw them getting their coats and I just ran out of the flat and ran home."

"Let's just deal with the injury to your hand. When you were first seen by Doctor Monkton you said this had been caused by smoking crack cocaine. Why did you say that?

"I was still shocked. I just couldn't remember how it happened and the Doctor was telling me I'd done it when I set fire to the place so I just made it up that I'd burnt it when smoking crack. I then remembered what had happened by the time I saw the next Doctor, which is why I told him."

"Let's go back to your journey home. How long did it take to get home?"

"It took about 15 to 20 minutes."

"Why so long?"

"I ran out of the flat but I was exhausted so I walked home."

"Your sister Christine has given evidence that you got home at about 7:30am. Is she right?"

"I don't know what the time was. I know I went straight there from Usman's flat."

"What did you do when you got there?"

"I was in a panic, I stripped off my clothes and washed them and had a shower to get the blood off me."

"We know from the phone records that you phoned your friend Christopher White at 12:32 that day and you were in your mother's flat at the time?"

"Yeah that's right, he's a friend I just wanted to chat to someone I trust, just to ask him what to do."

"We also have a phone record that shows your phone communicated with his phone at 5:21am?"

"I can't remember anything about that. I might have phoned him but I don't remember."

"There is a suggestion from the Cell Site evidence that you may have been in your mother's flat at the time of that call. Did you leave Usman's flat in the early hours of the morning and go to your Mother's flat and then return to Usman's?"

"No way, I was at Usman's flat from the time I went there before midnight until the Murder and then I left."

"What did you speak to Christopher about at 12:32 that day?"

"I told him what I'd seen, I told him I was scared and asked him if he thought I should go to the Police. He said I should."

"We know you did go to the Police Station at about 2pm. You were heard to say, "Why him? Why did it have to be him?" What did you mean by that?"

"Usman was a nice man, he was kind and I liked him. I just couldn't understand why they killed him."

"We have heard that you were interviewed by Detective Sergeant Monkton?"

Damien's mood visibly changed at the name of the Officer.

"Yeah, he was all nice at first. He asked me what happened and I told him. Then the female Officer came in with the tea and biscuits and handed him some papers. I didn't know what they were. He then told me he had to arrest me on suspicion of Murder but not to worry, it was just a formality and I didn't need a Solicitor."

"He told you, you did not need a Solicitor?"

"That's right, he said it would take a lot of time to get one and I might as well carry on. I thought there was nothing wrong so I just carried on telling him what happened. It was ages before he turned round and started accusing me of murdering Usman and setting fire to the flat. After that I told him I wanted a Solicitor and then the Solicitor arrived and told me not to answer any more questions, so I didn't."

"We have heard that you were charged with the Murder the next day and you said, "I didn't kill him." I want to ask you about that now. The Prosecution case appears to be, that in some drug fuelled craze you killed your good friend Usman Hussain. Is there any truth in that allegation."

Tears started to well up in Damien's eyes.

"No, none whatsoever, he was a good friend to me, I had no reason to kill him and I never did."

David decided that he had asked enough questions. It was just after 4pm so the case was adjourned for Damien to be cross-examined the following day. David and Charlotte shared a bottle of Claret that night. Both thought that Damien had been a good Witness so far. The question was how would he hold up under Joanna Glass's cross-examination?

CHAPTER 24.

DAY NINE, THE CROSS EXAMINATION OF THE DEFENDANT.

On Thursday the case commenced at 10:30am. David had not visited Damien in the Cells because Damien was now giving evidence and David was not allowed to speak to him until he had finished his evidence.

Damien returned to the Witness Box and Joanna smiled at His Honour Judge Tanner and then started to cross-examine.

"Mr Clarke, at the time of this Murder you were drinking heavily, smoking Cannabis and smoking crack cocaine, as you say on a social basis?"

"Yeah that's right."

"Things have changed for you over the last few months though haven't they?"

"I've been in custody since February so yeah they have changed."

"Yes, you've been in Belmarsh prison, presumably not drinking alcohol, not using drugs?"

"I am a lot more sober than I was."

"In February this year, were you a heavy drinker?"

"I was a very heavy drinker. I have been drinking since I was 14."

"Were you a heavy user of crack cocaine?"

"I wouldn't say heavy, it was a social thing."

"Mr Clarke, crack cocaine is one of the most addictive drugs out there, no one smokes it socially do they?"

"Have you ever tried it?"

His Honour Judge Tanner could not allow Damien to make comments like this and show disrespect for the Court.

"Mr Clarke, Counsel is here to ask questions of you, not for you to ask questions of her and may I suggest that you will do yourself a great disservice in answering questions in that style."

"Sorry Sir."

Joanna tried again,

"Mr Clarke, crack cocaine is one of the most addictive drugs out there, no one smokes it socially do they?"

"I don't agree. I did."

"Very well, how much did you smoke in a week?"

"I don't know the quantities, I'd have 20 quid's worth here and there."

"Did you drink most nights?"

"Yeah."

"Did you smoke crack most nights?"

"Not every night, a few nights a week."

"Life must have been almost a daze for you?"

"No."

"What effect did drinking heavily and smoking crack cocaine have on you?"

"It made me merry, happy."

"Did it make you aggressive?"

"No."

"At 11:17pm on 3rd February 2012 you sent a text message to Jenny Jones your ex- girlfriend, "You fucking bitch you led me on again." Would you not say that was aggressive?"

"No, I was just annoyed."

"And aggressive?"

"I wasn't aggressive."

"How did her clothes get torn?"

"It wasn't me, I don't know."

"Having consumed a large amount of alcohol throughout the day, having smoked Cannabis you moved on to crack cocaine?"

"Didn't that make you more aggressive?"

"No, it made me more tired, that's why I fell asleep."

"Really, we only have your word for that?"

"Yeah."

"You have told us you were in the flat with Mr Hussain, Babs or Babe and the two men, the Arab man and the Scottish man?"

"Yeah."

"You were all drinking and smoking crack cocaine."

"Yeah."

"You have told us that you were a Witness to the assault on Usman Hussain?"

"Yeah, that's right."

"You were then told to wrap a Duvet around his body?"

"Yeah."

"Did you know that Usman Hussain was dead when you wrapped the Duvet round him?"

"I knew he'd been stabbed but I didn't know if he was dead."

"When you left the flat did you think he was dead?"

"I didn't know, I knew he was seriously hurt."

"He was a friend of yours?"

"Yeah."

"You did not know whether he was alive or dead?"

"No I didn't."

"Why didn't you phone for an ambulance?"

Damien paused for a few seconds.

"I don't know, I was in a lot of fear."

"You're lying aren't you Mr Clarke?"

"No. I'm not."

"You knew Mr Hussain was dead when you left that flat because you had killed him?"

"That's not true."

"If you thought your friend was seriously injured you would have phoned an ambulance?"

"I told you, I was afraid, I was shocked, I didn't think properly."

"Did you set the fire?"

"No I did not."

"Were you even in the flat when the fire started?"

"No I wasn't."

"We know that Mr Feeley, a neighbour of Mr Hussain phoned the fire brigade at 6:57am?"

"Yeah."

"That means the fire had started before that time?"

"Yeah."

"How close are you to your family?"

"Very close."

"Does your sister Christine have any problems with you?"

"No."

"She gave evidence in this case, she had no reason to lie?"

"Yeah."

"She would have done her best to remember things accurately?"

"Yeah, she would."

"You told us you ran from the flat when the men were getting their coats?"

"Yes."

"That was before the fire started so it would be some time before 6:57am?"

"Yeah."

"It then took you 15-20 minutes to get home. I believe you said 15 minutes in your interview and 15-20 minutes in your evidence?

"Yeah."

"So on your evidence, the very latest you would have been home was 7:17am, and probably earlier?"

"Yeah."

"However, Christine, your Sister, who has no reason to lie and who you say would do her best to remember, says you got home at 7:30am?"

David interjected at this stage,

"Actually her evidence when she answered questions under cross-examination was that it might have been earlier than 7:30am although not much earlier."

Joanna glared at him but then smiled and continued.

"That is of course right. Nevertheless, I suggest that on your case the timings do not add up. Did you go anywhere else when you left the flat?"

"No I went straight home."

"Covered in Mr Hussain's blood?"

"Yes."

"Your sister Christine never saw any blood on you. Had you gone somewhere else, perhaps a friends and changed your clothes?"

"No, my clothes had blood stains on them that's why I washed them and that's why I showered."

"After Mr Hussain was stabbed there was a lot of blood around?"

"Yes."

"He was murdered in the living room or the lounge area as some Witnesses have described it?"

"Yes."

"You were close enough for blood to get on your clothes?"

"Yes."

"According to you, you were told to get a Duvet to cover him up?"

"Yes and I did."

"I suggest you have made all of this up. There was no one else in the flat when you murdered Usman Hussain?"

"No that's not true. I didn't murder him, they did, and they were there."

"Let's look at the evidence, shall we? According to your account, you would have to walk over his body that was pooling blood onto the Living room floor. You would then walk to the bedroom, get the Duvet, walk back, wrap the body into the Duvet, walk back to his bedroom carrying the body and then walk back to the living room. You were then given the knife, you walked to the kitchen, cleaned it and then walked back to the Living room. Eventually you ran from the Living room and exited the flat?"

"Yes, that's what happened."

"You must have got his blood on your trainers?"

"I probably did, there was a lot of blood around."

"However, none of the trainers taken from your flat had any blood on them, why was that?"

"I don't know."

"You would have blood on your trainers. You would have left some bloody foot prints in the flat?"

"I may have done."

"Yes, I suggest you did. In fact you left the **only** set of bloody foot prints that were found?"

"No they can't have been mine. They were left by a pair of trainers called Star 'D' Sprints, I never had any such trainers."

"I suggest you did and you got rid of them before returning to your Mother's flat?"

"That's rubbish."

"Really, if the prints found in the flat were not yours, where were your prints?"

"I don't know where my shoeprints were, they might have been the smudged prints."

"Those were near the curtains in the Living room. You would have left prints near Mr Hussain's body in the Living room, you would have left shoeprints in the Hallway, in Mr Hussain's bedroom and in the Kitchen. The only bloody shoeprints found in those areas were made by Star 'D' Sprints which I suggest belonged to you?"

"That's not true, those weren't my prints. They must have been made by the Scotsman or the Arab."

"I suggest they were made by you after you stabbed Mr Hussain with a knife."

"That's not true."

"It wasn't the first time you stabbed someone with a knife. As we have heard you stabbed another man with a knife in the past?"

"Yeah but that was different."

"How was it different?"

"He started on me, he was always threatening me. I used that knife in self-defence."

"No Mr Clarke, if it was self-defence you would have fought the case as that would have provided you with a Defence. You pleaded Guilty to the criminal offence of Wounding a man with a knife. What happened, did you lose your temper on that occasion?"

"Yeah, I'd been drinking and I lost my temper with him."

"That is what I suggest happened this time as well. You had been drinking all day, you were smoking crack cocaine, something happened to make you snap and lose your temper and you stabbed Usman Hussain to death, didn't you?"

"No that's a lie."

"How long passed between Mr Hussain being stabbed and you leaving the flat?"

"I don't know, it was some time because I had to move his body and clean the knife and I had to wait until I could escape."

"Less than an hour?"

"Probably, I don't know."

"The Paramedics arrived at the flat at 7:15am and from their experience they believed he had been dead for possibly two hours by that time. You are lying to us aren't you?"

"No I am telling the truth."

"Why did you phone Christopher White at 05:21am that day, almost exactly two hours before the paramedics arrived?"

"I don't remember phoning him."

"Was it to tell him you had just murdered Mr Hussain?"

"No."

"Where were you when you made the call?"

"I don't remember making the call."

"Had you gone home arriving at about 5am and then left again at 6am to go back to set fire to Mr Hussain's flat in order to destroy the evidence?"

"No."

"And you set fire to his flat didn't you?"

"No I didn't."

"That's how you burnt your hand, whilst you were setting the fire?"

"No they burnt it when they held the lighter under my hand."

"Why did you first lie and say you had burnt it whilst smoking crack cocaine?"

"I told you, I was in a state of shock. I couldn't recall how I burnt it. It was only later that I could remember."

"I suggest the reason you lied was because you had not thought of a good reason for the burn. It was only when the Doctor pointed out that your injury did not look like an injury caused by smoking crack cocaine that you changed your story?"

"That's not true."

"You set fire to the flat to destroy any evidence of your being in the flat?"

"No, I didn't."

"That is why you washed your clothes and showered, in order to destroy some of the evidence?"

"No."

"And whilst in drink and high on crack cocaine, you killed Usman Hussain?"

"No I never."

"You stabbed him in the lounge and he backed up into the Hallway where you stabbed him again, that is why we had the airborne droplets of blood in the Hallway. It was from you thrusting the knife into the already bleeding body of Usman Hussain?"

"No that's wrong."

"You murdered your friend that night and you simply will not admit it?"

"No I never".

Joanna sat down giving Damien as contemptuous a look as she could. David did re-examine on a few issues but did not ask many questions and Damien was allowed to return to the Dock. It was now near to Lunchtime and the case was adjourned as David's next Witness had been warned to attend Court to give evidence at 2:05pm. David and Charlotte went to visit the Cells as they were now allowed to talk to Damien as he had finished giving his evidence. He was interested in the answer to one question. How had his evidence come across? David told him that he had clearly done his best. Although there were difficult areas in his evidence he had answered every question fully and not sought to evade any question.

In reality David wondered himself about the effect Damien's evidence had on the Jury. He had answered every question put to him but Joanna had made some very good points. Damien had also not been the most sympathetic of Witnesses. His demeanour had been surly when he was cross-examined and his tone had been aggressive when he answered some of the questions. Had he acquitted himself by his evidence or made his position worse?

CHAPTER 25.

DAY NINE, THE FLAT SUPERVISOR.

At 2:05pm the case re-commenced and David called Robert Davies into the Witness Box. Within a few minutes he had established that Mr Davies was the Flat Supervisor at Cambridge Gardens and he lived on the ground floor in flat 1. It was his job to deal with any problems that occurred in the flats, arranging for the fixing of any problems such as Central Heating or the front door locking system or any other issues. He also interviewed all the prospective Tenants for the Landlords and would deal with any complaints made by the Tenants. David then moved onto the relevant evidence.

"Mr Davies, did you know Usman Hussain?"

"I did."

"We have heard that he lived at flat number 6 on the first floor, the floor above you?"

"That's right he did."

"It was a two-bedroomed flat and he lived with another Tenant Gillian Banks?"

"Ms Banks was not a Tenant. Mr Hussain was the Tenant. He rented the flat. It was up to him who stayed with him but Ms Banks was certainly not a Tenant."

David noted how vehement Mr Davies was in making his denial. He was probably aware of Gillian Banks' occupation and did not want the landlords of Cambridge Gardens to face a potential "brothel-keeping" charge on his watch!

"I want to ask you about Mr Hussain. Was he a good Tenant?"

"He paid his rent on time and he was a friendly bloke, but I wouldn't say he was a good Tenant."

"Why not?"

"He was very noisy. Loud music and voices would be heard from his flat at all times of the day. I received many complaints from other Tenants and I had to speak to him frequently. The Landlords were thinking of giving him notice because of the noise and the number of people he used to invite to his flat."

"Did you know that crack cocaine was smoked in his flat?"

"Certainly not. If I had known, the Landlords would have evicted him."

"I want to ask you about some visitors to his flat. You tell us he had many people visiting his flat?"

"Yes, he did."

"Did you ever see those visitors?"

"Frequently, I live on the ground floor and I would see most of them coming in through the main entrance which I can see through a spy hole in my door. I'm not being nosey, I just think it's important to check who comes into the building."

"Can you help us with the types of people who would visit?"

"There were all sorts. Men, women, different Nationalities. Most looked scruffy like they could do with a good wash and a feed."

"Did you ever learn the names of any of them?"

"No, I never had any interest in their names."

"Did you learn their Nationalities?"

"Not really, I remember White, Black, Asian people frequently visiting."

"Did you ever hear any accents?"

"I remember an Irishman frequently visit and a Scotsman."

"A Scotsman?"

"Yes, he had a Scotsman visit a few times. He was very loud, very aggressive in the way he talked."

David decided to pause to allow this remark to sink in with the jury.

"Sorry just give me a moment to note that comment, 'The Scotsman was very loud, very aggressive in the way he talked'. Thank you, I want to ask you now about the 3rd February 2012, the day before Mr Hussain was killed. Did you see any visitors to his flat that night?"

"I did see quite a few visitors come during the day."

"Let's deal with the night, did you see any visitors during the night?"

"Yes, I did. At about 11pm I heard really loud noises, someone was shouting up to Mr Hussain from outside his window. I could tell it was the Scotsman from his accent. I looked through my spyhole and saw him come into the building. He was arm in arm with a young girl I had seen visit many times. They were also with a Lebanese looking man, who I had not seen before."

"Did you know the names of any of these visitors?"

"No."

"Did you see them leave?"

"No, I went to bed at about 1:30am and they hadn't left by then."

"Did you see anyone else come to Mr Hussain's flat that night?"

"Yes, I saw him."

He pointed at Damien in the Dock and looked at him with a look of utter contempt. He had performed what was referred to by lawyers as a "Dock ID" which was strictly inadmissible, but David was not objecting. He rather liked Mr Davies look of contempt, it demonstrated that he was not here to give evidence on behalf of a friend and therefore was more likely to be telling the truth.

"You have just pointed towards Mr Damien Clarke in the Dock. Had you seen him visit before that night?"

"Yes a few times."

His expression of seething dislike remained on his face. There was clearly a history between them which David decided to avoid.

"Can you recall the approximate time he visited the flat on the evening of 3rd February?"

"Yes, it was about 40-45 minutes after the others. I knew then we would all be in for a noisy night."

David decided again not to enquire further into this aspect of the evidence.

"Did you see what time he left?"

"No, he had not left by the time I went to bed at 1:30 am. None of them were around when the smoke alarms went off at about 7am on Saturday morning, which woke me up."

"We have heard that the Fire Brigade, Paramedics and the Police arrived shortly after that time. Did you see them?"

"Yes I did, I even let some Police Officers in later on."

"Did you ever speak to any Police Officers?"

"Yes, I did, I spoke to a young Officer and told him what I'd seen. He took my name and address and phone number and said someone would be in touch but no one was until a Solicitor contacted me a few days ago."

"That would be a Mr Rooney of the Solicitors Rooney Williams LLP, who instruct Ms Williams and I in this case?"

"Yes, that was his name."

"Did the Police ever contact you again?"

"No, never."

"Thank you Mr Davies, will you wait there, there will be some more questions."

David sat down and looked towards Joanna who was busy in conversation with her Junior, Tim and DS Monkton, the Officer in the case. David knew she would be furious that the Police had missed this Witness, particularly as she had put the Prosecution theory to Damien that no Scotsman or Arabian gentlemen were present in the flat that night. DS Monkton made a hurried exit from Court as she rose to her feet, adjusted her gown and turned towards Mr Davies.

"You have told us that you spoke to Police at the scene on 4th February 2012?"

"That's right."

"Did you think your evidence might be relevant?"

"I thought it might be important."

"Clearly, this was a Murder investigation and you had seen four people enter the victim's flat and not seen them leave. The Police did not come back to visit you though?"

"No."

"Did you not think that strange?"

"Not really."

"You had important evidence to give, why didn't you go to the Police Station to give it."

"I never really thought about it. I knew they'd arrested that man ...."

Again he pointed to Damien in the Dock.

."... so I didn't think my evidence was that important anymore."

"You never saw any of the persons you mentioned leave the premises?"

"No."

"It follows that the lady you mention, the Scotsman and the Lebanese man could have left at any time between you going to bed at 1:30am and the time the fire alarm went off at approximately 7am."

"I suppose so."

DS Monkton returned to Court and briefly spoke to her. Joanna nodded and then turned to His Honour Judge Tanner.

"My Lord, a matter has just arisen which I need to consider. Could we have a short adjournment as I need to ask the Officer a number of questions? It may affect this Witness and I ask that he remain in case I have any further questions."

His Honour Judge Tanner could clearly see the importance of this Witness's evidence to the Prosecution and he readily agreed to a half-hour adjournment until 3:30pm.

David and Charlotte left Court and sat outside on the benches placed there, quietly pleased with the evidence of Mr Davies. After 15 minutes Joanna came up to them.

"We've found the Officer's notebook who spoke to this Witness and it's only right I disclose it to you. It was a complete oversight that it was not referred to in the Unused Material. I certainly would have liked to have known about it! The officer did not hand his notebook in straight away and then went on leave. When he returned it was just overlooked."

David's immediate reaction was to question how evidence of this nature could be "overlooked" but he decided to keep that to himself.

Joanna produced a copy of the notebook which referred to speaking to Mr Davies. It listed his address and telephone number and brief short hand notes about what he said. It simply listed that Mr Davies said there were many visitors to the flat and there had been some the night before the killing, he did not say how many, what sex the visitors were or anything about Nationalities or the number of visitors or when they had arrived.

"David, I've spoken to the Officer. We can call him if you wish but he says he can remember nothing more than is in his notes."

"Thank you Joanna, I don't think we need trouble him."

David did not want the Jury to see some fresh faced officer explain he was incompetent and obtain the Jury's sympathy. He preferred that they make their own minds up as to why this evidence was "missed."

"What do you propose to do now, Joanna?"

"I shall just put the contents of the Officer's notebook to Mr Davies and leave it at that."

They all returned to Court and Joanna put the contents of the notebook to Mr Davies, suggesting he had said very little to the Police Officer on duty that night. Mr Davies maintained he had given details of how many visitors there were, the fact that one was a girl and that there had been a Scotsman, a Lebanese man and later Damien had gone to the flat. Mr Davies was then released and David announced that was the end of the Defence case.

His Honour Judge Tanner dismissed the Jury for the rest of the day announcing that he had to discuss matters of law with Counsel. Once the

Jury left the Court he discussed the legal issues with Joanna and David and told them the Directions on law which he proposed to give the Jury during Summing Up. The case was then adjourned for the day. Tomorrow it would be Speeches, the last opportunity for both the Prosecution and the Defence to sway the Jury into accepting their respective cases.

CHAPTER 26.

DAY TEN, THE PROSECUTION FINAL SPEECH.

The case re-commenced the next day, Friday at 10:30 am. Joanna had spent the evening putting the finishing touches to her Speech and had predicted that it would last about an hour. It was now her time to tie all the threads of the Prosecution case together and discredit the Defendant's account. She began by reminding the Jury that it was for the Prosecution to prove their case and not for the Defendant to prove anything. She then moved on to the Prosecution case in detail.

"It is the Prosecution case that this Defendant was the killer. He came to Police probably because of fear. He had time to make up a story and he had already thought of one before he arrived. We say you can totally reject that story because it is totally incredible and does not fit the known facts.

Firstly, what mood was he in when he arrived at Usman Hussain's flat? We know that he was out that day with his ex-girlfriend Jenny Jones, the girl whose clothes were torn at some stage in some unknown way. He was drinking and smoking Cannabis. Did this make him aggressive? Certainly the text message he sent her at 11:17pm sounded aggressive,

"You fucking bitch you led me on again."

Does that help you with the mood he was in when he arrived at Usman Hussain's flat?

What did he do to calm himself down from this pent-up anger? He smoked crack cocaine.

Did that make him more aggressive? Did some slight by Usman Hussain cause him to explode ferociously stabbing and causing the death of Usman Hussain?

Secondly, who was in the flat at the time of Usman Hussain's murder? We know Usman Hussain and the Defendant were there, but was anyone else? Of course we have been told that others were in the flat at some stage that night. There was Babs or Babe and it appears from the evidence of Mr Davies that the Scotsman and a Lebanese gentleman were there as well, **at some stage**. You may want to consider Mr Davies' evidence closely. You may find it strange that he never attended the Police Station to tell anyone his version of events when he knew he had relevant evidence, why leave it so late to come forward? Let's assume in his favour he was telling the truth about these men. We have no idea what time they left the flat, it could have been any time after 1:30am.

The Defendant states that Mr Hussain was killed by these men. However, there are a number of problems with that version of events. There is no independent evidence that they were present at the time of the Murder. What evidence there is leads us away from their being present, namely the Forensic evidence of the bloody shoeprints. Those prints, you may think, lead to one conclusion. The Defendant was the only other person present when Usman Hussain was murdered.

Where did the Defendant go when he was in the flat after the stabbing took place? In the Living room, the Hallway, the Kitchen, in Mr Hussain's bedroom. He would have left bloody footprints just as anyone else present would have. However there were only shoeprints from one type of trainer and those were in the locations the Defendant admitted to going to. There were only one set of prints because there was only one person present in the flat at that time with the dead or dying Mr Hussain.

Thirdly, there is the Defendant's version of where the stabbing took place. He states it was in the Living room. However, there is a problem with this evidence. It does not account for the aerial blood spots in the Hallway. Mr Brant in cross-examining the Forensic Expert Mr Albright valiantly tried to suggest a number of ways this may have occurred and to be fair Mr Albright said it may be possible. However, the most realistic way in which that blood was caused was by someone thrusting a knife into an already bleeding Usman Hussain in the Hallway and that fact does not accord with the Defendant's version of events. It is consistent with the stabbing first occurring in the Lounge and Mr

Hussain retreating into the Hallway where he was stabbed again.

Fourthly, the perpetrator of this crime was someone willing to plunge a knife into Usman Hussain. We know from the Defendant's previous convictions that he has a penchant for knives and has, in the past been willing to use one to plunge into the body of another person.

Fifthly, there is the evidence of the phone call to Mr White at 5:21am. Both the Defendant, and his good friend Mr White, claim they cannot recall that call. Is that because they don't want to? The Paramedics arriving at 7:15am stated they thought Mr Hussain had probably been dead for two hours or so. That would be just around the time the Defendant called Mr White, or maybe the Murder was slightly earlier at say 4:30am when the neighbour, Annabelle Lyons, heard a scream. Did the Defendant make the call to Christopher White to explain to him he had done a terrible thing, killing Mr Hussain? Where was that call made from? It appears to have been made from the vicinity of the Defendant's Mother's flat. There is of course, according to the Cell Site expert, Mr Rollins, a possibility it was made in the vicinity of Mr Usman's flat, but making it from his Mother's flat is consistent with the evidence of the Defendant's own Sister, Karen, who recalls hearing a noise at around 5am that sounded like someone coming into the house. She heard a similar noise at 6am that sounded like someone leaving the house. Was that the

Defendant, coming home after the Murder, phoning Mr White and then returning to Mr Hussain's flat to set fire to it in order to try, unsuccessfully, to destroy the evidence?

Perhaps the most telling evidence against the Defendant is his version of going home. He stated he could not recall when he left Mr Hussain's flat. He ran away to avoid the assailants. It took 15-20 minutes to get home. That, you might think, was a long time to travel under one mile, particularly if he was running, which is what he initially told the Police. That would mean on his own evidence, he left Mr Hussain's flat no earlier than 7:10am. However, that simply cannot be true. The Fire Brigade were called by Mr Feeley at 6:57am, thirteen minutes earlier. The fire was already set and you may think that whoever set it would have left pretty quickly. You may think it would take some time for the fire to take hold. Sometime before the alarms went off, sometime before Mr Feeley saw the smoke. This puts the time the Defendant left the flat at some time before 7-00am. Did he go somewhere and get rid of his Star 'D' Sprint trainers before returning to his Mother's flat?

Finally, there is the evidence of the fire and the injury to the Defendant's hand. Someone set fire to that flat. You may think that setting deliberate fires can be a dangerous thing for the person setting the fire. He might get injured and we know that the Defendant had an injury to his hand that according to Dr Monkton could have been caused whilst trying to commit an arson. You will have noted that the Defendant gave a false account to Dr Monkton as to how that injury occurred. Was that because he had not thought that part of his story through? Days later he said the injury was caused by the men torturing him using a lighter to burn the palm of his hand. We heard the injury could have happened that way. He said he had forgotten this when asked by Dr Monkton. However, is that really plausible? He supposedly remembered so much when questioned by Police. Would he really have forgotten being tortured? We suggest that is nonsense.

Ladies and Gentlemen, it is our duty as the Prosecution to prove the case against the Defendant, we say we have done that. We say his version of events was a lie from first to last. We say he lied to the Police and he has lied to you and that in fact, for whatever reason and we do not have to prove it, he lost his temper and killed Usman Hussain.

There is only one proper verdict in this case, that the Defendant is Guilty of Murder."

Joanna smiled at the Jury, thanked them for listening to her Speech and sat down.

CHAPTER 27.

DAY TEN, THE DEFENCE FINAL SPEECH.

After a short adjournment for everyone to have a coffee, it was David's turn to address the Jury on behalf of Damien.

He commenced by stating that they had heard an excellent speech from Joanna Glass, piecing together all the parts of the Prosecution case and making an attractive and able final submission. He then moved on to remind the Jury that the burden of proving the case fell solely on the Prosecution's shoulders and the test was a high one. They could not convict unless they were satisfied so that they were sure of Damien's guilt. He then continued,

"This is an unusual case in that both the Prosecution and the Defence agree on a large number of the basic facts. This is a case where it is not so much the evidence that is disputed but the interpretation of that evidence.

For example:

There is no doubt that in the early hours of 4th February 2012 Usman was stabbed to death.

There is no doubt that Damien Clarke was present when Usman Hussain was killed.

There is no doubt that he handled the knife that killed Usman Hussain and cleaned it.

There is no doubt that there was a fire in his premises.

There is no doubt that Damien Clarke went home after the stabbing and indeed put some of the items that he was wearing into a washing machine.

We therefore have a broad level of agreement between both the Prosecution and the Defence.

However, the Prosecution go further, they say he alone perpetrated this Murder, wielding a knife repeatedly, intent on killing or causing really serious harm to Usman Hussain, for some unknown reason.

Damien Clarke is adamant it did not happen like that. Yes he was at the premises at the time the stabbing took place but he was not the person doing the stabbing, he is not a vicious killer but a terrified Witness to this violent assault.

This is now our opportunity to address you on behalf of Damien Clarke. We want you to look at the evidence carefully with us, we know you will, when carefully analysed one proposition stands out:

The Prosecution case is based entirely on assertion and guesswork.

The Prosecution say it is based on circumstantial

evidence, namely a chain of evidence from which you can infer that Damien Clarke was the Murderer. Circumstantial evidence can be powerful evidence but it is important that it not to be confused with speculation or guesswork. If there is a break in the chain then you cannot fill that gap with guesses. Here we say that is what the Prosecution have done. What the Prosecution have done from the very start in this case is jump to conclusions, often based on false premises.

If you look at the Chronology, the time line of the investigation you can see how quick the Prosecution was to jump to conclusions in this case rather than have a close analysis of the evidence.

The Murder took place undoubtedly before 6:57am, the time we know that Mr Feeley made the 999 call on 4th February 2012. The Police discovered the body just after 7:15am. At 14-00 Damien Clarke arrived at the Police Station, on his account trying to help them by telling them what he had witnessed, who the perpetrators were and the threats that had been made to him.

Instead of being grateful and looking into his story, the Police immediately checked his antecedents to see if he had a criminal record. Clearly this played an important part in the investigation for the Police.

Within 30 minutes of presenting himself at the Police Station, Damien Clarke was arrested on suspicion of Murder at 14:30. Within a single day, after being interviewed at length and not changing his version of events in any way, he was charged with Murder at 10am on 5th February 2012.

An almost indecent rush, before there was any time to properly investigate the case.

DS Monkton concluded that Damien Clarke's account was disjointed. Ignoring the obvious fact that Damien Clarke was distressed, had been drinking all of the previous day, had been smoking crack cocaine and on his own account had witnessed a horrific Murder and been threatened with a knife.

You may think in those circumstances it was fortunate he was able to give any account never mind one that DS Monkton thought was disjointed, but DS Monkton using amateur psychology decided he had got his man.

From that moment onwards, there was no proper investigation into this Murder, the only investigation was a biased one, aimed solely at trying to establish that Damien Clarke was Guilty rather than look at other reasonable possibilities.

What we say on behalf of Damien Clarke is that this is a weak Prosecution case and that when you look at the evidence closely and carefully, something the Officers did not do, the evidence does not point to Damien Clarke being responsible for the Murder. It in fact points away from him for a number of reasons.

Let's take the number of points made by Ms Glass in her speech, I counted seven points.

Firstly, the Prosecution rely on his mood, saying he was aggressive when he went to Usman Hussain's flat. What evidence is there for that? The Prosecution rely on a single text sent by him at 11:17pm probably 7 hours before the Murder took place. The comment uses a swear word, it does not make any threat towards Jenny, it is consistent with annoyance but is not the type of aggression that you might expect from someone with Murder on his mind.

A throw away comment was made by Ms Glass about Jenny Jone's clothes being torn. Remember there is no evidence that Damien Clarke tore them. He says he did not and Jenny cannot remember how they were torn. Perhaps not surprising considering how much alcohol she must have consumed that day. People who have consumed large amounts of alcohol fall over, they tear their clothes accidentally and cannot recall how the next day. We suggest you put aside this allegation of aggression, there is in reality no evidence to support it.

Secondly, the Prosecution rely on who was present at the time Usman Hussain was murdered. The Prosecution say that it was just Usman Hussain and Damien Clarke but there is no evidence that was the case. You will recall that Ms Glass cross examined Mr Clarke on the basis that the Scotsman and the Arabian man were never there. The Prosecution had to change their stance when they heard Mr Davies' evidence, evidence he had given to the Police and which had been ignored, possibly because it did not fit the theory that Damien Clarke was the perpetrator. Mr Davies had no reason to lie, you might think it was clear from his expression when he gave evidence that he does not even like Damien Clarke, he has no reason to lie about these men. He was adamant he saw a Scotsman, a Lebanese man and a lady go to Usman Hussain's flat that night. He also saw Damien Clarke go there. He never saw anyone leave. It is right they could have left before the Murder but there is no evidence either way. They could have been present at the time of the Murder and could have been the Murderers. Remember it is for the Prosecution to prove they were not the Murderers and Damien Clarke was.

The Prosecution try to make a point about the bloody footprints. There is no doubt that twelve prints were found. However, common sense tells us there must have been more than twelve steps. It follows that not every step left a bloody footprint. There is no evidence that the footprints that were found were those of Damien Clarke. There is no evidence he ever owned a pair of "Star 'D' Sprint" trainers. Those prints could have been made by one or more of the actual assailants. We know that the size range could have included Damien Clarke's shoe size but considering the range given in evidence it probably covers most of the adult male population of the UK. As we have heard there could have been two different size shoes making these prints. It is not beyond the realms of possibility that the two assailants both wore "Star 'D' Sprint" trainers of the same or even different sizes.

Thirdly, the Prosecution raised the issue of where the stabbing took place. Damien Clarke did say it took place in the Lounge. We know there is evidence that there were bloodspots in the Hallway that could have been caused by a further knife blow in the Hallway into the already bleeding Mr Hussain. However, as the Forensic scientist, Mr Allbright told us, that is not the only way that this could have been caused. It is possible that the stabbing only took place in the Lounge and not in the Hallway. In any event, why would Damien Clarke lie about this? He could have told a story that the Scotsman stabbed Mr Hussain in the Living room, Mr Hussain retreated into the Hallway and was stabbed again. He had no reason to lie about where the stabbing took place.

Fourth, the Prosecution rely on Damien Clarke's previous convictions. Yes he possessed a broken flick knife that the Prosecution accepted he had found one night and was stopped by Police before he had got rid of it. Yes he has a previous conviction for wounding someone who had threatened him and confronted him. That is completely different from the present case. There is no evidence of any problem between Usman Hussain and Damien Clarke, quite the opposite, Damien Clarke did not take a knife to the Usman Hussain's flat. The witness Christopher White who has known Damien Clarke all his life perhaps best expressed Damien Clarke's character when he was asked by the Police in Interview whether Damien Clarke had ever been violent in such a way that he'd be capable of killing anyone. His answer was "No way, Damien could never kill anyone, never."

Fifth, the Prosecution rely on the call to Mr White at 5:21am. It is right that neither Mr Clarke nor Mr White recalled this call. May it have gone to voicemail? Was it merely calling a friend or even an accidental call? We simply do not know and I suggest it would be wrong to suggest as the Prosecution do that there was something sinister in this call. We have no idea what the call was about and there is no evidence of what it was about. My Learned Friend for the Prosecution tries to suggest that the call was made at the time of the Murder because the Paramedics arriving at 07:15 am stated that Mr Hussain **possibly** had been dead for a couple of hours. Please be careful of such a statement. No tests were carried out by the Paramedics to determine the time of death, this was just a guess and there is actually no Forensic evidence of when Usman Hussain died.

Further, the evidence of where this call was made from is challenged. The Cell Site expert, Mr Rollins did accept that the call could have been made from the vicinity of Mr Hussain's flat. There is no evidence that Damien Clarke returned home that night at about 5am and left again at 6am. In any event if he was able to get in and out of the house at that time why did he have to get his Sister to let him in at sometime around 7:30am that day?

Sixth, the Prosecution rely upon Christine Clarke's timings of when she says Damien Clarke came home. It is right that she has no reason to lie and it is right that she undoubtedly was trying her best when she gave evidence. However, honest and convincing Witnesses do make mistakes about matters such as time. It could have been earlier than she said, it could have been nearer 7-00am. Murder trials do not usually turn upon Witnesses' fallible recollections of timings and differences of a few minutes.

Seventh, the Prosecution rely on the fire and the burn injury to Damien Clarke's hand. They say this was caused when he set fire to the flat. It is right the injury could have been caused in that way but equally it could have been caused as Damien Clarke stated, namely the perpetrators of this Murder held his hand and burnt him with a lighter as a warning. Ms Glass says that he would have recalled this. However, he had been drinking all day, he had been smoking crack cocaine, and no doubt he was in a state of shock from what he had seen. It is quite feasible in that state he had put this out of his mind and only recollected it later.

There is another problem for the Prosecution in this regard. The evidence does not point conclusively to a fire being deliberately started in the flat. No accelerant was used, there may have only been one seat of fire. You have heard this evidence from the Prosecution witness, Mr Wardle, the Fire Investigation Officer who accepted that this fire could have been started accidentally by a carelessly discarded cigarette. In a place where people regularly smoke crack cocaine you may think it not so surprising that there was an accidental fire!

What else is there? There is no other evidence that the Prosecution can rely upon. You however, have had the advantage of seeing and hearing Damien Clarke in the Witness Box. He did not need to go into the Witness Box, he could not be forced to. However, he chose to get into that witness box and deal with the cross-examination of Ms Glass, a very skilful and experienced Advocate.

It is for you to consider that evidence. Nothing changes just because he gave evidence. It is not his duty to prove anything. It is for the Prosecution to prove that he lied to you. When you consider that evidence, do bear in mind how nerve racking it must have been to answer questions when allegations like this were made in the course of the interview. Some of you may have been nervous reading the Oath out in this court, Court One of the Old Bailey, the most famous Criminal Court in the Country. It must be quite intimidating with so many eyes watching you. If you made a mistake in reading out the Oath, all that would happen is that you would have been asked to read out the oath again. Imagine how much worse it must be to give evidence for hours during a trial like this, Damien Clarke knowing that if he used a wrong word, Ms Glass would jump on him and suggest that there was something sinister behind the mistaken use of a word.

In fact, you may think he was never caught out in a lie despite the hours of questioning and that goes a long way to suggesting that he told you the truth.

Finally, what is missing from the Prosecution case? Simply this, they have not established any motive for this killing. It is right that the Prosecution do not have to prove motive in order to prove Murder. However, the absence of any motive you may think is a serious flaw in the Prosecution case. If the Prosecution cannot establish a motive maybe it's because Damien Clarke does not have one, maybe it's because he didn't kill Usman Hussain.

The Prosecution have put together a theory, but one that is missing essential elements including motive.

We submit when you consider the evidence carefully as we know you will, on the evidence you have heard there is only one proper verdict, Not Guilty to Murder."

Thanking the Jury for their attention, David smiled at them and sat down. Throughout his speech he had tried to get eye contact with each member. He had noted one or two refused to look at him but most had returned his eye contact. One or two had smiled and nodded at points he had made and at least two had made notes of some of what he thought were his best points. Of course it meant nothing in reality. He had seen Jurors convict his clients in the past after nodding furiously at him about certain points. He had also had Juries acquit who had not shown any interest in anything he had to say. He knew after thirty years in the job he could not read a Jury. It usually amused him to hear young Barristers say they could as he was firmly of the view no one could.

He had finished now, there was nothing more he could say to help Damien. There was just the Summing Up from His Honour Judge Tanner and then they would retire. He had expected an awful time in front of His Honour Judge Tanner and had been surprised how fair he had been. He now expected a fair Summing Up and the Jury would soon be out to consider their verdict.

CHAPTER 28.

DAYS TEN AND ELEVEN, THE JUDGE'S SUMMING UP.

After the lunch break His Honour Judge Tanner commenced his Summing-up. He dealt first with the points of law he had discussed with Counsel. He reminded the Jury of their respective functions, he was the Judge of law and they must take the law from him but they were the Judge of facts. He warned them that if he made comments on the facts they should ignore them unless they agreed with him. He reminded them that the burden was on the Prosecution to prove the case and not for the Defendant to prove anything, also that the burden was a high one, that they could not convict unless they were satisfied so they were sure of the Defendant's Guilt. He pointed out this was the same standard as proving Guilt beyond a reasonable doubt. He directed them on the definition of Murder, informing them that the necessary intent was an intent to kill or cause really serious harm. He told them the use they could make of Damien's previous convictions and how to treat Damien's lies such as the lie he admitted to about how his hand was burnt, and how to deal with circumstantial evidence. He then moved on to summarise the evidence they had heard from the various Witnesses.

At 4:15pm he broke off his Summing-Up and explained that he thought the Jury had heard enough for one day and he was now sending them home for the weekend. He asked if anyone would mind him starting at 10am on Monday so he could finish his Summing-Up early giving them more time to deliberate on their verdicts. No one complained about an earlier start and the case was adjourned until 10am on Monday. He warned them that their deliberations were now at an end and they must not discuss the case with anyone over the weekend, including each other. He then wished them all a good weekend.

David and Charlotte went to a local wine bar and enjoyed a bottle of Claret. Both agreed the case had gone well but there were still difficulties in the Defence case and they expected a Guilty verdict. They both agreed that His Honour Judge Tanner's Summing Up had been fair and there were no obvious grounds of appeal so far.

David had a relaxing weekend. He had done all he could and the result of the case would make little difference to his career.

The weekend went slowly for Damien. He knew that this could be his last weekend before starting a life sentence with no knowledge or guarantee that he would ever be released.

On Monday the case did not start until 10-15am as one of the Jurors was late. His Honour Judge Tanner nevertheless thanked them all for being there earlier and continued with his summary of the evidence.

Finally, he reminded the Jury of a summary of the points made by both sides.

"You have heard two excellent speeches from Counsel. Those speeches were made to assist you in your deliberations. You are of course not bound to adopt any of Counsel's suggestions or comments and can accept or reject any point they make.

Ms Glass for the Prosecution states that there are seven points in favour of the Prosecution case, Mr Brant for the Defendant states that all of those points can easily be explained away.

The points that Counsel made are that:

Firstly Ms Glass argued that there is evidence that the Defendant was in an aggressive mood when he went to Mr Hussain's flats. She relies on the aggressive words of the text he sent to his ex-girlfriend who, having spent a day with the Defendant, somehow ended up with her clothes torn. Mr Brant points out this must have been hours before the Murder took place, that it was only an offensively worded text and that there is no evidence the Defendant tore Ms Jones clothes.

Secondly, Ms Glass relies upon the evidence of the bloody shoeprints, evidence you might think is crucial to understanding this case. She points to the fact that there was a great deal of blood around and whoever was present in the flat after the Murder of Usman Hussain was likely to leave bloody shoeprints. She of course points to the fact that apart from two smudged prints by the curtains in the Lounge, there were ten shoe prints in the Lounge, Hallway, Mr Hussain's bedroom and the Kitchen which were made by the sole of the same trainers, a "Star 'D' Sprint" trainer. She also points to the fact that the Defendant on his own admission, visited all of those areas after the Murder took place. Mr Brant reminded you that there is no evidence the Defendant ever owned a pair of "Star 'D' Sprint" trainers. He also made the comment that it may be the Defendant's trainers left no print and the two assailants may have been wearing the same type of trainer and the prints found could have been made by both of them. Of course members of the Jury it is for you to put as much weight as you think fit to that suggestion, remembering that you are not expected to live in cloud cuckoo land just because Senior Counsel makes such a comment!

Thirdly, Ms Glass points to the forensic evidence of the bloodstains in the Hallway and how the forensic evidence suggests these resulted from someone thrusting the knife into an already bleeding Mr Hussain in that area. If that is so, that differs from the account the Defendant gave the Police and to you about where the stabbing took place. Mr Brant points out that the Forensic Scientist, Mr Allbright conceded that it was possible that the blood in the Hallway got there in a different way.

Fourth, Ms Glass points to the Defendant's previous convictions for possessing a flick knife and being willing to use a knife to wound another. I have already directed you on what use you can make of those convictions. Mr Brant points out the facts of those convictions differ to the facts of this case and no doubt you will want to consider this carefully. The Prosecution case is that the Defendant repeatedly thrust the knife into Mr Hussain killing him. The Defendant's case is that it was not him. You may think the evidence about the knife is important in this case. The Defendant does not deny holding that knife. He states he was given the knife and told to clean it which he did. No doubt you will want to consider that evidence carefully. According to him he was being threatened by the men who enforced this threat by wielding the knife. If his version is correct, the men then handed over the only weapon we have heard anyone possessed that night. Would he still feel threatened now that he was the only one with a knife in his hand? That will be a matter for you to consider.

Fifthly, Ms Glass points to the call made from the Defendant's phone to Mr White's phone at 5-21 that morning. There is an issue of where that call was made from. Was it made from the Defendant's mother's flat or Mr Hussain's flat? That will be a matter for you to consider bearing in mind the evidence of the Defendant's sister Karen who believed she heard him return to the flat at about 5am and leave at 6am. Both the Defendant and Mr White claim they cannot recall that call. There is no suggestion anyone else made that call so you may think that it must have been the Defendant who phoned Mr White. What was the call about, a call that lasted over two minutes? I have warned you already that you should not speculate or guess in this case and only draw proper inferences from the evidence. Ms Glass, relying on the evidence of the Paramedics suggests that the call would have been made around the time Mr Hussain was killed. Mr Brant counters and states the Paramedics evidence only deals with a possible timing of death and we have no idea what the call was about. This of course will be a matter for you to consider and how the call fits in, if it does, with the evidence the Defendant gave to you.

Sixth, Ms Glass relies upon the evidence of the Defendant's other sister, Christine who recalled the Defendant returning to her flat at about 7-30am. She points to the evidence of Mr Feeley's call to the Emergency Services at 6-57am, meaning that, on the Defendant's evidence he must have left the flat sometime before 6-57am. According to the Defendant, it would only take 15-20 minutes to get to his Mother's flat from Mr Hussain's flat. You have copies of a map showing these locations and you might think it would take a lot less time if he was running away from two Murderers. Ms Glass suggests this indicates he must have gone somewhere else, possibly to change clothes and discard his trainers. Mr Brant in answer to this point, states that Witnesses can make mistakes about timings, which is of course true and that there is no evidence of the Defendant going anywhere else.

Finally, Ms Glass relied on the evidence of the burn on the Defendant's hand which we know from the Doctor's evidence, could have been caused whilst setting fire to Mr Hussain's flat. Mr Brant points out to you that it could have been caused the way the Defendant said a few days after he had been arrested, when he said the men deliberately burnt his hand with a lighter. You have Ms Glass's point about, how could he have forgotten that if that is how the injury occurred? You also have Mr Brant's argument that the fire may have been accidentally caused by a discarded cigarette, although it was not clear to me if a discarded cigarette was found at the seat of the fire. Again this will be a matter for you to consider.

Having summarised the points for both the Prosecution and the Defence in his own way, His Honour Judge Tanner told the Jury it was now time for them to consider their verdicts. He advised them to elect a Foreman or Woman to assist their deliberations and give the Verdict in court. He told them they were under no pressure of time and finally warned them that they may have heard of majority verdicts but to put such matters out of their minds. The only verdict he could accept was a unanimous one and that would be the case for some time to come. Should it change, he would send for them. They should not send a note to him saying they could only reach a majority verdict as at this stage he would have to ignore them. Finally he told them they had heard all the evidence they were going to hear in this case, they were not going to hear anymore and should not ask for anymore.

The Jury Bailiffs were then sworn to keep the Jurors in a proper place and not to speak to them or allow anyone else to speak to them about the trial other than to ask them what their verdict is. With that the Jury left Court at 12-05pm to consider Damien's fate.

CHAPTER 29.

DAYS ELEVEN AND TWELVE, THE JURY'S DELIBERATIONS.

The Jury moved slowly into their room, each sensing that they might be there for some time. They provided the Jury Bailiff with their mobile phones just in case they should be tempted to phone someone during their deliberations. Their first task was to elect a Foreman. Two members of the Jury offered to do this, David Williams and John Wilson, both had taken copious notes throughout the Trial and both felt themselves best suited to the task. David Williams was 45 years of age and a banker, although he had hidden the latter fact from the Jury and simply said he worked in Investments. John Wilson was aged 39 and worked in the Administrative side of an Eco Glass company. A vote was taken which resulted in a deadlock and so as a solution, Katherine Fairhead who was aged 42 and worked as a Manager in a Catering Company, offered to do the task instead. In order to progress the matter, her suggestion of becoming Forewoman was accepted by the majority much to the annoyance of both David Williams and John Wilson.

Little had been achieved when the Jury Bailiff knocked on the door at just before 1pm to take the sandwich orders for lunch. Already a few members of the Jury had shown themselves to be more vociferous than others and some had barely said a word. It had been decided to start with the Judges directions on the law, a suggestion made by Carl Smith, a nineteen year old law student who had suggested it would be a good idea before considering the evidence in detail. Few members of Jury had actually found it very useful and wanted to move on quickly to consider the evidence.

David Williams, still inwardly seething that his obvious acumen for the position of Jury Foreman had not been seen by the ingrates around him, was one of the most vociferous speakers. He was trying to make his position clear, it was obvious that Damien was guilty of Murder and no real discussion was needed. John Wilson, who was less offended by being rejected for the role of Foreman, but still annoyed, was equally vociferous in arguing the case for an acquittal, partly because in the last two weeks he had taken a dislike to David Williams and could not accept anything he said in his dogmatic and dictatorial monotone.

The afternoon passed slowly with the two sides beginning to polarise. The Jury were almost equally divided on those in favour of a conviction, those in favour of an acquittal and those who had no idea one way or the other.

At 4-15pm the Jury were asked to return to Court. They were not asked any questions about their deliberations and were simply told that they should be ready to resume on Tuesday at 10-00am. His Honour Judge Tanner then wished them a good evening and adjourned the Court until Tuesday.

On Tuesday the Court resumed at 10-10am. Jude Davis, the Juror who had been late on Monday, was late again. He was an unemployed twenty year old who felt that going to bed much before 3 am was a waste of his personal time and getting up before 11am should be discouraged if at all possible.

The deliberations resumed with the leaders of the opposing sides becoming more adamant about how right they were. David Williams consistently referred to the bloody shoeprints as being the key to the case.

"It's clear the Judge believed that was the most telling point in the whole case. His comments about the cloud cuckoo ideas of the defence Barrister said it all. The Defendant left a trail of bloody shoeprints in every room he visited. If there were others present there would have been more shoeprints."

John Wilson was equally adamant that the shoeprints were not the most important evidence.

"The person who killed Usman Hussain was likely to be the one with the most blood on him. He would surely have left bloody footprints. We know the Defendant didn't have much blood on him because his sister Christine did not see any. It's quite feasible the Defendant did not step in any of the blood and therefore did not leave the prints. They could have been left by the killer who followed him into the rooms he visited."

David Williams could not accept this point,

"That's ridiculous, anybody in a room where a Murder has taken place is likely to step into the blood. The absence of more than one set of bloody footprints is because there was only one person around to make the prints, only an idiot would think differently."

John Wilson's anger at this insult was noticed by all, he was about to launch into a tirade of abuse when Katherine Fairhead intervened.

"I don't think it's going to help anyone David, making comments like that, can we all try to be polite to each other."

There was general agreement with this comment, making David Williams convinced that he was in a room full of morons.

Susan Hargreaves, a thirty two year old divorced housewife, who had been relatively quiet during the discussions joined in with her views.

"I think we should concentrate on what the Defendant said in evidence. We know he has a bad criminal record but I think he was telling the truth when he told us he had not stabbed Mr Hussain."

David Williams could not help himself when he added,

"You have to be joking, did you expect him to tell the truth. He's hardly likely to say he stabbed the old man. Damien Clarke is a low life. He's carried knives in the past and used them, of course he used one this time."

Carl Smith decided to rely on his limited legal training.

"I think we have to be careful about his previous convictions. The Judge warned us about the use we could make of them but we shouldn't place too much reliance on them."

Susan Hargreaves agreed with him,

"I think we should put them aside, a lot of young men carry knives these days, it does not mean they are all Murderers. I think Damien Clarke has had a rough life, he is no Angel but I don't believe he's a Murderer."

The deliberations continued with opinions being expressed on the evidence, views taken from their own life experiences and little progress was actually made. Before long it was time for the Canteen's to offer its latest Sandwich delights and at the suggestion of the Jury Foreman, Katherine, time for a rest in the deliberations to let the air cool.

At 2:05pm, Members of the Jury were called back into Court and Katherine as Foreman, was asked if they had reached a unanimous verdict. Upon her saying that they had not, His Honour Judge Tanner now directed that he could receive a majority verdict, namely a verdict on which at least ten of them were agreed.

They returned to their Jury room a little more disheartened. They had hoped for more assistance and they did not seem to be close to a situation where ten of them would agree.

The deliberations continued with Katherine suggesting that they look at the major parts of the evidence again considering the points made by both the Prosecution and the Defence. There was an audible groan at this idea but as no useful alternative was suggested they adopted the suggestion.

David Williams having exhausted the shoe prints point moved on to the phone call at 5-21am to Christopher White.

"I have no doubt that Christopher White guy was lying. He remembered what was said to him at 5-21 in the morning and the only reason he didn't want to tell us was because he was protecting his friend. It was obviously about the Defendant having committed the murder."

John Wilson decided this was another opportunity to cut this Williams guy down to size.

"I don't think he showed any sign of lying. He probably gets all sorts of calls like that from his coked up friend in the early hours of the morning and doesn't remember any of them."

There were a few sounds of agreement around the room so David moved on to the burn injury.

"Well what about the burn injury? It's unbelievable that he didn't remember how that was caused when the Doctor asked him."

Carl Smith interjected at this point.

"I've been thinking about that point. He would only have lied about the burn if it was caused when he set fire to the place. However, the evidence for a deliberate fire being set is very weak. I read somewhere that most arsons are caused by someone using an accelerant, petrol, white spirit, lighter fuel etc. There was no evidence of an accelerant here, the evidence of there being two seats of fire is also weak, it could have been one and the Forensic scientist said it could have been an accidental fire. If it could have been an accidental fire I don't see how we can be sure it was deliberate. If we can't be sure it was deliberate then we cannot be sure the Defendant was lying about how his injury was caused. If it wasn't caused by setting fire to the place and wasn't caused by smoking crack cocaine we are only left with his explanation that he was deliberately tortured."

Carl was quite proud of his logical argument which met with approving nods from several areas of the room. He had decided before starting his law course that he wanted to be a Barrister. That wish had been enforced by being involved in this trial and he considered he had put together a persuasive argument that was better than the Defence QC had mustered.

"What a load of rubbish," responded David Williams, who was coming to the view that he was rapidly losing the room. Clearly he had to be more forceful otherwise there was a danger that a Murderer would be freed.

"Of course the fire was deliberate, it can't be a coincidence that a person is murdered and their flat set on fire accidentally on the same day, which just happens to have the effect of destroying evidence. We know the Defendant went home and tried to destroy further evidence by washing his clothes and showering."

Susan Hargreaves was becoming increasingly annoyed at David Williams' patronising voice and she immediately came to the Defence of the young, good looking, Carl.

"I think Carl made a very good point and it really is wrong to keep attacking other people's arguments by saying they are "a load of rubbish" or calling people Idiots."

Katherine had to re-establish her control of the Jury, so she added.

"I agree, David, it really does not help to keep making such comments and I ask that you stop and just give us your opinions and arguments without insulting others."

David saw the others nodding around the room and decided he had had enough. If these woolly eyed liberals wanted to acquit a guilty man so be it.

John Wilson returned to the discussion re-enforcing Carl's point.

"I agree with Carl's analysis and of course it goes one stage further. If these men tortured the Defendant, what was their reason? It could only have been to threaten him. The only reason to threaten him would be because of what he had just witnessed, the murder of Usman Hussain."

Again there were murmurings of agreement around the room.

Jude Davis looked up at this comment and wondered whether to voice an opinion, but as he had not listened to much of the deliberation and even less to the evidence in the case, he decided it was better not to show any ignorance and he remained quiet.

Geraldine Webb, a retired civil servant aged 68 had also kept quiet for most of the discussion. However, she liked David Williams and had listened intently to his theorising throughout the trial when they had coffee together. She felt now was the time to show him some support.

"David has made some very good points and it's not surprising he is vigorous in making them when so many people are so dismissive of his views."

People around the room looked surprised at her interjection but most rapidly ignored it as motivated by frustrated lust.

One by one it became clear that the majority in the room was beginning to agree with the Defence version of events. John Wilson put forward his final opinion with customary force.

"I do think the Police did not properly investigate this matter. Why didn't they go back to Robert Davies when they had taken details from him? They decided with indecent haste that Damien Clarke was the Murderer and they ignored all other possibilities. It's clear that a Scotsman and a Lebanese man were in the flat that night. No one can say when they left. If they were there at the time of the Murder, they may have been the Murderers. In those circumstances I cannot be sure that Damien Clarke committed this crime and I am not going to convict him of Murder."

At 3-45pm the Jury returned to Court and upon being asked if they had reached a verdict, Katherine announced that they had. When asked whether it was a unanimous or majority verdict she stated it was by a majority. She then gave the verdict, Damien Clarke was Not Guilty of Murder. As it was a Not Guilty verdict she was not asked what the majority was. In fact it was 10-2, David Williams had refused to "acquit a guilty man" and Geraldine Webb had supported him to the end.

Upon hearing the verdict, Damien let out a loud, "Yes!" which could be heard by everyone in Court. Joanna turned to David Brant and said, "Well done," and David smiled an acknowledgement at her. David's remaining task was to ask for Damien to be discharged which was acceded to by His Honour Judge Tanner who then proceeded to thank the Members of the Jury for their commitment to the case, reminding them how important the Jury is to our system of justice. He then gave a perfunctory thanks to Counsel for their assistance and left the Bench feeling that David Brant might actually have learnt something during his pupillage with him. He still would not give him a reference though.

David and Charlotte went down to the cells to see Damien. Although acquitted and "discharged" there was still a degree of administration before Damien would be released from the clutches of the Prison Service.

They were both feeling good. Although every lawyer is told that results are unimportant and doing your best is what matters, it is human nature to feel elated at an acquittal, particularly in a Murder case.

Damien was in a good mood. He no longer faced a potential lifetime in jail and would soon be released to resume his life of drinking excessive amounts of alcohol and smoking crack cocaine, both of which he had missed in prison as although illegal supplies of drugs and alcohol, were available, they were expensive.

David smiled at him when he said,

"I bet you're feeling a lot better today?"

"Yeah, I am but I knew I'd get off. You didn't really have to do much did you. I knew I was innocent and everyone would accept that."

David looked at the ungrateful youth before him. He had worked incredibly hard for this ingrate who had almost thrown the case with his evidence. It never ceased to amaze him how Defendants who were convicted we're often more grateful than those who were acquitted.

David and Charlotte did not spend much further time in the cells. They left Damien wishing him well, although in view of his lack of gratitude, neither really meant it.

CHAPTER 30.

DRINKS WITH THE SENIOR CLERK.

Two weeks later on a Thursday night in October, David Brant and John Winston were seated in El Vinos pouring their second bottle of house Claret. David had not been in Court since the Damien Clarke case but he was not that concerned at the moment. He had heard from Charlotte that Damien had been released but arrested a week later after meeting Jenny Jones again and during an alcohol and Cannabis-fuelled celebration he had given her a black eye. The only positive point that could be made in Damien's favour was that he kept the legal profession busy, although, on this occasion, it would be a Pupil Barrister and not a Silk representing him.

Chambers had instituted a new system of what was expressed as a "checks and balances" on the Clerks and David headed the Committee that introduced them. Although John Winston had objected to "repairing a system that was not broken", he had found the new system imposed on him of keeping records of meetings with Solicitors, records of where he was and records of follow-ups, to be quite useful to answer complaints about, "where was he?" and "what was he doing for Chambers?"

He did not resent David's heading the new Committee as he had heard what David had said at the "confidential" Chambers meeting. He had not survived as a Senior Clerk so long without having allies amongst the Tenants who told him everything that was discussed in Chambers meetings. In these Chambers his source of information could not be any higher.

David and John discussed the new system and whether improvements could be made. It was during the third bottle of Claret that David moved on to the subject of his own practice.

"John, I am grateful for the Damien Clarke brief, it filled a large gap in my diary, but obviously I need more work than one Murder case every few months. I don't want to have to leave Chambers, but if work doesn't pick up I will have to."

John took another sip of Claret and munched on a wafer biscuit. Here we go again, he thought to himself. Fortunately Charles Rooney had been impressed with David's victory in the Damien Clarke case and had picked up a Fraud case that he wanted David to conduct.

"Of course Sir, we don't want to lose a Senior bod like you and there is no reason to. Work is starting to pick up and there is even a little more Silk work out there. I've been offered a VHCC Fraud case that will take place next year. It's a wine fraud, you know Sir, where fraudsters contact investors telling them that large amounts of money can be made from investing in wine. Then they get them to invest large sums of money only to find months or years later that the wine never existed and their money has disappeared."

David knew what a wine fraud was and did not need this description but he chose not to interrupt what was clearly good news.

"There should be at least a thousand hours preparation in it for you and a six month trial. I thought of you the minute I was told the brief existed and you will be getting the papers in the next week."

David sensed that John was not telling the whole story, but so what, a good brief was on the way and that is what he needed. He thanked John and mentioned the prospect of yet another good lunch in the near future.

David picked up his glass of Claret and took a further sip. The ruby red liquid swirled as he gently turned the glass in his hand. He looked at it intently noticing that he had already consumed half the contents. He smiled as he looked at what remained, and right now, it definitely seemed half full to him.

Books by John M. Burton

THE SILK BRIEF

The first book in the series, "The Silk Trials." David Brant QC is a Criminal Barrister, a "Silk", struggling against a lack of work and problems in his own chambers. He is briefed to act on behalf of a cocaine addict charged with murder. The case appears overwhelming and David has to use all his ability to deal with the wealth of forensic evidence presented against his client.

US LINK

http://amzn.to/1bz221C

UK LINK

http://amzn.to/16QwwZo

THE SILK HEAD

The second book in the series "The Silk Tales". David Brant QC receives a phone call from his wife asking him to represent a fireman charged with the murder of his lover. As the trial progresses, developments in David's Chambers bring unexpected romance and a significant shift in politics and power when the Head of Chambers falls seriously ill. Members of his chambers feel that only David is capable of leading them out of rough waters ahead, but with a full professional and personal life, David is not so sure whether he wants to take on the role of *The Silk Head*.

US LINK

http://amzn.to/1iTPQZn

UK LINK

http://amzn.to/1ilOOYn

THE SILK RETURNS

The Silk Tales volume 3

David Brant QC is now Head of Chambers at Temple Lane Chambers, Temple, London. Life is great for David, his practice is busy with good quality work and his love life exciting. He has a beautiful partner in Wendy Pritchard, a member of his chambers and that relationship, like his association with members of his chambers, appears to be strengthening day by day.

However, overnight, things change dramatically for him and his world is turned upside down. At least he can bury himself in his work when a new brief is returned to him from another silk. The case is from his least favourite solicitor but at least it appears to be relatively straight-forward, with little evidence against his client, and an acquittal almost inevitable.

As the months pass, further evidence is served in the case and begins to mount up against his client. As the trial commences David has to deal with a prosecutor from his own chambers who is determined to score points against him personally and a co-defending counsel who likewise seems hell-bent on causing as many problems as he can for David's client. Will David's skill and wit be enough this time?

UK LINK

http://amzn.to/1Qj911Q

US LINK

http://amzn.to/1OteiV7

THE SILK RIBBON

The Silk Tales volume 4

David Brant QC is a barrister who practices as a Queen's Counsel at Temple Lane Chambers, Temple, London. He is in love with a bright and talented barrister from his chambers, Wendy, whose true feelings about him have been difficult to pin down. Just when he thinks he has the answer, a seductive Russian woman seeks to attract his attention, for reasons he can only guess at.

His case load has been declining since the return of his Head of Chambers, who is now taking all the quality silk work that David had formerly enjoyed. As a result, David is delighted when he is instructed in an interesting murder case. A middle class man has shot and killed his wife's lover. The prosecution say it was murder, frustration caused by his own impotency, but the defence claim it was all a tragic accident. The case appears to David to be straight-forward, but, as the trial date approaches, the prosecution evidence mounts up and David finds himself against a highly competent prosecution silk, with a trick or two up his sleeve.

Will David be able to save his well-to-do client from the almost inevitable conviction for murder and a life sentence in prison? And what path will his personal life take when the beautiful Russian asks him out for a drink?

UK LINK

http://amzn.to/22ExByC

USA LINK

http://amzn.to/1TTWQMY

THE SILKS CHILD

This is the fifth volume in the series, the Silk Tales, dealing with the continuing story of Queen's Counsel (the Silk), David Brant QC.

Their romantic Valentine's weekend away in a five-star hotel, is interrupted by an unexpected and life-changing announcement by David's fiancé, Wendy. David has to look at his life afresh and seek further casework to pay for the expected increase in his family's costs.

The first case that comes along is on one of the most difficult and emotionally charged cases of his career. Rachel Wilson is charged with child cruelty and causing the death of her own baby by starvation.

The evidence against Rachel, particularly the expert evidence appears overwhelming and once the case starts, David quickly notices how the jurors react to his client, with ill-disguised loathing. It does not help that the trial is being presided over by his least favourite judge, HHJ Tanner QC, his former pupil-master.

David will need all his skill to conduct the trial and fight through the emotion and prejudice at a time when his own life is turned upside down by a frightening development.

Will he be able to turn the case around and secure an acquittal for an unsympathetic and abusive client who seems to deliberately demonstrate a lack of redeeming qualities?

UK

https://goo.gl/YmQZ4p

USA

https://goo.gl/Ek30mx

THE SILKS CRUISE

The Silk Tales volume 6

This is the sixth volume in the series, the Silk Tales, dealing with the continuing story of Queen's Counsel (the Silk), David Brant QC.

After a difficult, exhausting but highly remunerative fraud trial, David and Wendy decide to take their young daughter Rose on a cruise to Norway to get away from cases, chambers and city life.

A chance meeting leads to David being instructed in a particularly difficult murder trial. The case appears straight forward at first, even though the defendant's own friends give evidence against him. However, a series of surprising developments in the case make David wonder what his strategy should be and whether he should ever have taken the case on in the first place.

UK LINK

https://amzn.to/2VD6bPh

US LINK

https://amzn.to/2VfZoMo

PARRICIDE

VOLUME 1 OF THE MURDER TRIALS OF CICERO

A courtroom drama set in Ancient Rome and based on the first murder trial conducted by the famous Roman Advocate, Marcus Tullius Cicero. He is instructed to represent a man charged with killing his own father. Cicero soon discovers that the case is not a simple one and closely involves an important associate of the murderous Roman dictator, Sulla.

UK LINK

http://amzn.to/14vAYvY

US LINK

http://amzn.to/1fprzul

POISON

VOLUME 2 OF THE MURDER TRIALS OF CICERO

It is six years since Cicero's forensic success in the Sextus Roscius case and his life has been good. He has married and progressed through the Roman ranks and is well on the way to taking on the most coveted role of senator of Rome. Meanwhile his career in the law courts has been booming with success after success. However, one day he is approached by men from a town close to his hometown who beg him to represent a former slave on a charge of attempted poisoning. The case seems straight forward but little can he know that this case will lead him on to represent a Roman knight in a notorious case where he is charged with poisoning and with bribing judges to convict an innocent man. Cicero's skills will be tried to the utmost and he will face the most difficult and challenging case of his career where it appears that the verdict has already been rendered against his client in the court of public opinion.

UK LINK

https://goo.gl/VgpU9S

US LINK

https://goo.gl/TjhYA6

THE MYTH OF SPARTA

A novel telling the story of the Spartans from the battle of the 300 at Thermopylae against the might of the Persian Empire, to the battle of Sphacteria against the Athenians and their allies. As one reviewer stated, the book is, "a highly enjoyable way to revisit one of the most significant periods of western history"

UK LINK

http://amzn.to/1gO3MSI

US LINK

http://amzn.to/1bz2pcw

THE RETURN OF THE SPARTANS

Continuing the tale of the Spartans from Sphacteria, dealing with their wars and the political machinations of their enemies, breathing life into a fascinating period of history.

UK LINK

http://amzn.to/1aVDYmS

US LINK

http://amzn.to/18iQCfr

THE TRIAL OF ADMIRAL BYNG

Pour Encourager Les Autres

BOOK ONE OF THE HISTORICAL TRIALS SERIES

"The Trial of Admiral Byng" is a fictionalised retelling of the true story of the famous British Admiral Byng, who fought at the battle of Minorca in 1756 and was later court-martialled for his role in that battle. The book takes us through the siege of Minorca as well as the battle and then to the trial where Byng has to defend himself against serious allegations of cowardice, knowing that if he is found guilty there is only one penalty available to the court, his death.

UK LINK

http://goo.gl/cMMXFY

US LINK

http://goo.gl/AaVNOZ

TREACHERY – THE PRINCES IN THE TOWER

'Treachery - the Princes in the Tower' tells the story of a knight, Sir Thomas Clark who is instructed by King Henry VII to discover what happened to the Princes in the Tower. His quest takes him upon many journeys meeting many of the important personages of the day who give him conflicting accounts of what happened. However, through his perseverance he gets ever closer to discovering what really happened to the Princes, with startling consequences.

UK LINK

http://amzn.to/1VPW0kC

US LINK

http://amzn.to/1VUyUJf

Printed in Great Britain
by Amazon